MARISA

And the Enema Fetish
3rd Edition
By

J. G. Knox

Love, Truth & Life Publishing
PO Box 65130
Vancouver, WA
98665
1-360-690-0842

©

Copyright 2010
by
J.G. Knox
All Rights Reserved

No part of this book may be reproduced by any mechanical, photographic or electronic process, or in the form of phonographic recording, nor may it be stored in a retrieval system, transmitted, translated into another language, or otherwise copied for public or private use, except brief passages quoted for purposes of review, without the written permission of the author.

Contents

The Tent 1
My Enemas 7
English & Working Men 15
Judaism 21
Other Enemas 25
American Cossacks 29
Nurses 35
The Orpanage Infirmary 41
Daddy Valik 53
Scars & Coming Home 61
Where is She? 73
My Hero 85
The Villain & the Farm 97
The Werewolf 103
Care and feeding of Werewolves 109
The Priest on Education, Sex & Obedience 117
Our Wedding 139
Our Honeymoon 149
Confessions and Confidences 157
Pleasing my Husband 165
The Visitor & the Werewolf 173
The Legacy 183

Dedication

Home from war, heroes, men who charged machine guns, men who killed men, honored with parades, medals on their chests, slaps on their backs, minds still at war, blood still on their hands, their acts of heroism crimes in peace time---are they home? Can they come home, live in peace? War breeds hitting, killing, hating; peace requires touching, living, loving.

Trained to kill, men in uniform innately wanting to be touched by women in dresses, wanting to be loved, home; the rules of engagement change.

The right woman's touch transmutes nightmares: the silence of the dead, the screams of the wounded, and the color of bayonet blood red become restful sleep in her arms: the color of paring knife peach pink and the songs of children playing: sweet dreams.

This book is dedicated to all the right women: the ones who kiss heroes obviously wounded, who kiss heroes less obviously wounded---the women whose touch loves away war and make heroes live.

Chapter 1
The Tent

A cold day, late afternoon, October 10, 1913, two weeks before my eleventh birthday, I am Russian, from St. Petersburg, the daughter of a mathematics teacher and a librarian. I stand on a piece of flat in the mouth of a canyon in Colorado, buttoning my coat and watching a layer of clouds blow over us from the east. Smashing into the mountains, trying to follow the wind over the peaks, all day clouds came, wave after wave of them, mountain peaks visible above, mountain slopes visible below, clouds in between, no cloud making it over the wall, their water, their ice, and their lives sucked out climbing the mountains, becoming part of glaciers, and part of ice covering cliffs, cliffs that in morning shine like a hundred miles of cathedral windows catching the sun, reflecting the image of the mountains back to the plains.

The plains, endless horizons, endless hope; the mountains, endless crests, endless faith, looking toward the plains, holding Daddy and Momma's educated hands, I am warmed by endless love. They taught me to walk on paved city streets and to read in a park near the university. My parents always learning, sharing, and teaching me, I yearned to walk the halls of the Imperial Public Library again.

Why were we in mountains with no colleges, no other scholars?

Daddy saw the missing in me, the clouds in my eyes.

He said, "Marisa, what is the square of three?"

"Nine," I said.

"The cube?"

"27"

"There, over the horizon is Wichita, Kansas. Is it colder there or here?"

"We're higher. It's colder here," I said.

"How much," he asked.

"We're at 7,300 feet. Wichita is below two thousand, isn't it?"

"Around that," Daddy said.

I said, "Ok, more than five thousand feet difference, at 5 degrees per thousand feet, its more than twenty five degrees Fahrenheit colder here. Right, Daddy?"

"If the same conditions are here, as there, yes," he said, hugging me.

I was his girl, his only student. We kept walking.

Momma never asked me questions like that. A librarian at the Imperial Public Library, she read Russian literature. Daddy made me compute and think. Momma made me read and remember. She brought books home for me. Three million books on the shelves, more than can be read in a lifetime, what could be more permanent, more lasting than studying, learning forever in a city with unlimited knowledge in the public library? But in my ten years, only my parents and their lives intertwined in mine lasted, was permanent, geography changed, learning changed.

No Russian books here, not even enough to keep me reading for an afternoon, I missed the reading. I missed my teachers smiling at me, thinking of me as brilliant, but not really brilliant, the daughter of two well educated people teaching me at home. Here my teachers saying I was stupid, all the Russian children were stupid, understood nothing, we were not able to follow the simplest instructions in English. There were no paved streets in the coal mining camps of Colorado, no libraries, no colleges, and no Russian speaking teachers in schools.

Holding my parents hands in St. Petersburg by the sea, an ancient city, it was their love that made it beautiful. Their books in my head, I felt their hands. I closed my eyes---St. Petersburg, home. The Baltic Sea alive with waves to a horizon, like the plains, always changing, always there, physical reality balanced culture and intellectual reality. My eyes opened---Colorado, America, no words to read, no books or ballet to balance natural grandeur, beautiful, spectacular sights filling my eyes, more than can be seen in a lifetime.

Momma looked east seeing a two thousand feet drop onto the plain, across eastern Colorado, into Kansas, endless fields of wheat, flat land, the heartland of America, where horizons never end, where the fairy dust of hope makes the most distant dreams come true, where children grow up to mount horses and ride the world, be ridden over, or plant their feet in the earth with the wheat and live forever free, and never hungry.

Daddy looked west, unmistakable, the Colorado Front Range, a wall of more than ten thousand foot tall mountains, impenetrable, a block to travel even now, roads and trains go north to Wyoming, around these mountains. To us, close enough to touch, close enough to see snow on ground, in trees above our camp, a permanent white glacier higher in the canyon, a gravelly creek near camp with the best water Daddy ever tasted, and always cold, just above freezing in August, He breathed in cold, crisp air, breathed in faith in the mountains, the work, the future---in America, the place he, Momma, and I, not noble born, could rise to be all we could be. Daddy saw mountains to stand on, to touch sky from their peaks, but not this late in the season, another warmer season, when English was no longer an impenetrable wall of words, when we were ready, when the snow retreated far enough up the mountains to make them climbable again.

I looked at us, felt my father's strong hand, coal dust imbedded in the cracks between hard calluses; felt my mother's smaller hand, once soft, a librarian handling books, now hard from washing laundry and household work, she was alive with love, endless love, radiating to my father, to me. Love is the thing that lasts, not mountains, plains, St. Petersburg, or this material world, love, love lasts. We hugged as we stood together in the mountain's shadow, as sun still lit the plain, filled with love, our last sunset together. We walked back to our tent on a darkening trail, with well lit memories in our souls.

Night came, men, women, and children talking around an open flame, children herded to beds on cold ground called for their mothers to warm them. Talking quieted. Men crowded closer to the fire, and, one by one, join their wives, their families. Glowing under burned black wood, the fading red of embers below, ringed by frosted grass, our campfire, no longer a warm spot, no place of warmth except under blankets, cold bit us with ice teeth.

Predawn light, dark figures and warm breaths in the tent, I watched Daddy, sleeping, breathing, his hot air condensing into mist, rising clouds against the tent top, clouds that drifted above his head, turned to ice, disappeared, precipitating as snow on the Front Range, sticking to the underside of freezing cloth before reaching the top of the tent. Thin glaciers coated canvas hanging above us, most covering ribbed thread patterns, brown cloth now white. I saw spots directly over our heads, ice thick enough to be imagined as alpine lakes frozen over, a first layer of winter snow blown in patterns on their smooth surface, the pattern of threads surrounding them like a snowy shore.

Daybreak igniting ice crystals radiated into our tent. The sun emerged sliver by sliver from the prairie's oceanesque horizon. Velvet white shoreline threads turned brown and lakes melted, rivulets slithered down the canvas. Our tent thawed. And, as every good winter camper knows, the enemy is not ice, but water, water permeating coats, blankets and other insulating materials chills to freezing, thirty two degrees: Daddy's back and shoulder against the tent damming the flow, cold water soaked into his coat, shirt, and long johns, a rude alarm clock woke him. Day started.

Pushing tight against me, Daddy's arm over me holding Momma's waist, drawing us tight into a single bundle of flesh, shielding us from cold, yet trying to get more of himself under the blanket, a blanket too small for three people, Daddy sleeping partially covered, protected us, kept Momma and me completely covered, warmer than he kept himself.

Closing my eyes, trying to sleep, sandwiched on my side between Momma and Daddy my body was warm, and my left foot, but my right foot, still under a blanket, in space, touching neither Momma nor Daddy, it felt cold, unloved, and left out. My foot ached.

Daddy moved bringing his leg down on my foot, resting his toes on Momma's toes, the warmth of his leg eased the pain of my foot, as his shivering vibrated me more awake.

Before shaking hands buttoned his coat and he left Momma and me, he tucked us both tighter under the blanket.

"I love you, Sarra," he kissed Momma, then me, "I love you, Marisa."

Momma said, "Love you, Alexi," and dozed off again.

Lifting the tent flap, a whiff of frozen mountain air, he let in light, the reflection of a pink face of ice on a snow capped peak. The far side of the valley, the ice's mirror image lit the interior of our tent enough to see faces, and welcomed daylight reflecting back into the plains for a hundred miles. Daddy saw me smile, knew I was awake and kissed me again. Ice from his beard left wet streaks on my face.

Daddy fumbled with his boots, laboriously covering his triple socked feet, stiff, not with age, but with frost, hypothermic arthritis. He was thirty; he needed heat, even the white in his beard healed blonde again with five minutes thawing before a fire. First up, he rekindled the campfire and added billows of gray smoke to the mist of morning. Standing close to the flame, he shivered in a circle of men, drying the cold wet spots on his back, all the men warming similar cold spots, their beards darkened, their shivering eased with the fire's warmth.

I didn't need to say I loved him. He didn't need to see it in my smile. He knew I loved him. Nevertheless, I was glad he saw it that morning. In the light outside the tent, I remember his smile beaming down on me in the early light. Closing the tent flap, he was gone, huddled with other men by the fire. Both my feet against Momma, and warm, I dozed off. Momma and I slept an hour more.

Sleeping between them, my back scrunched tight against Momma and my head on Daddy's shoulder was a different warm, a loving warm, Daddy not working, Momma not keeping house, with them living in that tent was the best time in my life, and the worst time in my life.

I liked sleeping in our house. Sleeping alone under three blankets and a goose down comforter, and a pot bellied stove glowing in the living room, I never woke in my bed with a cold foot, but did I ever wake feeling so loved? The love I felt that week in an old tent, made for two, sleeping three, was something defining, something that warmed my soul through the decades, whenever I thought of my Momma, my Daddy.

I thought of out house in St. Petersburg, a nice house; I thought of our house further up the canyon, smaller, simpler, but a nice house. Why were we camping in the cold? Two weeks ago, Daddy in the mine when it started, a man ran through yelling, "Get out!"

Men at the entrance shouted strange noises in English, did Daddy and the other Russians have any idea what they were talking about?

Mikhail shoved a sign in Daddy's hand, for him to carry. He could sound out and pronounce what the strange looking letters said: "On strike!" What did it mean?

When we came to the mine four months earlier, a man stood on the platform by the train with a sign that said, "Welcome Mine Workers of America."

How would we know what it said? If Mikhail had not shouted into the box car in Russian, we would have stayed on the train.

Daddy said, "What's a strike?"

Mikhail explained it to him.

Daddy said, "Cossacks will kill us!"

Mikhail laughed, said, "This is America. No Cossacks. The Union will protect us."

The Union hired Daddy, brought us here, and made sure the company paid us. The Union hired Russian men at the boats in New York, Daddy one of them. He trusted the Union and Mikhail, the gang boss. He liked the idea of a union, of the people having someone to represent them, to look after the interest of the workers.

Daddy said, "Russia would be better with unions."

Russia had a Czar, peasants, and Cossacks---not unions, the Czar communicating with the peasants through the Cossacks; the peasants communicating with the Czar through God. If God heard the peasants, God would speak to the Czar directly as he sipped French wine standing by a marble fireplace in the Winter Palace. If the peasants persisted in screaming for help from God, and the Czar didn't hear God, the Czar sent more Cossacks.

My father had no faith in God hearing peasant screams, nor in God-deaf Czars; he had faith in the Union, Mikhail, and a man in New York speaking directly to the capitalist owner for him. Daddy carried his sign and looked down the road, over the hills, and into the valley below--- no lines of Cossacks marching toward them.

Quietly my Daddy looked to heaven and said, "Thank God, we're in America."

At dawn, a week ago, sleeping in my bed, a noise started, a neighbor screamed. Other shouts came in English. Momma grabbed me, my clothes, and pushed me out the door in my night gown.
Men in brown uniforms stood with rifles in a line. What were they saying? One was yelling. The others pointed their rifles at us. Momma hurried me away in the direction the man in front pointed.

"Momma, what's happening," I said.

"Cossacks, American Cossacks! Run, Marisa, run!"

I ran.

Company thugs forced us from our homes and into tents the first week of the Front Range Coal Strike.

Chapter 2

My Enemas

Momma got away with the things she stuffed in a bed sheet: two blankets, coats, a few clothes, a pan, a pot, and my enema bag. She couldn't leave my enema bag.

Enemas useful for all children, with the prevalence of colds and other childhood diseases, as well as, constipation accompanying growth spurts and high levels of growth hormones, she saved the bag for me. But, more important, I have a problem. I never go on my own---never since I was born. I need my enema bag.

Momma told me, my uncle Boris, a doctor, delivered me. A few days after I was born, I had a huge bowel movement releasing all the waste built up in me during nine months inside my mother, a normal occurrence in newborns, my last normal bowel movement. Within a week I was fussy and constipated. He gave me a high enema. Constipated the next day, and the next, three days later with no bowel movement, he gave me another enema. After a few weeks with no improvement, my uncle told my momma: "Give her a high enema every day."

Every morning, I had one. Momma never missing a day, an enema is part of waking up to me, part of my life since I was born.

Giving me enemas was convenient for my mother at first---no dirty diapers, and toilet training was simple, me learning not to wet myself. Giving me an enema and putting me on the potty got consistent results. Did she need to say, "Good girl!" and reward me for that? She was the good girl, whether I went potty or not wasn't up to me, it was up to her, unless I had diarrhea.

Momma worried.

Uncle Boris didn't have any good answers. Some of our people, other Ashkenazis, having constant problems with constipation, not going for days, then going profusely, but no one like me, I never had a bowel movement without a high enema.

Uncle Boris said, "I don't understand, Sis. She's normal in every other way---except this. It's a curse---but there are worse curses. Having an enema every day will only make her more healthful over a lifetime, reduce the amount of toxins held in her system. As long as she has the enemas properly, increasing her elimination, the enemas will slow her aging rate."

"It's inconvenient, Boris," Momma said.

Half an hour every morning giving me an enema, without an end in sight, was not what Momma expected of motherhood.

Uncle Boris said, "What do you want to do?"

Momma said, "What can I do?"

Prunes, why don't I like prunes? Was it the week Momma fed me prunes with every meal? Three-years-old, I made a mess of myself. Never having a bowel movement on my own, when it started flowing out, it was a unique experience; I didn't try to stop it.

Momma said, "Thank God, she's alright!"

True, with enough prunes, I got diarrhea. As soon as Momma stopped feeding them to me, I stopped going.

Momma tried roughage, laxatives, and rubbing my belly. Anything that gave me diarrhea worked---as long as the diarrhea lasted, then I was back to my usual complete blockage.

My ears perked up anytime I heard of a treatment for constipation, particularly if Momma was part of the conversation. If anyone gave her a new treatment, she tried it. Most of the time, I got diarrhea, but nothing improved my condition.

By the time I started school, Momma's experiments growing rare, I got up, ran to the toilet to empty my bladder, went back to bed, and waited for Momma to give me an enema: every morning before school. Every Sunday and every Sabbath, this was our routine.

She was getting my enema ready the morning the company thugs came. The water warm, she was about to pour it in the bag---screaming started. Instead, looking outside seeing what was happening, the water spilled. She put the bag and the few things she could carry into a bed sheet and grabbed me. We ran. I was fine, no bullet holes, but by afternoon I got cranky. That evening, as soon as the tent was up, Momma warmed water over a camp fire and gave me an enema.

Three weeks later, after Daddy left for the picket line with the other men, I peaked under the tent flap at the pink glow on the cliff face beyond the valley. Dawn light sprinkled the top of a big pine down the clearing, silhouetting it against the dark further below. The tree, golden green against black, welcomed day, needles and branches of life in light, guns of soldiers hired by the company in edge of night below.

Momma would do our laundry on a rock in the creek then help the women fix lunch. After Daddy finished his turn walking the line, we would explore the canyon higher up the mountain, to where big trees ended and only short ones grew. But before any of that, Momma would take care of me. Waiting for my enema, I closed my eyes and snuggled in a ball under two blanket in our tent.

Cold, under two blankets in a tent was not like waiting for my enema in my room, on my bed, under my feather comforter, and my three blankets. Being filled by an enema is best when warm and snuggy. Being warm and snuggy laying on the Fall alpine ground under two thin blankets and no stove takes imagination: remembering Daddy's warm smile as he closed the tent flap, remembering Momma's warm smile as she closed the tent flap, remembering sitting in our living room by our warm stove as an icy wind fluttered the tent flap---lots of imagination. The tent, warm and snuggy mentally, my foot was numb with cold, I made believe I wasn't shivering, and pretended to be relaxed, pretended I was home, warm and snuggy, in our company house.

Our home in the mine's village, was it our home? Not our house, provided to us as long as Daddy worked in the mine, it was our home, the company's house. A common ploy from share cropping to mine working to textile mills, employers own houses. Employees make them homes. In any dispute the first thing employers do is clear the homes, leave families homeless or cold in tents.

My warm bed, I missed my warm bed with a stove in the living room radiating heat through the house, floating in my door and filling my lungs. A living room, a bedroom for Momma and daddy, a storage room big enough to make a bedroom for me, and a kitchen, it was our home, a home with an outhouse in the back that I ran too every morning before and after my enema. Doing what I needed to quickly in the icy outhouse, I hurried back to the warmth of our living room.

Momma in her overcoat climbed in the tent like a three legged Saint Bernard carrying my faithful enema bag in one hand rather than a flask of brandy around her neck. She laid the warm bag on my cold foot. That felt good. My foot not hurting any more, I stopped pretending. I relaxed. Momma moved the bag, hanging it from a nub of a small branch Daddy left on our tent pole for just that purpose. Climbing under the blankets with me, her coat over both blankets, and her body pressed against my back, Momma probed for my anus with the enema nozzle. It went in.

Is there anything like being cold and being heated from inside with a warm enema? Enema water heats like the pot bellied wood stove in our company house filling every room. With no place else to go, heat fills everything inside. Not shivering, I felt vibrating warmth in my anus, then a puddle of warmth in my rectum, then a warm swell moving up my left side. Cold of the ground outside of my abdomen and warm enema inside factored out the cold, made me feel like a turtle lying on a sun warmed flat rock on a summer day.

Relaxed, warm, good feelings of good enemas, there is more than that. Good enemas give strong urges. Strong urges are to relaxed as pot bellied stove hot is to seventy two degrees Fahrenheit. Warm and relaxing, putting me back to sleep, the first part of my enema loosened me. Strong and urgent, surges tightened me, as they tighten everyone. But, different from everyone else, these were my only colonic urges.

My enemas, my only number two toilet training, Momma taught me to hold my enema urges, then go potty. Easy to teach, easy to learn, I only had to remember to hold on during the enemas. Holding on for less than twenty minutes every day, I was out of diapers before I was two years old, except at night to keep the bed dry.

Other kids had to learn to pay attention with urges coming morning, noon, and night. But strong urges send all scampering for the toilets whether driven as designed by nature or pushed by an enema. Having an enema, I was the same as other children having enemas. Diapers changed to toddlerhood, we were the same. Now at ten years old, other than having an enema, other children went on their own, had privacy, didn't need their diapers changed. My enemas, a form of diaper changing, never ended. Momma cared for me as other mommas cared for babies. I couldn't grow out of this stage.

A baby has no thought of this. They go. They are changed. A toddler goes to please mommy, grows up. A ten year old, every morning Momma spread my cheeks, filled me, changed me. I didn't grow up. Dependant on her to have a bowel movement, I needed my Momma more than other children needed theirs. Dependant on her, a closeness between us, a love special and different, an infant-mother bond frozen in time, I was lucky to have a mother like my mother. Like other children with a handicap unshakeable, my wheelchair was my enema bag. Every morning Momma cleaned my colon. The rest of the day I was like any other girl, playing, talking, running, walking, being a kid---but every day is followed by morning, another enema.

With an enema healthful colon waves of urges come and go and ideally don't reach intense levels until the colon is nearly full. With every good enema I have two sets of intense urges: one when the water reaches a spot in my left side, a second when my colon is completely full. With both, water stops flowing up. My rectum and descending colon up to my spot bulge. Would an enema stopped at this point work for me, not filling the rest of my descending colon, my transverse colon, my ascending colon, and my cecum? An easy fill, it would come back as only water. Below this point, my colon is always empty, easily filled. A small, low enema comes back clear, no waste, no effect. One day without a good enema filling my entire colon is uncomfortable, but livable. I feel a growing pressure above the point in my side. By the second day it is a painful bulge. If I go longer pain begins to hurt, sharp pains, a constant ache. Having a high enema, water surging, I squeeze the nozzle until the pressure pushes through the spot in my left side. Once that happens, water gushes higher in me and the urgency passes.

Momma kept it pouring until she felt the enema fill my right side, my cecum, low in my abdomen. Once my entire colon, was completely filled, it was over, the enema worked. It cleaned me out.

All this might have been very exciting had it happened once or twice a year, as enemas did with other children. Happening every day, my roller coaster ride of holding in the strong urges of a well given enema happened every morning. Exciting things that happen every morning aren't exciting---they're routine, like riding the subway in New York to other kids who do it every day.

We stayed in New York a week when we arrived in America. Riding the subway five times, Daddy's eyes sparkled as he hung on to the strap crushed among other men. Momma sat, awestruck, swaying in her seat. The first ride, I held her arm so tight I left finger prints. The fourth ride I watched rock faces in the tunnels race past and reveled in the lurches and sways of the car as it rocketed toward Manhattan.

Trying to stay awake, a boy watched me. Smiling, he asked in English, "Newcomer?"

Not understanding the word, I understood the yawn. This was routine to him.

Answering in Russian, I said, "Isn't it wonderful. In Russia, even in the circus, we don't have rides like this!"

Newcomer, he understood without understanding my words.

All the other people in our carriage were as bored with the ride as the boy, taking that ride every day. The subway exciting and unique to me, enemas not unique, surges and urges were my routine. No one else in my world felt about enemas as I felt: necessary, routine, boring.

Getting my enema ready on our stove was routine, better than the camp fire. Momma liked her routine: firing up the stove, pumping a pail of water from the well, warming a pan, enough for the enema, then waking and fishing me out from under my comforter.

Campfires warm the side facing them. Can ice form on the side facing away from the fire? Momma drank hot coffee, or hot water when there was no coffee, and spun around regularly thawing different curves of her body as the water in the kettle warmed on one side. By the time my enema was ready she had well done spots, and freezing feet. Camp fires don't warm feet when you have them planted on cold ground.

When she did her Saint Bernard impersonation coming in the tent, I drew up my feet keeping them away from hers, avoiding frostbite. I liked planting my cold feet on her warm thighs.

"Marisa, I don't know how you can get such cold feet with them under the covers," she said.

I didn't answer. Her legs were my hot water bottle for my feet. At home, on cold days, she would put a hot water bottle on my feet. Only the enema bag saved, there was no hot water bottle, and I liked my feet on her legs. Nice, touching her made me feel more loved.

The whole enema experience was more loving in the camp with all the intimacy. Waking up between my parents was nice; being held while being filled every morning was nice. At home, Momma held me, but not always. If she was in a hurry it was a bag on a hook, a little back rub, an order to hold it, and she was back in the kitchen. Here, there was time: time for me as there had never been before. Librarians have work to do. Miner's wives have work to do. Mothers in tents pare that down to taking care of a three feet by seven feet tent space and doing their share in the group of families, and spending time with children---one child in my case. I loved it.

The nozzle in me, she held me close to her, our bodies together keeping out the cold. Her arm around me, her breath on my neck, her enema surging in me, it was special, something so routine, so new, so loving that I didn't mind being different, needing enemas in a way no other child in the camp needed them.

"I love you, Momma," I said.

"I love you, Marisa," Momma said.

She held me until my calves began quivering and the enema filled me to the point that the surges became steady pressure, water behind a dam.

Momma kneaded into my right side with her hand and felt my colon. It sloshed, was full. She clamped the clamp, held me until it was time to go.

Enema time was a special, intimate time: a mother daughter time, a time of caring, feeling, surges, holding, and being held. Even if it was routine, it was special---special that day, special in a way I remembered all my life.

"Shoo, go to the toilet, Marisa," Momma patted me on my bottom.

Not looking forward to a trip to cold latrines, a cold board over a ditch in the ground, I didn't want to give up this beautiful moment with my mother.

Momma lifted the covers off me and gave me a nudge.

I slipped out of bed, grabbed my shoes and coat on the way out of the tent. My gown flowing down protecting my dignity as I opened the tent flap, I slipped my coat on. I looked back. Momma was smiling at me from under the covers. I ran for the toilets.

When I came out of the toilet the first time Momma was talking to one of the other women. They were sipping warm cups of water from a kettle on the edge of the campfire.

The other woman said, "Why does Marisa need enemas every day?"

Momma said, "I wish I knew. She was born this way."

The other woman said, "We're from the mountains, many old people. I know three women and one man who take enemas every day who are over 100 years old. It's a good treatment."

Momma smiled, "I'll be happy if my girl lives to be a hundred."

"She will," the other woman said.

I listened. I had another urge and scampered back to the toilet.

The women laughed.

My Mother shouted after me, "I love you, Marisa," the same thing Daddy had said on leaving me that morning.

When I came out again my Mother had gone to join my Father on the picket line.

Chapter 3

English & Working Men

Momma said to Daddy, "Why can't we stay in our home? Why can't you work?"

He thought about it, thought about working deep in the earth covered with black dust, struggling to breathe, the week ending, standing in a line waiting, counting out the money the company bookkeeper gave him; he thought about the last few weeks standing in a line breathing clean air, not working, no payday at the end of the week. He wanted to work, wanted payday. Every week three silver dollars in a can, a can getting heavier, every month he, Momma, and I practiced English. When we could speak English, Daddy and Momma would apply to teach in a school, maybe a college. Momma and I would read books not Tolstoy, but Washington Irving, Mark Twain, and Upton Sinclair, in English. Daddy would keep teaching me mathematics, the same in Russian or English, but in English he would be paid in dollars, more than by my smiles. Until then every week, three silver dollars in a can was savings, money to buy a train ticket to a school, a place where Momma and Daddy's hands would grow soft again, and coal dust would work its way out of his lungs.

Digging in the mine, breathing bad air, ten hours a day in the bowels of the earth, but Saturday afternoon, payday, greenbacks, and clean air, Daddy was ready to work and wasn't sure why the union said he had to strike.

Daddy, a working man in America, did what he was ordered, struck. It was a cause. Following a cause, something inside Daddy, inherited from his father, inside his paternal great-great-great grandfather, a tall, blonde Nordic peasant heard a call. That boy standing tall, marching straight, and meeting the enemy head on, Peter noticed. Peter the Great noticed my ancestor, Daddy's ancestor, made him an officer, a nobleman, one of hundreds who rose with the cause, made Peter, Peter the Great, and created the Russian Empire. He never questioned Peter the Great; he obeyed, marched, stood in lines facing enemies, rose on the coattails of his czar, and the blood of his czar's enemies.

On the picket line, others carried their "on strike" signs like crosses, as if on their way to executions, bearing them, on their shoulders, shovels, not a rifles, not a flags---shovels. Watching Daddy on strike, I looked at him, standing tall, marching; on his shoulder the sign was a rifle, carried for the cause; by his side it was his saber, carried for the cause. It was his time to be like his father, his father in dress whites, gold braid, standing at attention awaiting the order of a descendent of Peter the Great. It was Daddy's time to stand and be what he wanted to be, what his father wouldn't let him be, a military man with a cause, even if he didn't understand what the cause was.

Working people didn't have education, and didn't need to be told why they were striking, any more than a soldier needs to know why he is fighting, unless they are officers privy to information, and they speak the language of their leaders, English in America. Irish miners, knowing English, knew why they were striking; Poles and Russians didn't. Daddy, the son of a long line of military men, stood in line, carried his sign and followed Mikhail as if he were Peter the Great, as if he knew what they were doing.

Mikhail told the men to strike. Daddy struck, did anything Mikhail asked him to do. Mikhail understood some English, but not enough to know why the union leader said they were striking.

In the meeting with Mikhail and the Russians, he said they talked about mini-fits. The union wanted us to have better mini-fits.

One of the men asked, "We're striking for mini-fits? What are mini-fits?"

"Not big fits, little fits, small fits," Mikhail said.

Daddy found the word in the paper handed out by the union. Benefits, what were benefits? He asked a Polish miner, Andre, on the picket line.

Poles and Russians, not natural friends, more often natural enemies: many Poles were refugees, leaving Poland after the failed 1904 Polish uprising. More Poles understood English than did Russians, and most Poles spoke Russian, the official language of Poland as a colony of the Russian Empire. Polish blood having been spilt by my noble ancestor many years earlier making them a colony, keeping them a colony, it was spilt by cousins of my father nine years ago.

Andre smiled at my father, as he once smiled at upper-class Russian officers before answering them.

Andre said, "Alexi, benefits mean a guaranteed ten-hour work day, no more working till you drop at a boss's whim, and one day off every week, and a company doctor treating mining families."

Benefits worth having, one day a week for Daddy, Momma, and me to walk in the forest together, more story time, and good health care, Daddy was striking for Momma and me: benefits, a righteous cause.

All Mikhail actually understood when the union boss talked was, "Here, carry this, and stand over there!"

Mikhail followed orders. Daddy followed him. He said strike, Daddy struck.

One of the men asked when Mikhail was getting his mini-fits. Pointing, laughing, and mini-fits was Mikhail's lot for a few days.

Then the men decided mini-fits were a downward look with the eyes and the face turning red, but Mikhail was their boss. They dropped kidding him the second week of the strike.

Used to work, Daddy missed it. Missing our home, Momma cried. Daddy promised her it would be over soon. He would go back to work, and we would go back to our house. Missing her blankets, her comforter, and time alone with Daddy, Momma hugged him, and cried.

Watching, could I stand and watch? I hugged Momma, and hugged Daddy, and cried. Ten years old, never more than a few feet from Momma and Daddy, when they were in bed, now, I slept between them. I wanted to go home, to sleep in my own bed. They wanted to sleep in their own bed, without me between them.

At home, if I were awake, I listened to them make love. Most of the time, I was asleep before they started, and walls muffled the sound. If I were awake, they didn't know. Privacy at home meant not being able to see, not being between them, interfering with nothing, and hearing everything. I didn't know what they were doing in bed after they put the lantern out, but momma liked it, moaned a lot. In the tent, being between them was wonderful for me, not for them. I saw the look in Momma's eyes as she looked over me at Daddy, and felt in the way.

Momma and Daddy, young, in their early thirties, wanted time to themselves. If Daddy got home early, they sent me with a friend of Momma's. Momma's friend told me not to bother my parents, and stay away from the tent. After they were alone for a few hours, Daddy came for me. Last night, dark before Daddy's face appeared in the campfire light, I was lonely---and cold.

Before the strike, Daddy worked long hours in the mine. Usually long past sunset when he came home, when I was awake, he would read to me by lantern light from Krylov's Fables, or tell me stories in the dark. Some about our homeland, life in Russia, others oral traditions of rabbits, wolves, and animals with human voices, my favorites were about him and Momma, their meeting, their love, their lives. In cracks between stories he looked in my eyes, when my eyes closed, he tucked me in bed. Supposed to be too old for stories, I never grew too old for Daddy's stories. I loved them. Listening to them now, snug between my mother and father; they melted the cold as we went to sleep together. Sometimes I would wake up having missed the end of one of his stories. Other times he would begin to snore before he finished.

He and momma taught me to read, to do math, and things that other kids in the camp never learned to do. We were different from the them, and the same. In the mines they recruited foreigners. My daddy's crew all spoke our language, as did the kids and wives in our section of the company camp, but not the way we spoke it. To Americans we were all Russian, dumb Russians.

At school the teacher said we were all uneducated bumpkins because we didn't know how to read or speak English. Most of the other kids never had gone to school before, but was I uneducated? Were my parents, or most of the other foreign kids, bumpkins? We wanted to learn English, we tried, but English is hard, a difficult language.

Our English teacher, not our school teacher, was Katrina, a teen aged girl who came to America three years earlier with her uncle, and rejoined her family when they came from Russia. She spoke broken English, could sound out American letters and was learning to read English, even though she couldn't read or write Russian, like me.

"Paseba is tank you," she said, writing out thank you.

Daddy said, "You said tank, but you spelled thank you. Th is thuh, not t."

"Yes," Katrina said thinking, Aristocrats, what are aristocrats, educated people, doing here?

My fault that she knew, I told her my Father and Mother both graduated from the university in St. Petersburg, and that Daddy was the son of a count.

Daddy having more time to read to me and teach me after the strike started, both he and Momma were far better educated than my teacher at school, but we weren't nobles or aristocrats. Raised among the academics at the University, both Momma and Daddy spoke with a university refined dialect. I was blending, becoming a peasant with the other children, a college graduates' girl in the tent with my Mother and Father, and not belonging anywhere. Daddy taught me mathematics. He taught mathematics before we came to America and was planning to start me on algebra next year. He already started me on word problems, like the one on temperature and elevation he taught me after the strike began.

"Mathematics is the same in any language," He said, "You can use it here, as well as in Russia."

Momma loved books, was always reading, and read books she got from the University library to me in our country. By the time I was five I could read simple books. At ten I was reading everything---in Russian.

Being in America, hard for us, with no books in our language, Momma and I wrote as much as we could, but only we understood what we were writing. The other Russians, the peasants, could not read---not even Russian. In the camp with no paper or ink to spare, not writing or reading anymore, Momma was lost, walking in circles; me following her.

I had friends to play with, but wasn't getting the social education my parents wanted for me. In Russia, among the children of teachers at the University, we talked about books, challenged each other's knowledge.

Coming to America, Momma let me carry a book, *Kriloff's Original Fables,* well it really wasn't Kriloff, it was Krylov, Ivan Krylov, he worked at the Imperial Public Library in St. Petersburg, the library where my mother worked before the pogrom, but not at the same time, he retired in 1841, died in 1844. My mother was born in 1882. I read from his book all the time. Olga, a girl living next door in the company camp, saw it.

Olga said, "What's this, a book?"

"Of course," I said, not realizing she hadn't seen many books.

"You have a book?" She looked for pictures.

"Here," I pointed to the first section, and started reading.

" '*The chest:*
It often happens that our brains
We rack, and take most wonderous pains
When we need only try, a guess
And use the simplest means to win success.' "[i]

Olga looked at me as if I were a hybrid, something between the Czarina, and a witch. "You can read?"

"Yes, my Momma taught me."

Olga ran home and told the other children. At first they would come to me and ask me to read something from my book, then they stayed away. An enema every day, and reading, I was strange, different, not like them. In America no one was like me.

Lonely, I stopped reading where they could see me, and tried to join in their games. After the strike one thing was easier. My book didn't make it, left in the house, I never saw it again. In the tent, not so different, we were all surviving, books, toys, and our past lives gone, cold days, colder nights, and survival. Read or not, we were in a foreign country, unable to talk, unable to read, and even our alphabet was unintelligible to Americans.

Following the academic passions of my parents was going to be difficult for me in America, at least until we spoke English enough so that my father and mother could get academic jobs, then it would be better for us.

Daddy saw our sadness and tried to make us happy and was paying special attention to us. Our minds unfed by the fountain of knowledge at the University, our stomachs rumbling from a diet of mostly potatoes since the strike began; my parents remaining hunger, their love, being fed with Daddy's shorter hours on the picket line, and longer hours alone with her in the tent.

The days, Daddy not working, we would walk into the woods to look at the trees, mountains, and beauty of the land, and each other. Walking our special time, Daddy, Momma, and I walked. In St. Petersburg there were parks beautiful parks, one with a statue of Ivan Krylov on a base with illustrations of four types of his fables, a memory I cherished as a school girl. My earliest memory, looking up at that statue, Daddy rocking me, Momma sitting by him reading from Krylov's fables; my fondest memory, following them in the woods, watching them holding hands, a ray of sunlight percolating through the pines lighting my Mother's face, my Father smiling down at her, Daddy kissed her.

Watching them, I listened to breezes in the trees, watched clouds roll into mountain peaks and felt leaves and pine needles give beneath my feet. I was happy. They were happy.

At night, after he and Momma had their time alone in the tent, Daddy came and got me. My feet already cold, they put me between them to sleep so I would be warmest. Daddy's feet like ice in the mornings, he always kept the covers thickest over me. As momma slept, I noticed Daddy ease more covers her, then scoot under the edge of those that were left. Is that why he woke me with his shivering in the night?

Living through the strike hard, living in the cold hard, living with my parents in love painted a picture of heaven only hardship can frame.

My parents loved me. They loved me and each other. This is what I remember most about them.

Chapter 4
Judaism

Calloused hands, a face covered with coal dust, and unable to communicate with Americans, Daddy was another stupid foreigner. No one, outside the Russian workers, knew he was educated. We were all stupid foreigners. Hard for my parents, as hard as learning English, we missed being treated with respect. English was alien, another world. Even the alphabet was different. My third alphabet, we used the Cyrillic alphabet in Russia and Momma's brother taught me Hebrew at Sabbath school.

Both my parents finished university in St. Petersburg before a wave of persecution, a pogrom. Anti-Semitism swept Russia in waves, every generation a new wave, every generation a new wave of refugees heading east, west, any direction rumors of religious tolerance filtered through.

My Father's job gone with the purge, he was sick of it, ready to leave. The best rumors, America: no established state church, freedom of religion part of the Bill of Rights, and welcoming immigrants, my Father wanted to be in America, not Russia. Yet, my Father always loved Russia. It was Russia that didn't want him and us.

Asking my Grandfather was easy. Daddy loved him and that love had drawn out my Grandfather's check book before. However, Daddy wanted to see him, to be with him, not to leave him and our homeland, to feel his father loved him, and was proud of him. Asking my grandfather was hard, not because my Father feared rejection of his asking for money, but because he knew my Grandfather would say, "Yes!"

My Father unwelcome at the front door of my Grandfather's house, he went to the servant's entrance and wait to be asked inside. My Grandfather visiting us in our home was more acceptable, but our family living in the same town was a conflict for my Grandfather and his ambitions. A son, one to be proud of living within sight of the top floor of his manor house, the commandant looked, but did not visit. A commandant hoping to be a fleet admiral, and well married, my Grandfather had enough money for three steerage fares to America, a place more distant, more suitable for us. Seeing us off at the boat, my Grandfather smiled and waved, never communicating with us again, despite my father's letters to him.

An established member of society, my Grandfather was an Orthodox Christian, a low ranking nobleman, a rising naval officer. Would he have married my grandmother if his family had let him? They didn't, better my father, their grandson, be a bastard than for their son to marry a Jew. I saw my grandfather three times. He gave me a gold chain when I was born. Daddy pointed him out to me riding in a parade, his uniform's gold braid sparkling in the sun, and he waved goodbye to me as the ship moved away from the dock the day we left Russia. My grandmother lived her life loving him, dreaming of him, wanting him. When she died he sent flowers, didn't come to the funeral.

My Grandmother told my Father about his Father, her love, the tall sailor, dashing in his officer's uniform, so brave in battle, and that he would come to see him when his ship was in port. He never came. My Father never stopped waiting. And at age ten he waited at the docks, watched the ships, and found his Father.

Daddy said, "Captain Stralinov?"

"Yes"

"I'm your son, Alexander, the son of Anna Jewinski."

The captain looked back, and around, was sure. He was alone. Then he took the boy in his arms, "Alexander, you're a fine looking boy."

Feeding him a hot meal, after meeting him, there was closeness for a time; then there was a countess, one with a large rambling estate south of St. Petersburg, a manor house in town, and a daughter in need of a husband. She came between them. Peasant bastards, a common occurrence among nobles of all nationalities, was tolerated, but open friendship, not so tolerated, especially when legitimate heirs were born, as three were over my father's teen years.

Misfortune coupled with fortune, my grandfather's rise into the higher ranks of nobility made it possible for him to provide more than had been available on his naval salary. Doors opened for my father: a good school with full tuition, an apartment for his mother, and the presence of a tall gray-eyed naval officer in the audience when my Father earned the prize for best in mathematics. The door that never opened to him was the door to his Father's home. Nor ever did my grandfather visit my Father as a boy, or come to our home when he became a man.

In class his teacher called out, "Mister Jewinski" then looked with incredulity at my father. Daddy didn't look like a Jew. He was tall and blond, with gray eyes, like my grandfather. The Russians said Jews should have black hair and eyes---and were short. My father would have been the Orthodox Christian he appeared to be, if anyone had asked, but they didn't. He was a Jew, a tall, blond-haired Jew.

My name is Stralinkov! Daddy muttered to himself every time he heard his name, Jewinski, but he never said it aloud. He was a Jew, who didn't want to be a Jew.

When Momma and Daddy married, she had to beg him to marry her in the synagogue. He wanted a civil ceremony.

At Ellis Island Daddy waited in line.

The immigration officer asked the man one ahead of him, "What's your name?"

"Feinstein!" The short dark man proudly said.

"Yours?" The officer said to the next man.

"Askenazi!" A taller man said.

"Another Feinstein!" the immigration officer said changing his name to one easier to spell and pronounce.

"Yours?" The officer said to my Father.

"Alexander---Stralinkov!" My Father gave them his father's name, not his Jewish name--- "and my wife, Sarah and daughter, Marisa."

The immigration officer said, "Alexander---Alexander Stratford, I like that. You like it?"

He looked at my father.

"It sounds English," Daddy said.

"It's English. You're tall, blonde, look English enough to me. Learn to speak the language and you will go further as a Stratford than a Stralinkov. If you're changing your name, you may as well do it right, Alexander Stratford."

"Alexander, Alexander Stratford---write it out for me, so I remember it."

The officer smiled, one of a handful who spoke our language, he knew the problems we would face and gave us a name to bypass them. Or was it the few bills he had been slipped by a ship's officer, a final gift from a Russian commandant, who wanted this chapter of his life closed with finality—and the best for his illegitimate son.

We were no longer Jews, and no longer Russians as far as my father was concerned. Momma cried, but didn't say anything. No one would know unless one of us admitted being Jewish. My father, a dogged student, would speak English like an American, if things went as he planned. Most of the people getting off the boat that day, like us, were Jews, remained Jews.

My father saw another tall, blond man recruiting for the mines with a sign in Russian. Gentiles were gathering around him, mostly burly

Russian peasants. The sign said: "Workers needed---No Jews!" Most of the men couldn't read the sign, only recognized Russian lettering and knew it had something to do with us.

The recruiter repeated every two minutes, "No Jews!"

As he said this some of the men would fall away. Not my father.

That was what my father wanted. We went with the Gentiles.

Momma obeyed her husband and never mentioned being Jewish to other people, but that day she cried all day.

I asked, "Momma, aren't you happy to be in America?"

"Of course, Marisa, I'm happy," she said, continuing to sob.

She taught me things privately that helped me know who I was. She understood my father, and the pain he suffered, but she was proud of our people, even if she couldn't tell anyone.

Once in the mining camp we were practicing reading and writing Hebrew and one of the other women noticed the lettering.

She said, "Jewish words?"

Daddy burned the papers, the smoke ascending from our chimney toward a gray sky framed by rocky wall of mountains scratching the lower clouds.

We didn't look different. I was fair, my hair was golden, and I had my father's gray eyes. My mother, people asked her if she were Jewish sometimes, but she was fair skinned, blue eyed, and people weren't sure. No one questioned that my father was American and Aryan. When we were in town, people smiled and spoke to him in English, and only began to show contempt when he couldn't answer them. The people we watched from the train going west looked so nice. It wasn't until they spoke to us, or we tried to speak to them that life was difficult for us.

If my Daddy had been able to speak English, we could have had a good life. Our good life was in a tent among other foreigners striking for better mini-fits on a cold fall day.

Chapter 5
Other Enemas

I was a skinny little kid, a skinny little Jew. No one in the camp knew the Jewish part. Everyone with eyes knew the skinny part. My golden hair bounced as I ran. The women knew I had just had an enema, having seen Momma take it in the tent for me. When I got to the toilets there was one place open, between two women. I took it quickly and relaxed again as the enema poured out.

One of the women asked me, "Another enema, Marisa?"

I nodded.

They knew I had a problem, but enemas were very common treatments among our people, and no different here. I relaxed and let it out.

At the end of the latrine tent, Katrina, the teen age girl who was teaching us English was waiting to have an enema. Being shy about it, she blushed every time any of the women looked at her.

The one sitting next to me on the toilets, motioned to her, and pointed at me. "She has an enema every morning!"

The girl blushed more. I put my legs up and pushed them into my abdomen to push more water and waste out of me. I had to do this too, without the extra pressure; it wouldn't all come out.

Katrina spoke to me, "You have an enema every day?"

"Unhuh," I answered. "Since I was a baby. I can't go without an enema."

She had a look, a sorry for me look. Did I see any reason to be sorry for me? I was healthy. I just had to have enemas to go to the bathroom. In every other way I was perfect. I didn't know what it was like to wake up and not have an enema. It was a normal way to live to me.

I told her enemas don't hurt, and they make you feel good. "You'll do fine!"

She blushed again.

Two minutes later, she was lying on a cot, her dress off, blushing more as the nurse worked between her bare cheeks, under a single wool blanket. She shivered. Nina, the lady giving the enema, a lady about the age of my mother, her husband had taken their children, as he usually did, to the picket line with him so she could give enemas to the other women.

I was taking a break from the latrine tent as my colon rumbled: the enema moving down from my cecum and upper bowel. Out of the tent, a thin layer of flannel over my bottom, I stood near the fire, the heat cooking my buttocks. It felt good. I rocked from one foot to the other and turned around to warm my front. Getting the rest of the water to come down so I could get it out, I went back in the latrine tent after cooking my rear one more time. A hot bottom on a cold toilet felt better than a cold bottom on a cold toilet. No one stayed longer in the latrine area than needed. The latrines were cold and smelled bad.

    Less crowded this time on the bench, I let the rest of my enema out and watched as the girl struggled to get in the whole bag. She was having a hard time of it, and was begging her nurse to let her go. Was it because she was too cold? She didn't have a momma to snuggle up to and keep her warm.

    The lady giving the enema gave many enemas. Why else would a cot be in the latrine tent? Seeing Nina in the camp heading to the toilet tent with one of the other ladies, she usually gave them an enema when they got there.

    I hadn't seen this young lady take an enema before, but I had watched many of the women have them from Nina. No privacy in the camp, if you had an enema from the nurse, it was always in the latrine tent, and anyone using it watched you struggle to get all the water in your bowels. Katrina breathed harder as Nurse Nina coaxed her. Eventually she got it all in and the nurse took the nozzle out of her bottom.

    I was one of the few who had never had an enema from her, momma giving me all of mine. The enema lady was good at it. Katrina was trembling and her tummy was bulging.

    Katrina couldn't wait, she sprang up and made a dash to sit by me and spew her enema out. The nurse would have to give her another one in a few hours. Right then she wasn't embarrassed, just desperate to let it out: she was thinking about the water she had in her and making it to the toilet bench to sit by me and let it out. As she did, I saw the wave of relaxation spread over her face, as the enema exploded out of her. Relaxed, she smiled at me. Relaxed, I smiled at her. I was done. She would be there at least twenty minutes getting her's out. I went back to the tent to dress, on my way stopping at the stove and getting in line with the others to have some bread and gravy. This morning there was a piece of jerky for me too! Always hungry after my enema, I gobbled the food.

    Dressed, I came out of the tent and eyed the company men on the rise above the camp. There were a lot of them, more than usual. Not paying any attention to them, I was licking the bowl of the last of the gravy. Katrina came out of the latrine tent and passed me. We exchanged smiles again.

"I do feel better," she told me.

The enema bags in use more since the strike. It was the food. All we had was flour and dried meat---no roughage in our diet. I never noticed the difference. I got washed out every morning, no matter what I ate, but others did. Virtually everyone was having constipation problems, headaches, and general grouchiness. Enemas were much needed by every one. Momma even gave daddy one the day before.

Chapter 6

American Cossacks

The company men, milling about more than usual, formed a line. A machine gun began to rattle as smoke rose from the hill.

They were shooting---shooting at us!

One woman and her baby fell on the ground, a bullet through both of them, blood gushing. Soldiers concentrated fire on the picket line where men were, but increasingly shot at the camp, women and children. Company men, on horseback, rode down on the camp. Katrina, who had just had the enema, stood, a look of terror on her face as a company man rode up on her.

She fell to her knees, started screaming, "Please! Please!"

He pointed his pistol, fired.

She fell, still screaming, "Please!"

People running, women and children bleeding and dying around me, what should I do?

I ran to Katrina and tried to help her up. She was hurt, but not too badly, a bullet in her arm. Running, stumbling, panicked, we ran to a cleft in the ground behind a bush, under a rock jutted out, providing a concealed place, a place I had used for hide-and-seek two days earlier.

Hidden, we watched---horrible. A group of children in the center of the camp huddled together in the open.

One of them, a small blond boy, stood, yelled, "Please!" in English, held his arms up.

Others shouted, "Paseba!" Please in Russian.

They killed them.

Company guards stopped and killed each of them, one at a time.

It didn't last long---minutes, but it seemed forever. Katrina and I were quiet as we saw our people murdered. If the company men saw us, they would murder us too.

The strikers and their families, wives and children, were foreign, alien. We were no better than Indians to the soldiers. None of us knew Americans would feel this way about us, but from books, I knew how they felt about Indians. A long tradition from the Indian wars: the killing of women and children, as well as men, unless the soldiers wanted the women for pleasure or to take as wives when there were too few white women for marrying, Indians were subhuman, excess sheep on overgrazed land, live stock to be culled.

Culling skinny or sickly cows is simple; people are different, not as simple. I was told by a teacher from the Cherokee reservation in Oklahoma, that this tribe survived in such numbers, not because they were intelligent. Their chief in the 1800s was a graduate of Oxford University in England. Not for their size or strength, but their appeal: nice smiles, beautiful eyes, women with curves and men with shoulders. The reason many Americans are part Cherokee, a more European look, Cherokees are a handsome people by Caucasian standards, both Cherokee men and women. When white settlers in early America had no source of white women, the Cherokee nation was a favorite hunting ground for wives, pretty wives. Settlers most often worked out an arrangement, or if no arrangement, killed the men, older women, and children, and, either way, took pretty young women home with them for wives. Other tribes, less attractive to white people, fared less well.

The guards felt the same way about us; they killed everybody, until they tired of killing. Nothing we could do to protect ourselves, no one in the camp had a gun, and even if we had guns, would it have made a difference? The company men were experienced soldiers, had pistols, repeating rifles and a machine gun. A few gray haired sergeants and officers had been in the Indian campaigns. The commander of the militia was with Reno at the Battle of the Little Big Horn and rode with Custer during the slaughter of the Indian women and children the year before Custer was killed.

Custer knew if you killed their families, the braves would lose the will to fight. But, how is Custer is remembered? Isn't it for bravery, not butchery? Indians who knew him remembered him differently than those who read dime novels about him in New York and Washington. Those stories were of a heroic soldier, physically courageous in battle, verbally courageous in peace time, making more enemies with words than he did with bullets. Leading more charges than any other Northern general in the Civil War, there was no question of his heroism, but neither *brilliant* nor *sane* appeared in communications about Custer.

No brilliant or sane general seeks out the opportunity to charge. Custer did. He got more of his own men killed charging than any other Union general. Spoiling the hopes of both men in blue and gray, expecting to see his lifeless body carried from the field with the legion of men he led to their deaths, Custer survived every charge unscathed. The Union almost lost the war because of a lack of such courage and charges by more timid

Union generals. His example and heroism inspired others and moved the Union cause forward. Union leaders considered him a fool---a brave fool, a useful fool.

Everybody in New York and Washington read about the long, golden hair of twenty-three-year old General George Armstrong Custer waving in the wind, as he charged Confederate position after Confederate position. But it was clear that if the Union had had more brave generals like Custer, the South would have won the war by sheer attrition. One Custer was good; two, and there would now be a Confederate States of America.

After the war, special places were needed to assign such reckless and less than brilliant heroes. The far western plains were chosen for him, mostly because we did not have Hawaii in our control at the moment and Nebraska was as far from Washington as he could be assigned and not endanger the interest of the United States.

He continued to charge; charging always working best against undefended positions, his most successful charges were against unarmed Indian villages when the men were away hunting. There, opposing not a nation armed, organized, and in sedition, but Indian nations, poorly armed, disorganized, and trying to survive, he is not remembered for heroism, wise or unwise. He is remembered for killing women and children, slaughtering villages, and destroying American worlds; worlds other Americans would never know.

The charge that worked most poorly is what is remembered of George Armstrong Custer now. He charged that last time when the braves were home at the Little Big Horn river. Even George realized near the end that charging thousands of armed Indians with two-hundred and eight soldiers was not his brightest idea. He tried to cut and run, but didn't make it. They caught up with him and what was left of his troops a few miles away on a rolling hillside. If Custer could have, he would have killed all the Indians, including the women and children. As it was, they killed him and his two hundred and eight men. Custer is remembered as a martyr and hero for this sacrifice! If he had succeeded in killing all the Indians and their families, it would have been remembered as another successful campaign on his way to being president.

We were lucky, the company men killed a lot of people but quit before they killed us all. Would Custer have been disappointed with them? After they stopped shooting from the distance and came in close, the men started walking away, one at a time---after they killed the kids at the center of the camp. Even bad men seem to be bothered by killing little kids, particularly when those kids are the same race and have the same blue eyes and fair skin as their own children. Easier for Custer's white soldiers to kill dark-skinned, flat-faced women and babies, they killed whole villages including all the squaws, children, and infants. Blue eyed, white children were different for blue eyed, white soldiers. And being white, we weren't looked on by the local people in the same way as they looked at Indians, either.

As we learned English, more of us had begun to make friends in the local community. And the labor movement was beginning to be accepted and supported by Americans. Labor views were printed in newspapers, and soldiers killing workers did not inspire the romance of the Indian wars, against people with no English-speaking writers telling their story. This murderous rampage was covered by the press. It was one of the last against union men and their families by soldiers on company pay.

As I watched the last man walk over the ridge and disappear, I didn't know what to do. Katrina had passed out. I got a blanket from a nearby tent and covered her. Leaving her, running, I had to find my Momma. Afraid, I ran to where I thought she would be, but I couldn't find her. There were dead people everywhere. On the picket line, there was a stillness, a quiet, no voices speaking, no Momma calling me. Two people tossed and groaned. One man, not hurt, sat on the ground, silent. I saw Nurse Nina's husband and her son, dead in a pool of blood. Nina ran past me, falling between them screaming, hugging her husband, her boy, and praying for them, begging God for it not to be them. She needed help, more than I, more than anyone could give.

I couldn't stay. I needed Momma. As I looked among the pile of bodies, I saw my father's coat. I ran.

I screamed, "Daddy! Daddy!"

He never moved. As I got to him, I saw why. His back was covered with blood. Underneath I saw my mother's dress. Neither of them moved. I stopped, held my breath. Then I lay down beside them. Wet in their blood, I held my mother's hand and huddled as close to them as I could, not crying. I wanted to be with them, between them, them holding me. No one noticed me for a long time. I closed my eyes not letting my parents go. My mother's hand, warm at first, cooled. They stiffened. They made rumbling noises.

Hours later someone touched me. I looked up. He jumped back.

"She's alive," he shouted, "I found a live one!"

He took me away from my mother, away from my father.

Holding me, the man, who survived on the picket line near my parents, told me: my father tried to protect my mother by covering her with his body. The company men killed him first, and when they saw Momma move, they shot through him to kill my mother!

A woman came and took me away.

"Momma, Daddy," I screamed, as I broke away and ran from her, back to where Momma and Daddy lay.

How could I live without my mother? My colon couldn't work without her. I should have died with her, beside her, under my Father trying to protect me too. Why was I alive without my mother? Without her who would teach me literature, Hebrew, to be a woman? Why was I alive without my father? How could I study, learn, be the woman, the intelligent woman he was raising, without him, without his questions, without his answers? Why did I live and my Momma and Daddy die? How could I live without them?

I wanted to be with them, wanted to go with them.

"Please Momma, please Daddy, take me with you!"

One arm around my Father, the other around my Mother, I had to be pulled away from my parents. My world was gone.

Chapter 7

Nurses

Buried in rows, no tombstones, a slab of wood with painted names by the first grave, I never saw my parents buried, never got to say goodbye, never knew which graves among the rows were theirs, nor did any of the twenty-two orphan children know the exact graves of their parents. Lost among forty seven graves, two were listed on the central slab as Alexander and Sarah Stratford, not Stralinov, nor Jewinski---Stratford. My Daddy was not a college professor, not the son of an Orthodox Christian, a naval officer and a Jewish mother; my Momma was not an educated woman, the sister of a doctor and a rabbi. Not Russian, not Jewish, Stratfords, buried in a foreign land without their real names on a group tombstone, they were American Christians buried among Russians and Poles.

I was American, a blonde Russian girl, my mother's blood in my hair, taken to town, the blood washed out, dressed in an American dress, and taken to an American orphanage. Twenty-two of us put on mats on the floor to sleep, some cried. Babies, older children, and teenagers cried for their parents, cried like wolf pups in Siberia winter, a minus forty wind blowing and no mothers to nurture us, no fathers to protect us. No mother to snuggle, no mother to warm away the cold, I never expected my mother to die---ever. My mother alive before my existence began, I expected her to live forever, couldn't believe she was gone. I didn't cry. I listened. Steady whimpers, howls against the cold, hopeless howls, peasant cries to God in heaven, to a Czar in Washington, did he hear?

Rattling windows, a Colorado wind off the mountains whistled in the eaves. The sound of agony was not heard one foot beyond the door. Tears froze in my blue eyes, a smooth surface like the mountain lake two thousand feet above our camp, tearless, I lay watching the wood stove in the center of the room. Stoked, glowing orange, it didn't heat this cold. I shivered. My heart was outside in our tent, the wind shaking the canvas, laying between my parents, huddled, growing colder with them. I felt ice, the cold of their grave. My heart a frost choked piston pumping Arctic blood, I cooled to a temperature no fire could warm. Not crying, under a brown army blanket, I covered my head, I didn't want to be in America. I wanted to be home in St. Petersburg, Russia, going to sleep with my mother reading me a story from a book from the Imperial Public Library.

Forced to get up, I curled in a corner wrapped in my blanket, my head covered. I greeted the first day of my life without the reflection of the sun in Momma or Daddy's eyes, without running to the toilet and coming back, waiting for Momma to give me an enema. I drew into a knot, not functioning, not wanting to function, not wanting to live, but living.

The second day, the physical pain began, cramping, a bulge, the knot of my whole body shrinking to a knot in my left abdomen. I needed an enema. Yesterday, not thinking about enemas, I had a routine. I woke up, went to the toilet, and urinated. Momma prepared the enema. I came back to bed. She gave it to me. Yesterday was the first day I missed having an enema in five and a half years. An enema was part of every morning, like the sun coming up, like the smile in Momma's eyes. She gave me enemas. Who else would give me an enema?

Katrina, the girl I had helped lay beside me when we slept. I had touched her hand. Asleep, her arm in a sling, she winced and turned away from me. Now she watched me sitting in a corner, holding my side, rocking.

She asked, "Have you had an enema today, Marisa?"

"No!" I said wincing.

"Can you go to the toilet?"

I looked at her, didn't answer.

Didn't she know I couldn't go without Momma---without an enema?

I had to go to the toilet, and soon, the pain crept down my side, fading, then coming back in waves.

Katrina said, "Go to the nurse."

I had watched the nurse in the camp give enemas. In the orphanage, would a nurse give me my enemas, of would I sit in the corner, remain silent and let the pain swell until my bowel burst and let them bury me with Momma and Daddy?

Katrina took my hand, led me. She read the signs, found the infirmary.

A gray haired nurse in a white uniform waited.

I explained I was constipated, but she didn't understand Russian. All the kids were traumatized; she assumed, without understanding anything I said, that I was constipated. I found out later that when a kid came to her infirmary, she always gave them an enema. She got down the enema can. I recognized it. She was going to give me an enema!

"Dah, Paseba! (Yes, Please!)" I said out loud in my language, grateful she was taking care of me.

She turned, looking at me with an evil stare. Swinging her hand back, she hit me. I flew across the room and bounced off the wall. My mouth hurt. My mouth bled. One of my teeth was loose.

Why?

Katrina screamed, "She said, yes, please!" at the nurse in English.

A woman, I don't know who she was, stood at the door.

I didn't understand any of it. I was trying to hide under a table from the evil woman. The other woman said something I didn't understand. The other woman took me and the nurse to the dining room. A big man in a suit sat in the chair at the head of the table eating with a group of men. Putting down his carving knife, he chewed a bite of beef as he listened to the woman. He wiped his mouth with a napkin. He had fire in his eyes. He approached the nurse, towering over her.

One of the men in the room would tell me the words that were spoken years later.

The director said, "She said yes, please! Then you hit her?"
He bent down and looked at my mouth. My tooth was broken. He was angry. I saw it in his eyes. I was shaking, afraid.

The nurse said something about me being a stupid, little foreigner. The big man looked at me. More fire in his eyes. Afraid, I tried to crawl away. He turned his eyes from me, stood up, and walked to the nurse.

His big hand came back. I saw it hit as he backhanded her in the mouth knocking her to the floor. Blood dripped from her mouth, and one of her teeth lay on the floor. His Masonic ring hit it, knocking it out.

The anger in his face didn't fade. She stayed on the floor. She was afraid.

It was a memorable event without knowing the words. Knowing the words later helped clarify what happened.

The director of the orphanage told her with the cool of a winter sea breeze in St. Petersburg, "You're fired!"

Fired, and her severance pay used for my dental bill, she had no money to leave town. The director helped. He had a plan as she made her exit, two of the men holding her arms. The director sent another man to clear her room, stuffing all her things in a potato sack. That night, they tossed her, and her belongings, in an unused cattle car at the freight yard and helped her to travel to another state as a hobo.

The sheriff told her never to come back again. The director advised her that if she gave him as a reference: he would swear out a warrant for her arrest for stealing the potato sack.

The big man had been to the camp a few days before the massacre. He had played chess and lost to a little boy, who could not speak one word of English. The boy's father had died of pneumonia a few days earlier. The orphanage director wanted to take him to the orphanage, but his mother, crying, kept him and her other children.

He and his sisters were among those killed when the company guards surrounded the children in the center of the camp and executed them. The big man found them, was outraged, but the company had left no one for him to confront except one lieutenant, one slow getting out of town. The big man and sheriff had found him on the street, and literally kicked him out of town. The officials had blood on their boots as they poured the lieutenant on the train with multiple broken ribs, a broken arm and a boot print where his front teeth had been.

Not all Americans as heartless as the nurse and company goons, orphans were taken in, protected. The goons fired and sent away, not one of them went to court, or paid for what they had done to my mother, father, and the other people they murdered.

But the days when men like Custer could ride through the West murdering women and children and be proclaimed heroes for it were almost gone. This time the people spoke to the Czar, the President here, and the company, shamed by the killings, settled the strike. This nurse's abuse of me came just as the men were discussing this over lunch.

The nurse had done the wrong thing at the wrong time and said the wrong thing to the orphanage director.

The next day, Nina, the nurse from the camp, was in the nurse's station. She hugged me when she saw me walk in. I wrapped my arms around her neck, not letting her go.

She said in Russian, "Marisa, you need an enema?"

I said, "Dah, Paseba!"

She understood.

A half a quart into the enema, I was full: my side stuck.

She said, "Is that all you take, Marisa?"

"No, I have a spot in my side. It doesn't work unless the water gets above here." I pointed. "Let me hold it a minute---till it opens up."

I breathed deep, tried to relax. Three days of no enema and it was hard to get my spot open. My colon was not letting the enema go up.

Nurse Nina reached around, felt my abdomen, felt a soft fullness of my ascending and transverse colon, felt the lump in my descending colon. A hard, painful bulge on my left above my spot and bulging with water below it, I couldn't relax.

"You are different, Marisa." She began rocking me.

It hurt at first. As I struggled to hold the enema in, a cold shiver ran into the bulge and up into my side below my ribs. It opened. I felt the enema flooding higher in my colon. The urgency to go shifted to a pain in my colon as the water stretched my already dilated colon above my spot. I shook with pain. It eased. I relaxed. The water move further up, mixing. The pressure in my rectum dissolved. She started giving me more water and filled me until I thought I would burst, my legs quivering.

She didn't hold me or make me feel loved like momma, being very businesslike about it, as she had been in the camp. She knew what she was doing. Afterwards, I felt better. I don't know why it happened then, but after the first enema, as she prepared my next one, I had to be close to her.

I walked behind her as she mixed cold and hot water in the enema can, adjusting the temperature. I wrapped my arms around her, and started to sob. I hadn't cried after the murders. Now I couldn't stop.

She turned.

I sobbed out, "Momma! Momma!"

She held me.

"My baby!" she said.

I wanted my mother, my father. I cried. She held me. She wanted her dead children, her dead husband. She cried.

I stayed in the infirmary and wouldn't leave her that day. The director tried to take me to class. I cried. Nina held me. The director patted me on the head, letting me stay.

Two days later, Nina asked the director if she could have me.

I moved into Nina's room permanently, was her girl. Another day with her and she walked me to my class; letting her hand go, I stayed.

Momma Nina was waiting for me outside the class when the door opened.

Chapter 8

The Orphanage Infirmary

Momma Nina had a room adjoining the infirmary. We shared it. I slept in her bed for weeks, then she got me a single bed and set it up across from hers.

At first, English sounded awful, a language with odd sounds. Momma Nina talked to me in Russian, as did Katrina and the other Russian orphans. There were twelve of us, the first few weeks we ran to each other and formed a knot, not speaking to the other children. But we were different ages, assigned to different dormitories and classes. In my class, the one Russian boy, Igor and I became friends. The teacher noticed, moved him to one end of the classroom, me to the other. Neither of us had anyone to talk too.

I learned *hello* and said it to everyone who spoke to me. I already knew *stupid Russian*. The more I said *hello*, the more I heard *stupid Russian*. *Hello* is not a good response to *how are you*, and every other question, at least that's what Katrina told me.

"If they say *how are you?* say *wonderful*," Katrina said.

I learned a new word, a new string of words. I was the *wonderful, stupid Russian girl*.

Putting together a few things, I came up with *I not stupid! I smart!*

The teacher put it on the board.

She said, "This sentence doesn't have a verb. Sentences need a verb. Marisa say *I am not stupid! I am smart!*"

Even the crazy alphabet with the funny shaped letters was beginning to make sense.

I learned *I can play tag, You're it,* and *duck.* If you are playing tag in the same area the boys are playing ball, you can get a knot on your head if you don't know *duck.* I learned that. Momma Nina couldn't fix the knot; but it was gone in three days.

Three months after my first horrendous night at the orphanage, I understood most of what was said, and could give simple, if not grammatically correct, answers.

By spring I spoke, read and heard English. I didn't even speak Russian unless someone spoke Russian to me first.

We Russian kids shared a common and horrible past, it bonded us, and we never forgot, but being kids, we grew out of it, became Americans, English speaking Americans.

Katrina already spoke English and was our unofficial leader through that first winter. Almost old enough to be a mother, she took that role more often than any fourteen-year-old girl should have to. From class to class she was the go between for the school and the Russian students and an unofficial mother to most of the Russian kids, especially the little ones, who couldn't speak any English.

America was, and is, an immigrant society. The orphanage and the region had a mix of European settlers. The Indians who once owned all the land were herded into reservations. We never saw them. Their languages were dying, unheard, disrespected even on their reservations. Less than two thousand Indians lived in Colorado. In our towns grownups spoke German, English, Danish, Russian, and Polish: the full gamut of European languages. Some areas became gathering grounds for different groups. Where ever they settled, like the Indians, their languages faded and were replaced by English. Our town might have been a Russian had it not been for the massacre. The word spreading, Russians avoided immigrating to ground wet with Russian blood, but about 20 families made us a good minority.

I felt sorry for others. One boy, a Dane, was alone. His mother died on the boat coming from Denmark. His father was killed three days before the massacre. A lone Danish speaker in a foreign country, he learned English faster than I or my group because no one could understand him in his mother tongue. Fortunately for him he understood German, there were some Germans, but they didn't speak German, they spoke English, and, for some reason, the Danish boy did not want to talk to them. In class or out they would speak a few German sentences to give him an answer and go back to English.

Katrina felt sorry for him, and was always trying to talk to him. With a Russian accent, Katrina had a harder time speaking with him than native English speakers, or Germans, but she didn't give up. She kept smiling at him. He understood smiles.

Months went. We all understood each other by the time brown earth appeared between snow blankets. We understood the word *cold*. It was cold transiting to hot. Cold days mixed with warm, kids went out without coats: feet dry in arctic cold became wet in melting snow. These transitions, times of increased infection, kids got colds. Beds filled in the infirmary. Momma Nina worked harder. I worked harder.

I didn't get sick that year. I didn't get sick most years. Was it the regular enemas? Maybe I was just healthier than other kids. Whatever, I went years and never have a cold.

Katrina, lucky too, was not sneezing or feverish. Her dorm mother sent her to the infirmary, constipated again. The Danish boy, with a cold, had taken up residence in the bed next to the girls beds in the infirmary the day before.

A one room infirmary, girls on one end and boys on the other, what sort of building was the infirmary in? Built for a school, the orphanage was an afterthought. The classrooms were big rooms, eight of them with two grades in some rooms, standard classrooms. The dormitories were houses with kids stuck in every available place for a bed, and the infirmary was a long enclosed porch on one of the houses.

A single room, girls and boy's toilets were added at opposite ends and the long, skinny room shared by all. Girls filled the cots on the right end with the girls' toilet, boys on the left end. Divider curtains were draped between the cots and were put back during the day or when privacy wasn't needed.

The beds overflowing with the surge in colds, Katrina got the last cot, three feet from the Danish boy's bed. Usually Momma Nina would use an end bed for a couple of enemas, but another girl with a cold was in it.

Then, as now, the most effective treatment for a cold is bed rest, drinking plenty of fluids---ideally fluids with plenty of vitamin C in them---and a series of good, warm enemas to alkalize and hydrate the body, to remove foreign proteins from the colon and activate the immune system.

The Danish boy, at fourteen, having never had an enema, was embarrassed by this part of the treatment of his cold. Momma Nina gave him the first enema with his face red. Almost three quarts later, his ears pink, his face pale, his legs quivering, embarrassment was replaced by urgency. Momma Nina made him hold it for five minutes before letting him run for the toilet. The next three enemas, his ears turned red, but apprehension was gone, replaced by something else. A woman's touch, Momma Nina's gentle hand on his back and hip, he loved her care. Loving Momma Nina's attention, he missed having his mother's touch. Years since her death, no women cared for him, touched him. Like many orphans, he found maternal love in the infirmary. Every time Momma Nina told him he was having another enema, he headed for his cot, no resistance, knowing the enema would warm his belly and make him feel better, knowing the enema meant Momma Nina's touch, her soft electric charged hand on his skin, the electric energy of a woman caring for a boy. His soul longed for such a touch, and if an enema was the price to have this love, enemas were a part of his boy heaven.

Most kids stayed three days, had a series of enemas on the first day, one a day after that. On his second day in the infirmary, Lars had one enema, the usual pattern for kids with a cold.

Breathing deep, concentrating on relaxing his abdomen and contracting his anus, Lars was coping, holding in his enema when Katrina, his smiling Russian friend, talked her way through the door. Lars couldn't understand what Momma Nina and Katrina were saying, something in Russian.

Katrina said, "But Nurse, I can't take an enema with all these girls watching. It won't work."

Momma Nina said, "It'll work. An enema given on stage with the whole school watching works. That's not your problem. You're too tense. What doesn't work is your not having bowel movements because you are inhibited about going with three other girls next to you in your dormitory's toilet."

Katrina said, "How's having enemas going to help that?"

Momma Nina said, "Simple. I give you an enema till your colon is completely full and you'll have to go to the bathroom. Use the releasing of the enema to educate yourself into relaxing when you need to be relaxing, and I won't be giving you enemas so often."

Katrina said, "I really don't want an enema!"

Then she saw Lars, the Danish boy.

"Nurse, I really can't have an enema here, not today. Can I come back tomorrow---when he's gone?"

Momma Nina said, "No."

Holding his breath, seeing her, the embarrassment returned for Lars too. Momma Nina working with his quivering, naked flesh, a boy's need, something a boy would do for a mother figure was not what he wanted with Katrina. A surge rippled through his colon. He blushed. Struggling, him holding an enema was not the image he wanted this Russian girl to have. But for Katrina or Lars, both kids, privacy was a luxury the orphanage did not offer: bunk beds in the dorms and enemas by the row in the infirmary.

The Russian boy next to Lars had understood Momma Nina and Katrina's conversation. He said quietly to Lars, "This'll be interesting. She's a moaner."

Momma Nina giving enemas every morning, up and down the row of children filling colons, was an engine of interest. When she wasn't giving enemas, kids talked, a chatter back ground in the infirmary. When she gave an enema, silence, nothing but silence, every child listened. The child having the enema was the focus of interest. Moaners made more interesting listening. A privacy curtain between the girls and boy's parts of the room during the giving of an enema prevented watching a child of the opposite sex have an enema, but sound tip toed down the aisle, heard in every bed. An enema, one of the most exciting and embarrassing things that usually happened in the infirmary, every child might have one, might be the one moaning, holding on, trying not to make a mess.

A fear, a hope, a possibility of it being your own anus squeezing the nozzle as an enema flows in makes hearing an enema given stop all other activity in the room. Children in their beds, their pajama bottoms on, listened with intensity as others got enemas. Adult hospital patients in pajama bottoms listen intently as their ward or roommates receive enemas.

Katrina would be starting a series of enemas to treat her constipation. Momma Nina, more than not wanting to give her privacy, wanted to embarrass her into being more conscious of the need to go to the bathroom, to stop her from taking up treatment time. Giving her enemas only because she had obstipation, constipation caused by holding on and not answering the call of nature, was a waste of nursing time.

Momma Nina pulled the curtain between Lars and Katrina's cot then said, "Katrina, take everything off and put this on." She handed her a worn slip of a hospital gown.

Lars suppressed the urge to run to the toilet, suppressed it with less embarrassment with Katrina out of sight, even though she were only feet from his bed.

He wondered, *Can she hear my belly rumbling?*

Through the curtain, Katrina said, "Are you all right, Lars?"

He didn't answer.

Momma Nina said, "Lars, time to go."

He dashed.

Katrina said to Momma Nina, "You gave him an enema?"

"Yes, and now you," Momma Nina said.

Katrina blushed. She wanted Lars to see her smile, to hear her voice, but having him in the room made having enemas as bad for her, as it was for Lars.

Lars came out of the boy's bathroom, his bowel empty, and headed for his bed.

Crossing around the end of his bed, the privacy curtain didn't give privacy: a long thin tear, a slit dangled between the curtain. Katrina on her side, her nightgown up to her waist, her smooth white bottom and legs completely uncovered, a red hose between her cheeks running up to an enema bag hanging from a stand, she was naked, exposed. The soft flesh of her hip moved. She tensed. She relaxed. She sighed. Rocking to and fro like fresh dough under Momma Nina's kneading hand, she slowly straightened her lower leg. Neither Momma Nina nor Katrina saw Lars stop to absorb the view. The view stopped him. Katrina stopped him. Not wanting to move, not wanting to be caught, he hesitated; he slipped in his bed shaken.

The vision of Katrina's bare bottom on his mind, he could still see it, would be able to see it for all the years to come, but couldn't see it. She was beautiful with her clothes on. She was a goddess with them off.

He worshiped. He listened.

Curtains within reach of his hand, Katrina less than a yard and a foot away, Lars heard her breathe, heard the rustle of Momma Nina's skirt, could almost hear the rumbling of the enema moving up her side. He heard what none of the other boy's could hear, and what they all heard.

"Oh, oh, oh, mmmh," Katrina gasped!

Katrina was a moaner.

Momma Nina brushed her back against the curtain; the imprint of her back clear, Lars saw her black uniform top block the slit.

"I've got to go!" Katrina said.

Momma Nina leaned forward away from the curtain. "I'll stop the flow for a minute, Katrina. Breathe deep, relax into it. How many enemas have I given you? It was a lot worse in the camp. Here your feet are warm," Momma Nina said.

Her feet resting on a hot water bottle wrapped and under the covers with her feet, it was much nicer here, nicer than in the cold of the camp trying to take an enema with goose bumps from cold covering her back and legs. The enema was still hard to hold, but Momma Nina was intent on giving her every last drop.

In the moment of silence that followed, Lars mind quivered in his bed. Was he having new feelings, feelings that went with the new hairs growing on his pubic bones? His ears locked to the goings on in the next bed: a beautiful girl, no panties, a hose up her bare bottom, and Momma Nina's hand rocking her. This was new. He was not interpreting it as anything he had ever heard before.

He heard the little click. Silence continued for no more than a minute.

Katrina said, "I'm so full!"

Another click, "We'll wait a minute, Katrina."

"Passeba (please)," Katrina said in Russian.

Another click, more water flowed.

"Oh, Oh, Oh---I---Oh," Katrina said, in English or Russian. Moans are the same in either language; Lars heard them in Danish.

"Breathe deep, keep breathing," Momma Nina said.

There was no click.

Katrina kept moaning.

Lars felt something, a tear in a curtain opened in his brain, he was changing. It was time, his season for change. He didn't understand what was happening. He understood his interest in Katrina's enema. All children, having experienced the urges, surges, and most of all the sense of lack of control associated with an enema, were drawn to others going through the same experience. Aren't adults? Fear of losing control of the bowels is universal. Fear creates interest, pathological interest.

As Katrina moaned, he changed, his body changed. Suddenly he wasn't just listening to another child in the middle of an enema, something was happening to him. He was much larger than he had been. The sheet stood up. Trying to hide the new him, he rolled to his side, pulled the sheet and blanket taut covering him. Now his abdomen rumbled. Lars had more enema flowing from higher up into his rectum, needed to go again, but he couldn't get out of bed like this!

He held it.

Momma Nina said, "Katrina, you've done well for the first one. We'll leave it at that for now. I'll tell you when you can go to the toilet."

A privacy curtain between them, they lay, she holding an enema, her bowel swollen with water, he with another organ swollen with blood, both embarrassed. Not naked, covered with a sheet and blanket, she wanted to see him. Momma Nina wanted him to see her, to ad to her embarrassment. The nurse slid the privacy curtain back after she put a sheet over Katrina's bare bottom.

Lars, excited, expected to see Katrina on her side facing away from him still naked.

She looked directly in his eyes. His face glowed red.

Not ready to see him looking into her eyes, she turned redder.

Katrina giggled slightly, closed her eyes couldn't look at him. Lars smiled at her and looked away.

She was a nice girl. Ashamed of what he was thinking, feeling, Lars lept up, headed for the bathroom, forgetting what he was hiding. His night shirt fell to the side as he sprang for the floor revealing his---More red faced, he ran for the toilet.

Katrina's eyes wide, her mouth open, she didn't move, didn't blink. Katrina said, "He—he didn't, did he?"

Momma Nina came back in five minutes. "Katrina, you can go to the bathroom now."

When she came out and went back to bed, Lars was in bed.

"Hi," she said.

"Hi," he said.

Lars done with his enema, didn't say anything more to her, only blushed. They kept exchanging glances, trying not to meet each other's eyes. He had seen her naked. She had seen him---

Ten minutes later, Momma Nina came back in with a full enema bag. Lars listened while Katrina took it. She begged, pleaded, quivered and took the whole bag. They lay in beds facing each other, Lars covering a bulge that wouldn't go down and Katrina holding her bulging enema.

The second enema Momma Nina gave Katrina, a bigger one, a warmer one, one she had to hold for fifteen minutes. The enema in, she was back on her side, covered, facing Lars again.

"Talk to me, Lars," she said. "Take my mind off---" Katrina blushed.

Lars blushed. He tried to talk. He opened his mouth, nothing came out.

Katrina kept looking at him.

Time passed. The enema passed. Katrina walked slowly back to her bed looking at Lars.

Ashamed, he couldn't look at her. He looked down. He looked to the side. He glanced at her. She was beautiful.

As she walked within inches of his bed she swayed. He could see the curve of her hip through her hospital gown.

She looked demurely in both directions. Momma Nina wasn't in the room, the other kids were asleep or looking away. Katrina pulled the privacy curtain beside Lars bed part way to the foot of the bed, walked around and pulled hers all the way, then slipped in on his side.

She turned, her young, pert, developing breast hanging over his face.

"Lars," she said. Then suddenly she leaned into him. Her lips touching his, lingering for a second then fleeing into the air.

Lars said, "Why did you do that?"

She blushed.

"Do it again!" He said.

She did, then sprang around the curtain to her bed.

"Nobody ever kissed me," Lars said.

"Nobody ever kissed me either," she said.

Looking toward the door, being sure Momma Nina was somewhere else, Katrina, now dressed, slipped around the bed, and kissed Lars a long lingering kiss, pushed his privacy curtain back to the wall and walked toward the door.

Momma Nina walked in

Katrina said, "Thank you, I feel so much better!" and hugged her as she walked toward the door. She was gone.

Momma Nina fussed with her dress, crinkled a smile. Difficult for her to show the emotion Katrina always showed, she needed the hug, would be there the next time Katrina needed her.

Lars lay back in his bed, the sound of Katrina's voice in his head, the *thank you, I feel so much better* ringing in his ears. The pleading, the filling, the warm gentle hand of Momma Nina on his hip, on her hip; Momma Nina's voice encouraging him, encouraging her; helping them take it, Lars knew the feeling, but listening to her have it was something special. Hearing her in need, in the panic of taking it, holding it, taking more, begging, wanting, not wanting, the sounds rambled to places in his brain never entered before. Seeing her eyes coming out of the toilet, knowing her relief and ecstasy after emptying and returning to the room with that post enema glow, it was something he had felt and wanted her to feel. An observer, a child learning becoming a man, Lars wanted to touch her, wanted to hold her quivering hip in his hand, to give her ecstasy. That would be something special. She was something special.

Then he remembered, *She kissed me!*

One more day and he was discharged. Katrina smiled when he walked into class.

Her smile meant much more than it had a few days earlier. Lars melted, couldn't take his eyes off her, barely remembered anything of the teacher's lecture, only Katrina's face smiling.

Lars dreamed about her every night. She dreamed about him every night. He thought about their enemas. She thought about their kisses. Both teens, excited teens, her node of sexual awareness a few months passed, his not yet a week old, they were in love, erotic love.

They stole more kisses. At school dances they only danced with each other. Slow dancing was their favorite. Every waltz, Lars rushed to ask her. Every dance, no matter what they tried, they excelled in doing.

Katrina small, delicate, an hour glass figure, both fourteen year olds, they were royalty, a dancing pair, a beardless boy, with wavy red hair and a fairy tale princess. They danced, others noticed. They were special.

Katrina, like many girls, difficult to tell her age, stopped growing after her fifteenth year, and could have been a woman in his arms as he spun with her around the dance floor. Unlike most girls when she became an adult she never lost her hour glass figure, she stayed teen age thin, always looked royal, like a star, a princess.

Most teens are all legs, arms and disproportionately small bodies. At fourteen, almost five feet and nine inches tall, slender with wide shoulders and a man's appearance, Lars was perfectly porportioned. Those who didn't know him thought him to be a man, a handsome man. But like most men at fourteen he was beginning to grow. Starting his teenage years taller and wider than most men, he kept growing through high school and beyond. His legs and arms remained the same length, but grew in girth. Once in perfect proportion to his limbs, his body grew. By then end of their senior year he was five inches taller, all back and body, one hundred and fifty two pounds heavier, no longer thin, as broad and strong as a bear, a graceful, dancing bear.

A Russian girl, once shot, always afraid, she needed him, her massive, Norse warrior. With him protecting her, in his arms, she was safe. He needed her. The nurturing, mothering Momma to eleven other kids, she wasn't little to him. She was as tall and strong as the sky on the Kansas Plains. High school love affairs, common, usually not lasting, Katrina and Lars were different. At fifteen they were in love forever. At eighteen their love was broader than his shoulders and stronger than the beating of her heart. It engulfed them. He was her mother, her brother, her father. She was his father, his sister, his mother. They were everything to each other, no longer orphans, they were family.

Two orphans, alone in the world, they had been friends, and became lovers holding hands. The dorm mother's watched them to be sure that holding hands was all they did. An occasional kiss, occasionally caught. They were paddled twice for inappropriate touching, but couldn't stop. Only their lack of knowledge of sex kept them pure: feelings powerful and unfocused, neither Lars nor Katrina knew the feel of sex, what it was, or had the experience to lead one another astray.

Katrina fell dancing, sprained her ankle. Crying in pain, she looked to him. Lars gathered her in his arms, picked her up like a toy doll and ran with her in his arms to the doctor's office.

"She'll be all right," Doc said.

Lars shook, cried because she cried, gripped Doc's hand in a vice grip almost breaking his fingers.

"Thanks Doc," Lars said.

Lars slipped her a note, "Katrina, I will love you till the day I die. If in the rage of battle I die, I will die loving you. If I die old and in bed, I will die loving you. I will always love you."

She wrote back. "I won't live without you. The day I die, I'll be holding your hand, loving you. Without you, I don't live. I can't live."

The teacher saw the note being passed, started to get mad, to get her paddle out, then she read it.

"Lars, Katrina, I should discipline you. I---I want you to make a copy of this note, one copy each. I'll keep the original. The copies are for you. They are special. I think someday you will look at those notes and know you have a special love, when you are both old and gray, like me. This note will make you remember, will bring your love back to you again."

She didn't paddle them.

Katrina, the only source of discipline he feared, she mothered him, fussed over him to keep him in his coat in winter and made sure he didn't get wet in summer rains. She knitted socks and scarves for him, and in a sewing circle made shirts and a coat for him when he grew too big to buy them in the local store. She hovered over him like a mother bear with a single overgrown cub. Katrina, a natural momma, a woman born to care for babies, had her baby, a big baby bear.

Lars picked wild flowers for her every spring, summer and fall, any day he saw blooms. A bear standing in fields of flowers above the school, he brought her a full bunch every day before class. She kept them in a vase on a wrought iron night stand he made for her. Her favorite was Mountain Gold flowers, a wild flower of the northern plains. Lars found them in the field. In May he went with a baseball team for a game in the mountains. They brought back a victory. He brought back White and Blue Columbines, a huge bouquet of them mixed with sage to make her room smell as pure and innocent as she herself.

Three years later, they kept holding hands. Everyone expected them to marry. Only two months left of school, Lars planned to work full time with the black smith in town after graduation and rent a room, a room big enough for a big man and his little wife.

Momma Nina watched them, smiled, said to me, "Marisa, Lars is going to ask Katrina to marry him."

Chapter 9

Daddy Valik

Three years later I spoke English like any other teen, with very little accent, and was a freshman in high school, an honor student again. Momma Nina met and married the butcher, Daddy Valik, a widower with three children: a boy three years younger than me, a girl two years younger than me, and a girl a year older than me. We moved from the room in orphanage into town and lived in a two story house with an unpainted picket fence and a mongrel dog named, Vladimir, named after the owner of the estate where my step father grew up as a boy.

A long stick lying beside the house, I threw it. I watched the dog, expecting him to run after it. He hid under the porch. If I approached him he put his tail between his legs and slinked away.

The next day I saw Daddy Valik beating him with the stick.

Daddy Valik said, "Stupid dog!"

Vladimir was Daddy Valik's whipping dog. Everything that went wrong ended up with Vladimir being beaten, then in penance being fed a piece of meat from Daddy Valik's butcher shop. Vladimir slinked, hid under the house, waited to be beaten then fed. He was useless: he never showed the courage to defend us, our home, nor was he fun. Any time anyone paid attention to Vladimir, he assumed he had done something wrong, and, within the bounds of his chain, tried to hide, as Daddy Valik, a peasant serf, tried to hide every time Count Vladimir needed his whipping boy.

Momma Nina, the lady of the house, moved into the master bedroom on the main floor with the master, Daddy Valik. I moved into a remodeled piece of uninsulated attic. Before the wedding, Daddy valik stood on the rafters and checked the height of the roof. At the center it was a foot above his head, tall enough for him, tall enough for me. At thirteen, I was an inch shorter than him. He had his girls scrub out the cobwebs and dust, after that, I had to keep it clean. He put used, grade two, pine planking on the rafters so I wouldn't fall through, and had his boy, Ivan, sand them for me. He got me a curtain for the window, and bought a bed for me, but it was too tight to put a regular bed through the ladder hole. The bed went back to the store, traded for a cotton tick. The narrow space was as long as the house, but I lived in the last eight feet sleeping on the cotton tick pushed to the west wall, a throw rug between me and my books on the north side.

Three weeks after moving in, I checked out Cinderella and reread it. Cinderella lived in an attic. Was I Cinderella, the unwanted step-sister? Was my mother running the house, or was Daddy Valik? Were my step sisters wicked? They were trying to be nice to me, so was my step brother, so was Daddy Valik. I wasn't Cinderella. I was happy, no not Happy, one of the seven dwarfs or Snow White, happy, happy the feeling.

Having to climb a ceiling ladder into my room from the hallway of the second floor, I had complete privacy for the first, and only, time in my life. I read completely uninterrupted. Anytime and place I could read uninterrupted, I was happy. I loved my room.

The last thing I saw at night, as I lifted the glass of my lantern and blew out the light, was my books. Waking as reflected daylight filtered into my room in the morning the first thing I saw was my books. A glimmer of ice in the distance reminded me, not of books, but our tent. Like camping, like being with Momma and Daddy, only waking to Elizabeth and Mr. Darcy, Jane Austen's heroine and hero, talking, not my parents. Dream words at first from across the floor from a book cover, the voices moved to my hands and talked to me from ten or eleven pages before I got up.

A pattern, I yawned, slid out of bed, and retrieved my book, sliding back to my warm spot under five thick wool blankets, and a goose down comforter. No heat reached me from the fireplace or kitchen stove. In winter only the kitchen and living room warmed enough to take my coat off in the house. In summer my room was an oven. I took a book with me and slept on the porch if there were clouds. If there were no clouds I left my book on the porch and slept in the back of the wagon by the stable. Pelted by rain, I got wet a few times each summer, but never got a book wet.

A disadvantage to my room on what would have been a third floor, it was too high, too long a walk to the outhouse. I couldn't have enemas in my room. Waking up early, I went down to the pantry and lay on a mat beside the chimney, to warm and wait for Momma Nina. I had my enemas downstairs in the cool of the morning, before anyone except Momma Nina and I were up.

Coming out of the outhouse, I always walked around five minutes to help the water come down, if it didn't I had to have another enema.
On one of these walks, I noticed our dog looking at me. I rubbed Vladimir's ears. Expecting me to hit him, he shivered in fear, slowly

thawed, and licked my hand. Making him sit each day to have his ears rubbed, I made a friend. Slinking around the house, if Vladimir saw me coming, he wagged his tail and strained at his chain to reach me. He was happy, alive when I came near him.

Living in my own room for two months now, I regularly retreated there to read, study and live in my books from the library, and the few I owned. Before in the orphanage, I was lucky. Living with Momma Nina, I had a place, a private place. In our room I could read uninterrupted, unless Momma Nina needed me. Coming in our room she would find me, my eyes glued to a page, unaware of her opening the door.

She said once, "Why is reading so important to you, Marisa?"

I said, "I don't know. Momma always read to me, and with me. Every day we read. Every day since I learned to read; I read one book; she read another. She worked at the library in St. Petersburg, you know. We always had books."

As my grasp of English let me make out the words, I could read again, and read every book in the orphanage library. Momma Nina took me to town when she went, and I read the signs on the buildings for her. One was the Carnegie Library. Mr. Carnegie, a rich American with no children, gave all his money to build libraries for the people all over America, one in our town. More than a thousand books to read, I was in heaven. A trip to town from the orphanage meant a trip to the library. Living in town meant the library five minutes down the street. A room of my own meant no one to interfere with my reading as I sat curled up with my back to the window sill in the afternoon sunlight, or at night lying on the floor with my lantern by my shoulder.

Sometimes when I didn't have a new book, I stayed downstairs, talked to my new brother and sisters. Daddy Valik took most of Momma Nina's spare time and left me my nights alone. Newlyweds, even mature newlyweds, need time alone. When she wasn't slipping away with Daddy Valik, she did housework, or her job, nursing for a doctor in town. Her nursing, a night job, babies, most born around 2:00 AM, Momma Nina stayed overnight at least once each week on a birthing.

At the orphanage she worked days, only going in the next room to check a sick child at night. Our life was different there. At the orphanage meals were provided, we ate in the dining room with staff. I never prepared meals or cleaned up after them on a routine basis. Momma Nina's daughter, I didn't share chores with the other orphans, I was her helper. Momma Nina had me clean our room. I cleaned the infirmary, made the beds, and learned nursing from her.

I worked on the farm with other children before school for less than an hour. I gathered eggs. The only time I went into the kitchen was to deliver eggs, three flats of them. Now, no long row of beds to make and straighten, no room full of sick kids to nurse, I was an ordinary girl in an ordinary house with a new and exciting ordinary life.

Momma Nina helping the town doctor, leaving me alone with Daddy Valik and my new brother and sisters, I learned family, my first time not being the only child, or one of fifty girls in a school. Living in a house with a full range of chores was different, more work. My routine job was to wash dishes. Momma Nina cooked, but wasn't there to cook many evenings. When she wasn't there, my new sisters cooked, and taught me cooking, but did I like taking orders from them? They were a year behind in school and barely read. Stupid girls, they thought they were smarter than me because I couldn't cook, but I had responsibilities. I washed dishes.

Daddy Valik came home every night reeking of blood. He took a tub bath then expected his dinner. The table set and food on the table, he sat down, said nothing, and ate. When Momma Nina was gone, he went to the saloon. When she was home, for the first month, he stayed home. After the honeymoon period, sometimes he went to the saloon, sometimes he stayed home. An old habit, he worked in his shop, slept at home, and lived at the saloon, keeping the same routine, coming home to bathe, then to the saloon to eat and drink. Momma Nina changed the eating part. Three or four nights a week Daddy Valik came home reeking of beer.

That night, I was reading *Pride and Prejudice*. I mentioned Jane Austen at dinner. Momma Nina gone, no one looked up, or said anything, except Daddy Valik.

He said, "Why are you reading?"

"I like reading. It's fun, and *Jane Austen* is a wonderful writer," I said.

Beginning puberty, I was devouring my first romance novel. I waited for him to ask me about it, as Momma Nina would have.

He cut another slice of beef, popped it in his mouth, and chewed.

After we ate, I put the dishes in the sink and hurried upstairs to my book. A few hours later the living room door banged open. Two minutes later, Daddy Valik bellowed calling me down stairs.

"You didn't do the dishes, Marisa," he said.

"Oh, I forgot. I'll do them now," I said.

I started pumping water from the pump Daddy Valik had installed in the kitchen.

"This is the third time this week," Daddy Valik said.

"I'm sorry, I was reading. It won't happen again."

"No, it won't. This time you must be punished."

He took my wrist, holding it tight.

Punished? "Why, Daddy Valik? I didn't mean to! I was going to wash them."

I remembered last week, he paddled Ivan. I could hear the popping of the paddle, and Ivan crying.

I cried as he pulled me toward the wood shed.

"Please, Daddy Valik, Please!!" I begged.

Momma Nina spanked me a few months after she took me in, but I had cried for hours. She never spanked me again. Only paddled once at school, I wouldn't stop crying then either. Neither my momma, nor my daddy paddled me. They spanked me once or twice when I was little, but as soon as I understood what to do, it stopped.

"Please!" I said again, quivering as he bent me over and told me to hold on to the chopping block.

This time I heard and felt the popping. He blistered my bottom with a leather paddle. I was on fire, sobbing.

Taking my wrist again he pulled me up. "Now, you will wash the dishes."

We were in the yard again heading for the kitchen. I wept with intensity, an intensity I last wept with when Momma Nina held me, after my Momma and Daddy died. My bottom hurt. Never had I been paddled like that, but more, I felt betrayed, beaten. I didn't deserve to be paddled. I hated Daddy Valik.

As Daddy Valik dragged me back toward the house we crossed Vladimir's chain. He didn't quit barking. He barked and growled. Snarling when we came out, he saw me crying. Daddy Valik yanked my wrist and pulled me along. He had no fear of the dog, paid no attention to him.

I saw rage in Vladimir's eyes.

I said, "Daddy Valik, don't!"

Too late, Vladimir tore into his leg, ripped the skin, and grabbed another chunk. Trying to reach higher, to get Daddy Valik down, to kill him, our big, cowardly dog, was no longer a coward.

Dropping my wrist, tearing away from him, Daddy Valik raced beyond the chain. His leg was bleeding. Vladimir jerked at his chain trying to reach him. Daddy Valik glared at the dog, who had positioned himself between us, protecting me, his dog protecting me!

Daddy Valik hobbled in the house coming back with his shotgun.

The explosion silenced savage barking. Vladimir was dead.

"You killed him!" I said.

"Get in the house," Daddy Valik said.

He slapped me hard on the face.

I ran to the house.

Momma Nina came home, and bandaged Daddy Valik's leg.

"Poppa, she's not been paddled. Her mother, nor father, paddled her. I did once when I first had her living with me. I paddled my own children, but she's different. Her parents raised her different. She's a good girl, does anything you ask her to do. You shouldn't have paddled her," Momma Nina said.

"She didn't do the dishes. I'm the man of the house. If she needs paddled. I'll paddle her."

Momma Nina said, "She's thirteen, a child who forgets. All she thinks about is school, reading."

Daddy Valik said, "Next year she will be old enough to drop out of school and work. That'll be good."

"I don't want to drop out of school. I want to go to school!" I began to cry again.

"She goes to school, Poppa. She wants to go to school. We have no need for her to work," Momma Nina said.

Daddy Valik rose to his feet, started toward me. I cringed in horror, my eyes flashing fear.

"Touch her again, Valik, and we leave you. Understand that," Momma Nina said with a cold stare.

Daddy Valik put his hand back to slap Momma Nina.

"Beat me or her, Valik, and I'll wait till you're asleep, and burn you to ashes."

Daddy Valik put his hand down and hobbled out of the house. He came back drunk in the early hours of the morning. I was asleep in the attic, too far to climb in his state of inebriation. On the first floor, easier to reach, he beat Momma Nina leaving her face and arms bruised with a small bone in her face broken, then he passed out and fell asleep on the living room floor.

There was a price to pay, punishment: Momma Nina boiled a pot of water until it was at a rolling boil and threw it on him scalding his shoulder, arm, and back. Very few spots of second degree burns, mostly first degree burns, in a week, he healed. Momma Nina nursed him. The doctor, who Momma Nina worked for, treated him.

And the doctor told us what happened at the saloon. Doc and the sheriff were watching him, sitting in a corner, having a couple of shots. They heard him talking.

Drinking again, slurring his words, Daddy Valik said, "I should kill her!"

Doc and the sheriff finished their drinks and took their bar stools beside him.

The sheriff said, "Valik, you beat Nina, whipped Marisa, and killed the dog. What did you expect?"

Doc said, "Nina is the best nurse I've had in years, Valik. A good woman, she has helped hundreds of people in our region. You helped anybody lately?"

Daddy Valik said, "I work. I do my job. I expect respect in my home." Then popped back a shot of whiskey, and chased it with a beer.

Doc said, "You should have it, and you do have it. Nina has nursed you like a baby since your burn. She listens to you, but you hurt her baby; you hurt her. Maybe, in Russia, things like that aren't noticed. Sometimes they aren't here. Treat her with respect. She'll treat you with respect. Hurt her, or the girl, and people will know. You want that?"

"In my house, I do what I want!"

The sheriff said, "Outside your house is a large tree, a good tree. Nina has helped many people, Valik. Hurt her, and those farmers and townsmen she has helped'll tie you to that tree and bull whip you till your back is beyond healing, unlike this little burn you have now."

Daddy Valik looked at the sheriff.

The sheriff said, "Kill her, and we will hang you from that tree. In fact, if she dies from anything suspicious, like your last wife, and we'll hang you."

"You can't kill me like that," Daddy Valik said.

Doc said, "You misunderstand us, Valik. We won't kill you: you'll kill yourself. You forget, I'm the county coroner. I say what's murder, and what's suicide."

"We will be watching, Valik. Be good!" the sheriff slapped him hard on his back where a second degree burn was mostly healed.

Howling in pain, Daddy Valik thought of hitting Doc, or the sheriff, but put his hand down when two big farmers flanked Doc on each side, and the sheriff smiled.

His rage, the anger he had for Momma Nina faded. She was a passionate woman, cooked, and cleaned. Learning to treat her with respect, Daddy Valik learned to be the man she thought him to be when she married him. The night Vladimir died was forgotten by Momma Nina and her husband.

I didn't forget. I slept less secure without the big dog in the yard. Daddy Valik needed Momma Nina. He didn't need me. He didn't like me. He tolerated me. We were chained to each other by Momma Nina's love of us both. Vladimir's chain rusted in the yard, Daddy Valik never having another dog in his life. The rusted chain that kept me in his attic wouldn't outlast either of us. I worked hard and made good grades and helped Momma Nina. I waited to grow up. Three more years of school and I would graduate, go to college, and never live in his house again.

Daddy Valik never hit Momma Nina again, nor did he paddle me again. Hitting Momma Nina wouldn't teach her anything, she was too old. He thought I needed the paddle. He could teach me with the paddle like he taught his own children, but he never liked me. To him I was like the count's family on the estate where he grew up, useless. All I wanted to do was read and think and learn. A serf girl was for working, not reading or thinking. Learning was for work, to learn to be a wife, to clean and cook, not reading books about rich people. I was useless, not worth the trouble to teach. We rarely spoke. He stayed downstairs. I stayed upstairs. But, I never left a dirty dish in the sink again.

My room, facing the mountains, in winter I saw the pink face of ice in the distance that was so clear from our tent. I remembered another father, my father. I remembered how gentle he was with my mother and me.

A flash of light through my window came from the mountain as it came though the tent flap long ago.

I cried, "Daddy!" and said, "The cube of 3 is 27."

Chapter 10

Scars & Coming Home

I went to school that day, a freshman, the first person from our household to ever be a freshman in high school, a freshman they wanted to drop out. Others had it hard too: Lars and Katrina.

Lars was working after school at the blacksmith's. Strong enough to lift wrought iron fences, the current rage, Lars strength was Biblical. Barely over six feet two inches tall, his body larger than other big men; his back longer and broader, his arms and legs shorter and more massive; he was approaching three hundred pounds: a human bear.

The black smith liked him, would have hired him straight away, only a black smith needs to figure things, think. A high school diploma doesn't prove you can think and do numbers, but it's an indication. Mr. Swenson asked Lars to stay in school a few more months and get his diploma. After graduation Lars had a job as an apprentice that would be full time in June, and the orphanage would pay his expenses until he graduated. He was saving almost the same money as working full time.

Working hard, saving money for Katrina, he put almost everything he earned in the bank, had his bank book in his pocket. Two hundred fourteen dollars and twenty two cents, he had enough for three months rent on the apartment above the saddle shop on main street, the one being vacated by the English teacher at the high school in June, the one that came furnished with a feather bed, kitchen, and sitting room, and a common bathroom shared with two other apartments at the end of the hall. An end apartment, it looked out on the street, toward the mountains. Lars had a key borrowed from the teacher in his pocket with a ring. After school today he and Katrina had a date, dinner at the hotel. He would ask her then show her the apartment, if she said yes.

Before school, Lars met Katrina as he did every morning with a few flowers and a smile. They held hands waiting for the school bell to ring, for school to start.

Karl, a classmate of theirs, one of the Germans, a boy once a string bean and unattractive when Lars was a prince, Karl was now the class prince. Lars, the class bear, knew he was too disproportionate, too ugly for a beauty like Katrina, and resented Karl's smiling at her, and Katrina nervously smiling back.

Not content with smiling this morning, Karl threw Katrina a kiss.

Katrina blushed.

Lars moved forward, between them.

Did Lars mean to do it? A big right arm, a big right fist, Lars crushed the side of Karl's face with a single punch.

Karl's first dalliance with pursuing a princess possessed by an ogre didn't end like a story book with the ogre slain. Karl fell bleeding in the school yard. Princess Katrina came between him and the ogre protecting the prince, a prince no longer interested in kissing Katrina, but worse, a prince no longer conscious. Karl lay unresponsive, his eyes open, his mouth ajar.

This was serious. An ambulance took Karl to the hospital. Did he ever heal? Did he wake up any day in the next forty years without headaches, facial pain, or partial loss of vision in his right eye?

What would have been a schoolyard scuffle with a visit to the principal's office and a paddling for a boy of normal strength became a felony for Lars. No principal's justice, he faced a superior court judge. Had his family been rich, bills would have been paid, compensation given, and he would have been back in Katrina's arms. A child from a state run orphanage, his fate was certain. He stood before a judge in 1917, the third week in April, two weeks after war was declared on Germany. Without the war, Lars would have gone to prison; with the war, the judge looked at him differently. America needed soldiers.

The judge said, "Lars, you crippled another boy, something you should go to prison for doing, but you're lucky. The Army wants you."

Lars, crumpled in the defendant's chair, "I can't go in the army, please. I can't leave Katrina. I can't!"

Irrational, crying, Lars wasn't a big man, but a big boy. If he had looked up he would have seen the judges scowl. Lars was a big coward to the judge.

"Alright, boy, I'll put you in jail for a week. It's the army for four years or prison for five. You make up your mind."

Limbaugh and Sam, his friends, talked to him in jail. Katrina talked to him. Lars remained irrational, unwilling to serve his country.

Limbaugh, a fellow lineman, who coach had put on the left every time Lars was on the right through their high school football careers, they were a team. Lars with raging courage, Limbaugh, a taller, heavier boy with less muscle and more fat than Lars, they were a formidable defense.

Limbaugh said, "Lars, I'll go with you. With the war, I'll get drafted anyway, and if we stick together, we'll be fine. You'll be home with Katrina in two years or less---when the War's over, they'll let us out. Come on, Lars."

Limbaugh punched Lars lightly on the shoulder.

Sam, a smaller boy, water boy for the team, the black smith's son, Lars his coworker, was Lars' friend, the one that sat by him in class when Lars didn't understand English and helped him understand, the one that stood behind him when there was trouble, watched his back; the one that would get in front of Lars and the object of his rage and hold Lars back to keep him out of trouble, the one who had overslept the morning Lars hurt Karl.

Sam said, "I'll go with you too."

Sam didn't hit him. He put his hand on Lars' hand.

Katrina gripped Lars' other hand, said, "I'll wait for you. I love you. I don't want you in prison!"

Lars cried more, "I love you."

Katrina said, "Let's get married, and I'll go with you, live near the base, wait for you to come home."

Lars said, "What if I don't come back? I don't want you waiting, hurt, bitter, alone with no one to take care of you, alone with a fatherless baby."

Katrina said again, "I'll wait."

When the judge came back, Limbaugh talked him into letting Lars finish high school with Katrina and him and Sam, then the three boys left together on the train east for basic training. But, Lars never mentioned marriage to Katrina, or her waiting again. When he looked at her he cried. When he was with her, all he wanted to do was hold her and look at her.

Lars said, "Katrina, I'm not a good man. I hurt people. I don't mean to. I do." His big hands shaking, he said, "I'm sorry."

Not the first time, Lars remembered the fall, seven months ago, the first game of their senior year. He was a lineman, first string on the football team, could plow through taller boys with his heavy muscles and short powerful legs. A football game, an accident, another team's player knocked his helmet off, bloodied his nose.

Lars, a finger brushing his nose, saw blood on his hand. In one motion, a dance move almost, his hand went down, he spun, pivoted, lifted the other boy above his head and slammed him to the ground, then he kicked him in the ribs, breaking two.

Lars said, "I'm sorry, coach. I didn't mean too."

The coach said, "Damn, boy, you were one of my best players!"

Lars was off the team for the rest of his senior year.

Katrina held his hand.

"I didn't mean to, it just happened. I saw the blood. It just happened, Katrina."

Katrina said, "I know you didn't mean too."

She kissed him.

She didn't see rage in his eyes. She saw love.

She wasn't descended from Celtic villagers living on the coast of Scotland, villagers whose mouths turned dry as paste at the word---Berserker. Was Lars an ancient Viking warrior, a Berserker? Nordic raiders, soldiers, naked men in bear skins running amok, men who shook, shivered, their faces swelling, and turning dark, people were afraid of them with good reason. They killed in an irrational rage. They slew till they collapsed among their victims exhausted or their commanders threw buckets of North Sea water on them to chill their frenzy.

Lars shaking with rage, his eyes had intensity that frightened teachers, students, and football players. Could he control this? Could Katrina's kisses control it?

Katrina loved him as the gentle boy he was, and the violent man he became. She loved him every day as they grew together. She saw anger, felt his rage, but as a woman, his woman, she felt it in a different way. It protected her. Toward her, Lars felt only love. Her loving touch like sun on fog, dissipated rage, made his anger vanish before it settled eyes on her. With her secure in his arms, he was a different man than without her. With her, he was a modern man, a good student, polite, and Scandinavian reserved, a lover with flowers in his hand. Without her, he was in the 9th century, a Berserk raider, a naked man in a bear skin loose in an enemy village with six inch claws in his right hand tearing human flesh. With her trembling, afraid, behind him, he was a berserker with claws in both hands tearing human flesh, defending her. He was as his ancestors were a thousand years ago in the Firth of Forth, near Edinburgh. There he existed in semen yet to be passed through millennia of Nordic warriors and the women they loved until it reached him, made him; or in semen passed to victims, raped Scottish maidens, passed to red haired cousins seen by those mothers as sons and daughters of Satan.

Katrina loved Lars. To her he was her teddy bear.

To others he was a real bear, a mortal danger.

Looking in the mirror, Lars saw himself. Growing, becoming the man he would be, he saw his face, saw the rage. How long would it be before he killed somebody, or tried to kill somebody who would kill him, as his father had done? He looked at Katrina's picture on his nightstand, held it to his chest, cried before he met her on their last morning before he went to the army.

Katrina kissed him. She didn't know what to say. She wanted to say she loved him, but was that what he needed to hear?

"You're a good man, Lars. I know you're a good man," she said.

"I don't know what to do, Katrina. There's a war. What if I don't come back? What if I get killed? What do you want to do?"

"I want whatever you want, Lars," Katrina said.

She wanted to go with him.

He didn't ask.

Katrina waited. A girl, could she ask him to marry her?

If he wanted to marry her, she would be waiting for him, wait for years, wait till the war was over, his enlistment over, till she died, whatever he wanted.

She thought, *Say it, Lars. Say it! Ask me to marry you. Ask me to wait. I'll follow you as far as I can, write to you every day.* But, she didn't say it. She cried.

Lars held her.

"Am I hurting you, Katrina? What I did is hurting you," he said.

"No, it's not you. It's me. I'm afraid to be without you. I need you!"

Not afraid of him hurting her, she was afraid of losing him, of him rejecting her. She froze in her fear, trembled, cried, but could not tell him to marry her.

She didn't ask.

He didn't ask.

Never a word about marriage, about their future, Lars kept his thoughts to himself. Confusing her, he crushed her to his chest, kissed her, cried, and got on the bus. Lars gave Katrina the money he had been saving for them, all of it.

I watched Katrina, watched her lose weight. She didn't eat. She didn't talk. She cried. Out of high school, no longer the state's responsibility she had to move out of the orphanage. Doc said he would send her to the state asylum if she didn't come around soon, but the way she was, she would be on the street before he could process the papers.

I looked at my friend, remembered her teaching us English in the camp, couldn't let her be put on the street.

"Momma Nina, can she stay with us. My place in the attic is roomy enough for two?" Momma Nina listened to me. Daddy Valik took monthly rent from the money Lars left her.

For two days I took soup and dinner to her. She wouldn't eat it, then Momma Nina gave her an enema.

An hour later she was hungry, sat in our kitchen eating. After that I was out of my dish washing job. Katrina did all the house work.

We talked, at first the weather, people at school, girl things---and Lars.

I tried not to talk about him, but Katrina thought about him. If I didn't let her talk, what would she do?

If she talked about him she cried herself to sleep.

If she didn't talk about him, she went to bed and in ten minutes was crying anyway.

She said, "I'll wait for him, Marisa. He will write me. I know he will write me."

In the mornings, she was up working, but as soon as we were all out of the house, and she knew the mail was in, she went to the orphanage.

She said, "Mr. Barnes, any mail?"

"No Katrina," always the answer. No one ever wrote a letter to Katrina, to my knowledge, except me, and I didn't need to write her then, she was sleeping curled up on a tick by my feet.

One month passed. The crying herself to sleep every night passed, maybe once a week, but not every night. If she heard music from a dance at the school or in town, she didn't go, she ran home and cried.

The next two months the tears dried up, the sadness in her face remained. The daily trips to school for mail remained, but she was living. She noticed the flowers of summer, put one in her hair and walked in the fields where Lars had picked them for her.

The third month she smiled; she laughed at a joke. She was alive.

The forth month, a surprise, Limbaugh came home, not in uniform, not with any fanfare. He slipped quietly back on the evening bus and walked carrying his duffle bag back to his father's farm.

When he and his father brought a beef to be butchered, Daddy Valik said, "What are you doing home?"

"Hurt my knee," Limbaugh said.

He didn't walk any different, but no one knew any different. Still he stayed out of town for months, didn't talk to anyone, except Katrina.

He wouldn't have talked to her either, except she couldn't be stopped from talking to him. Twelve miles to his father's farm she started out alone on foot on a brisk October day.

Daddy Valik saw her moving, stopped her, and looked at the dilation of her eyes, "All right, take the mare. You can't walk twenty four miles out there and back in one day---and take her with you."

He pointed at me.

Riding double, she made the horse trot. Hard enough to ride that far when you aren't used to riding, it is doubly hard behind the saddle. My legs and bottom hurt for three days.

When we got there Limbaugh was in the field thrashing the last of the wheat.

Katrina trotted our mare up to him, "Where is Lars, Limbaugh?"

"The army. Where else would he be."

Katrina said, "Is he all right. He's not hurt?"

"Yeah, he's fine."

"What did he tell you to tell me?"

Limbaugh looked at her, stared for three minutes, saying nothing, then said, "He didn't say anything about you, Katrina. He's going on with his life. He and Sam are through basic, must have been assigned somewhere. I don't know."

Katrina said, "Why are you home, and not him!"

"I hurt my knee." He looked down, didn't look at us.

"What did he say about me, Limbaugh?"

"He didn't say anything, Katrina. Like I said, he's going on with his life."

"But he must have said something---felt something!"

"If he did, he's keeping it to himself, Katrina. I'm sorry."

Katrina didn't dismount, turned our mare around and started back to town.

As we crossed over a low hill losing sight of the Limbaugh farm, I asked, "Katrina, I need a break. Can we stop and get off for a few minutes, let me go to the bathroom, walk a little?"

She stopped; I got off.

In stead of helping pull me up, she got off, handed me the reigns, and said, "Here, you go back. I'm going to walk."

"I can't leave you out here on the plains by yourself, Katrina," I said.

"Yes, you can. It's not even noon. I'll be back before night."

I left her. Her image, smaller with every canter of the horse, her head down trundling along, remained in my mind for years. I crossed over another hill and didn't see her again until she walked in the door an hour after supper.

She wasn't sad. If there had been tears, she cried them out on her walk.

The next day she went to the priest and talked, went into town and got a job working at the hotel in the kitchen.

She was there three weeks when she dragged in a slim young man dragging his own leg.

"I hurt my knee," he said.

Daddy Valik said, "In the Army?"

"No a car fell on me when I was changing a tire," he said.

"Guess you won't be going in the Army then, will you?"

"No sir, I tried. They wouldn't take me. I would if I could. It's my country."

Daddy Valik extended his hand, "I'm Valik."

"Abe, Abraham I guess, everybody calls me Abe."

Katrina was smiling again, not the same smile as she had for Lars, but Abe never knew the difference. He liked the smile she had for him.

Over from Denver, Abe was a master mechanic. Mr. Sraelenburg brought him to do some work on the machines he had at his ranch, had put him up in the hotel for a day before picking him up.

It was hard to keep Abe out of town once he met Katrina. They saw each other every day for two weeks. Five times Katrina borrowed the mare and rode out to Mr. Sraelenburg's house.

Abe over for dinner after finishing all the work at Mr. Sraelenburg's, Daddy Valik talked to him.

"Abe, why don't you move over here? We could use a good mechanic."

"Not really sir, I'm a specialist. I fix the things no one else can. I have to be in a city where the work is. I go out on assignment when someone with the money, like Mr. Sraelenburg, will pay me."

"We'll be sorry to lose you, Abe, and I'm sure Katrina will miss you."

"I---well, I hope not."

Daddy Valik raised his eyebrows.

Abe said, "Sir, you see---I want to marry Katrina, with your permission of course."

"Son, and I'm not going to call you that, Katrina is a boarder, not a daughter. She has no father, no family. Marry her if you want, but I'll not be paying for the wedding."

Abe said, "I don't need your money. I just want her. Suppose I should be asking her?"

Daddy Valik said, "That's right."

Katrina was in the kitchen. She and I were rushing with the dishes so she could get back to Abe.

He poked his head in, "Katrina, can I talk to you?"

"Go on, I'll finish the dishes." I shooed her out of the kitchen then slipped into the living room to listen to them on the porch.

Katrina said, "Yes, Abe. What do you want?"

"You," he said, getting down on his good knee, "Katrina will you marry me?"

Katrina didn't answer. She leaned down and kissed him.

He stood up. "Katrina, I'll be a good husband. I own a house and my own shop, have three men working for me. I can take good care of you. You'll like Denver. I promise."

"Abe, can I answer you in the morning?"

"I'm leaving tomorrow at one twenty."

Abe kissed her and limped toward the gate.

That night we talked.

"Marisa, he's a nice man, and he has money, is good to me. I think he'll be a good husband, don't you?"

"Do you love him, Katrina?"

She looked down. She said, "He'll be a good husband, Marisa."

"I think so too, Katrina."

She kissed me on the cheek. I was her maid of honor at their wedding, such as it was. Abe went back to Denver for two weeks, then came back for her. She had two suit cases, everything she owned in the world with her, except the wrought iron night stand Lars made her. And, she went through the few papers she had. She kept her high school diploma, but left me a note, one crinkled with tears and worn from reading and rereading.

Lars had wrote, "Katrina, I will love you till the day I die. If I die in the rage of battle, I will die loving you. If I die old and in bed, I will die loving you. I will always love you."

She had written back, "I won't live without you. The day I die, I'll be holding your hand, loving you. Without you, I don't live. I can't live."

I held it up to her.

I said, "Katrina, are you sure you don't want to keep this?"

Katrina said, "Marisa, if Lars comes home, will you take care of him?"

She started crying. A girl shouldn't cry on her wedding day.

I squeezed her hand.

I saved the note in my Bible. I put the night stand in the living room to put flowers on and stood by her with flowers in my hand at the judge's office. Mr. Sraelenburg stood by Abe. They got on the bus to Denver twenty minutes after the ceremony.

Three months later Katrina sent me a letter and some money. I went to visit them for a week. They had a nice house, and her husband was good to her.

Katrina had missed two periods and thought she was pregnant. She wanted a baby, as did Abe.

The next year World War I ended.

Lars didn't come home.

The Germans had not killed Lars, but the army had held him for three of four years of his enlistment. He might have been released early for good behavior and come home in 1919 with other conscripts, but his behavior was too good. A hero, a sergeant in the army, he won more medals than any other soldier from our entire region. Lars was coming home without a scratch. Before leaving Europe he spent a year and a month being shown off at every allied capital and many army posts, then home he was stationed in Washington, DC, for two months to rub shoulders with legislators and big wigs.

General Pershing asked, "Sergeant, what're you going to do now? Why don't you stay in the army? We've a place for you. With your Congressional Medal of Honor, nothing in civilian life will compare to the life you will have in uniform."

Lars said, "No sir, I'm going home, marry my Katrina, and raise babies in Colorado."

Spring brought columbines to the hills of Colorado before he was home, before he stepped down from the bus at the same place he kissed Katrina good bye. Three years without writing or receiving a letter, without letting anyone know where to write him, he was home with twenty two people waiting for the bus to greet him.

The sergeant that bought Lars ticket had wired ahead that Lars was on the bus. The mayor, a congressman, and every dignitary in our part of the state descended on him.

Marching in formation with forty-three other young men, most of who came home the year before, he was the tall red haired boy I remembered from the orphanage. He was the sergeant in the front of the parade with the Medal of Honor around his neck. No one gave him a chance to ask about Katrina. He kept scanning the crowds expecting to see her. She wasn't there.

Surrounded by men, he kept looking. No Katrina. A welcome home dance, I was in the crowd, one of sixty-two young women in our finest evening wear smiling at returning heroes. He saw me standing my nose, eyes, and forehead standing out above the other girls at the dance. He waltzed with me, tried to dance every dance with me, but the congressman kept putting his daughter in Lars' arms. Then there were others. All the girls wanted to dance with Lars, the hero, and if he wouldn't ask, their fathers asked. I waited, but wanted to dance while I waited.

Easier with my shoes off and closer to the height of the shorter men, and better in cowboy country where men wear high heeled boots, I danced. Well into the evening, cowboys drinking and dancing, my partner planted a boot heel on my little toe. I yelped. Lars, the hero, rescued me.

Lars said, "Jack, why don't you let me have a spin with the little lady?"

I said, "I'd love to, Lars. Can you let me sit the rest of this one out, and let my toe ease up first?"

He said, "No. Here, it's a slow dance. Put your feet on mine. I'll carry you."

Like nothing I had ever experienced, he was taller than me, he was broader than two of me, and he didn't seem to notice I was standing on his feet. Clamped to him by his arm around my waist, it took me one dance to relax into him doing everything.

I said, "I loved that, Lars. I'd love to dance every dance with you."

He smiled. "Marisa, it has been a long time. You're not the same girl you were."

"You mean I'm taller and two axe handles?"

He said, "There's nothing wrong with a woman having hips, Marisa."

None of the other men could move me like him. Being tall and full boned is not ideal for a girl when dancing. Lars was the first person to dip me since I was twelve. We danced. He didn't just lead. I didn't just follow. He carried me around the floor with as little strain as a smaller man carrying a beer stein.

Then he let me use my feet. I surprised him.

"Where did you learn to dance like that, Marisa."

I didn't answer.

Dazzled by him, his uniform, he was my hero, the whole state's hero, the one every girl was trying to dance with. My dance partner, he drew me, made me smile, made me want him. I closed my eyes, imagined the red haired boy who smiled at me at the orphanage. He was with me, me in his arms, but he was scanning the other girls.

A state senator started to drag him away before we could talk.

"Katrina taught me," I said.

Chapter 11

Where is She?

In uniform last night with all his medals, he looked heroic; in a plaid shirt and work pants, like the ones he wore at the orphanage, he looked better. He used to have a nice ambling gait. Marching, he didn't used to march. A drill sergeant in his head, I watched him come---Johnny was there when I left, Johnny was there when you left, your right, your right, one, two, three, four, one, two---and he reached the porch, came to parade rest, looked up at me. Resting my shoulder and head against the four by four holding up the porch roof, I wanted to look alluring, then looked. Lars standing on the ground, interesting looking down at him, what was that? A few red hairs, pink skin, was that a thinning spot on the top of his head? He needed to wear a hat. He would look good in a cowboy hat. Most of the men around town wore them, hair or not.

I smiled at him. "Hello!"

No smile, not even a hello, he said, "Where's Katrina?"

My heart dropped. I folded like a shot doe, collapsed on the steps looking up at him. He wasn't looking for me. He was looking for her.

"She's married, Lars. Lives in Denver. She has a boy who will be two next month and a little girl born six weeks ago."

Lars knees buckled like a shot buck. He fell by me.

"I've got to go, Marisa." Lars never stepped up on our porch, never looked at me; he turned and walked away, back to the boarding house.

Mrs. Ashford, the rooming house landlady, told me as I passed her on the street, "He sat alone in his room all day, didn't come out for lunch, then took a bath, packed his duffel bag and put on his uniform. He's going to the mountains. I've got to tell the mayor." She ran toward city hall.

I went to the boarding house.

I said, "Lars, why are you leaving?"

"I've got to get away, Marisa. I miss her!" His eyes got misty.

"She loved you, Lars. Why didn't you tell her?"

He cried. He interrupted. For the next two hours he poured out his story---

He cried for the entire trip East on the bus the days after he left. At camp he kept crying.

A little sergeant had enough.

He said, "Soldier, get up!" He slapped Lars. "You cry like a child, I'll treat you like a child." He slapped him again.

Lars took it, not fighting back.

The sergeant said, "You big, cowardly Dane. You don't have the heart to face a man. All right, be a coward, shoot off a toe, go home. We don't need boys in the Army. We need men."

If he shot off his toe, he wouldn't go home, he'd go to jail---and he wasn't a coward.

"I'll fight, sergeant. I can kill a man with my bare hands. I can kill a man with a gun. Germans killed my father and my grandfather. I'll fight, but they'll kill me!"

Lars stopped crying.

Katrina didn't know Lars' history, his memories. In three years of being his beloved, he told her only what he heard watching the man who killed his father get on the train leaving town.

Three days after his father was shot, and the day after my Momma and Daddy, and Katrina's family, were murdered; Lars heard something none of the other orphans heard, a single word. He was at the demarcation point when the soldier who killed his father was loading his duffel bag on the train to leave. A corporal called him. He didn't say *come on, move out* or *get out of here,* as an American might have said.

The corporal said, "Rouse!"

What is different between *get out* and *rouse?*

Lars didn't speak English. If he had said anything but *rouse,* Lars wouldn't have understood it. Lars spoke German, understood what they were saying. Three years before Lars was forced into the Army to fight Germany, he said to Katrina, "The man that killed my father was a German."

She held his hand, trembled, said, "Let's not talk about it. I don't want to remember all that happened to us, to our families. Thinking about it hurts too much. Please, don't talk about this with me, Lars."

He saw a tear roll down her cheek, looked down, and stopped talking.

He wanted to share the rest of his story, but Katrina was never ready, and as he boarded a bus going to war with Germany, with her crying all ready, this wasn't the time to tell her, to tell anyone.

He told me that afternoon in the boarding house. Lars earliest memories, those with his mother, his father, his grandmother, were painful. Katrina had been close to her parents, but ripped away when she was 11 and sent to live with her uncle in New York, she was a child, afraid of the dark. Afraid before the strike, afraid before the massacre, Katrina was afraid to go to the toilets alone, embarrassed to go and be seen by others going to the toilet. Maternal, nurturing, but filled with fear, Katrina hid away from things fearful, didn't want to hear about wars, death, or dying. Lars didn't talk to her about these things after he learned it frightened her.

He didn't tell her his grandfather had been killed in a war with Germany. Everyone at the orphanage knew his father had been killed in a gun fight with a soldier before the massacre, but little else about him.

His grandmother married his grandfather when they were teens, just before his grandfather went to war, a little war. Denmark, a little country, disputed two provinces, Holstein and Schleswig with Prussia, a big country. A lopsided struggle in 1864, the war was over in less than a year, one battle really, Dybbol. Denmark lost, and as most losers, lost more men than the winner, more than 3,000 Danes died. A war and battle, both small and insignificant, it was meaningful for Denmark, and for one teenage war widow.

Alone with a new baby, Lars' grandmother was home when her husband was killed. Broken hearted, she died of grief and left their son to her brother to raise. Was Lars' father half the size of Lars because of growing up without enough food, an unwanted nephew in the home of his uncle? Were all the scars in his father's soul from the death of his father before he was a month old?

Lars' father's hands shook as he pointed to the newspapers, "Germany wants Denmark, wants the world."

Lars' father hated Germany and Otto Van Bismark, the great German military leader. Bismark's first battle, the one that started the creation of the nation of Germany, was the one that killed Lars' grandfather.

It was over Bismark that Lars' father died. In town, a gun on his hip, he had argued with a German soldier, a man who idolized Bismark. Lars' father, a farmer, not a fighter was slower with his gun than the professional soldier, and wrong to try to shoot him. A fatal mistake, he lingered two days, then died.

Lars' grandfather and his father killed by Germans, Lars knew they would kill him too. Years of his father talking hatred of Germans, had had a different effect on Lars. His father talked to a boy as big as a man, but not a man. The surge of masculinity released when he kissed Katrina was in childhood dormancy. A child, told tales of terror, hides, runs away, is afraid to die, fears. A man, his masculinity pumping, gets his ire up, rants, sees enemies, attacks, hates. Lars growing, his manhood coming on line, was becoming a man, able to kiss girls and love one, but too much a boy to think as a man, too much a boy to hate with purpose.

Young men, not fully grown, fear enemies with guns, and making mistakes get killed in wars. In the Army he was going to Europe to fight as his grandfather had done---to die as his grandfather had done.

Katrina's protector, could he leave Katrina a grieving teenage widow, or explain his feelings to her?

He said nothing, kissed her lips feeling her warmth, smelling the clean of her dress, the clean of her hair. Breathing deep, he breathed his last breath of life holding her. In uniform on the bus he carried her memory, when the German soldier ordained to kill him blew a hole in his heart, the hole was already present before their kiss ended. He died in her arms before the war.

"I didn't expect to come home, Marisa. I didn't want her to die like my grandmother. I wanted her to go on with her life and forget about me, let me die like all the other men in my family died fighting Germany. I never expected to be alive---be here without her." Lars sobbed.

I stood up, and for the first time held his head to my chest.

"She still loves you, Lars. I still love you."

The sun moved from behind a cloud, came through the window like an open tent flap, lit my hair and face. He looked up at me. I smiled down at him. He heard me, but couldn't hear me, not with his heart full of her.

The mayor and Mr. Sraelenburg burst through the door.

The mayor said, "You're leaving us?"

Lars said, "I need to get away, have some time to myself, be alone for a while."

Mr. Sraelenburg said, "You want time alone in mountains, no people, time to think?"

"Yes," Lars said.

"I have sheep. Be moving them up the mountain in a few weeks. You want money? Want to take care of them for me? I pay good."

Lars smiled. "You pay good?"

"Damned good, per sheep, and you not see person till fall, except old Val, he bring you supplies every month. I got cabin there. Even put a heavy gauge door keep bears from hibernating in so it smell nice for you, like French hotels you tell us about with scented sheets---at least it not scented with *ode de bear*. One room, a bed, a stove, no out house. You no need. Go anywhere, even herd sheep naked if you want, no one see except a thousand wooly eyes. Keep sheep out of the cabin though or you be wishing for *ode de bear*. Old Val'l show you ropes and back you up first few weeks, then you got time alone."

Lars said, "When can I go up?"

Mr. Sraelenburg said, "Sheep moving up mountain now. Three days get your stores and Val ready, and I send you up. I soldier too, know how you feel. Come ranch with me. Talk me."

Lars started to unpack, he would need different gear.

Mr. Sraelenburg said, "Leave it. Bring bag. I got everything you need at ranch."

I smiled at Lars. "Come back when you're done with sheep herding, Lars. I want to see you."

The two men and I left together.

The mayor said, "Keep talking to him, Marisa. I'll have you and him over for dinner tonight. Will you come?"

Surprised to have attention like this from the mayor, could I say no?

The mayor said, "That was brilliant, Mr. Sraelenburg, how did you think of the sheep herding?"

"I soldier too, come home from two years at war, the Russo-Turkish war, 1877-78. My hand twitch all time. Lars in worst of fighting, need time let demons go. Best place mountains. Best company sheep. Lars need be alone, but not alone as he think. If he come apart, Val see him through. Val do that for me, long time ago in Urals. This man of mine give him space and be there if he need."

The mayor said, "Good, you need the help. It worked out well."

"My man do this every year alone. He not need help. Lars, need help. But, he useful. My man old, like me, too old do alone." Mr. Sraelenburg looked at me. "Marisa, no tell Lars what I say. I need him. He useful. He hero, our best; we take care him."

I smiled. Mr. Sraelenburg smiled. The Mayor smiled.

Lars disappeared into the mountains three days later.

During basic training, Lars kept saying to Limbaugh, "Katrina, I wonder what Katrina is doing."

Limbaugh said, "Write her, find out, and quit asking me about her. I don't know!"

I, unlike Lars, never let anyone go without writing them. I sent Katrina a short letter at least once each month. After Lars left for the mountain, I sent her my longest letter, explaining what happened, about his grandfather and all the other things Lars had told me.

Two weeks later she sent a letter back. Nice paper, good stationary, but wrinkled, it had spots where it had gotten wet. I didn't remember any rain. We were in a dry spell. She thanked me for the letter, and wished me luck with him, wanted him to be happy."

He came back in the fall. The nights getting cool enough for blankets, days were for sweating. In town, I saw him. I wanted to talk to him, but was having cramps, didn't want to talk to any man. I tried to avoid him, but seeing me, he came to me, touched my hand. His hand warm, mine cold, I looked at him.

He said, "Hi Marisa. How was your summer?"

"Long and hot."

He said, "Aren't you feeling well?"

I looked at him. Three days of PMS, now in the first day of my period, was I feeling well? Was he stupid?

"I'm Ok," I said, but I wasn't ready to talk to him.

"I'll get you dinner?"

"Ok," I ate with him.

That night Momma Nina brushed my hair. For more than a year before Lars came home from Europe, Momma Nina kept saying the soldiers are coming home and brushing my hair. Did she know one of the soldiers was for me? When he came home from the mountains, she was more fussy about my looks.

"Momma Nina, he's been with sheep all summer. I look better than a sheep!"

"I'm not worried about sheep, Marisa. I'm worried about other girls. Every girl in this town wants him."

In the mountains, Lars remembered his high school buddy, Sam, the one who enlisted with him, and missed Katrina. When he thought about a girl, a real girl, one he might hold in his arms, did he think of me?

Grown, no longer a kid idolizing an older boy, I wanted him in new ways, a real man, one I might hold in my arms, I thought of him, said to Momma Nina, "Make me pretty!" She kept brushing my hair.

Lars disappeared. Mr. Sraelenburg kept him at his house in the country, no one seeing him in town. Then the Sheriff offered him a job and moved him to town. Special treatment, he had a room on the top floor of the rooming house, an attic apartment with a private entrance, a long stairway attached to the side of the house. Was it special treatment or could anyone else staying there make the climb? Mrs. Ashford had a rooming house full of disabled soldiers, ground floor only types.

Two weeks passed, my mood changed. I was ready to see him, wanted to see him.

Did he come by my house, look for me? He had, but when I was out working with Doc, he disappeared again.

Our dance in my mind, sparkling teeth, being spun around the dance floor, his touch on my back, my hair fresh brushed, I wanted to see him. If he wouldn't come to me---I'd go to him. I took a book.

6 PM, page one: 7 PM, page seventy one: 8 PM, not able to tell the page numbers, it was too dark to read. Millard, the lamplighter was making the rounds, lighting the street lamps, fifteen of them, down Main Street. The boarding house lady leaned out from the front porch, saw me sitting on Lars' steps, and said nothing.

Young girls hanging around her boarding house was not acceptable, but the mayor had talked to her. Young ladies, or young women not considered ladies, could visit Lars. He needed company, and the mayor thought his life would be better if he had a reason to stay in town. Young women, is there another reason for young men to stay anywhere?

Finally, he showed up, alone walking down the street. Now he was ambling, his old gait, at a time I would have been impressed by marching, faster marching.

He smiled, said, "Hi."

What was I supposed to say, *I've been waiting for you for three hours!* with my fist on my hips.

Since he didn't ask me to wait for him, come see him, or anything else, that didn't sound right. Half the girls in town might have said that, but Katrina was a lady, soft spoken, didn't say things like that. Neither did I. Was that a reason he liked me?

"Are you all right," I said.

He asked me that at a most embarrassing moment the last time I saw him; it was fair play to ask that, and as close to being a fish wife as I wanted to play.

He said, "I'm fine, but I've already eaten. If I'd known you'd be here, I'd have come by here and asked you."

I said, "That's OK, I've ate too."

I lied. My stomach was growling. I wanted dinner.

Lars started up the stairs. I followed him. At the top, he looked back. I was behind him. Unlocking the door, he went in. I went in.

Turning toward me, he put his hand on my shoulder. "Do you think it's smart to follow a single man into his house?"

"Lars," I said, putting my hand on his.

It was hot, electric; there was energy in his hand. Holding his hand, I stopped moving. He moved closer, his hot electric breath ebbed and flowed on my neck.

"Lars," I said again.

He touched my face.

That breath, what was with his breath? It was hot, burning me. The electricity of his hand was tingling me. I looked up at him.

His lips descended to mine. He kissed me. I kissed him, withdrew a quarter of an inch and thrust my lips into his. The electricity tingled my whole body. My lips were tingling so much, I could barely feel his. Night coming outside, inside everything went dark.

I woke up. Lamps were on in the room. He was sitting by me. In his bed, a cold wet cloth on my head, I was afraid to touch my hip, afraid to look around the room, afraid I would feel my panties gone, or see my skirt dropped somewhere.

Still tingly, I said, "Did we?"

"No we didn't. You passed out! Marisa, how many times have you put yourself in this situation since I was gone? Don't you know it's dangerous to be alone with a man?"

"You're the only man I've been alone with, Lars."

"Marisa, if you keep following young guys like me around and into their houses, you won't keep your virginity."

I said, "You didn't, did you?"

"No, I didn't. You were lucky this time."

"I've never been alone with anyone but you, Lars."

"You've never kissed anyone but me?"

"Not like that kiss. I kissed Roger after the junior-senior prom, but it wasn't like---"

"Nobody, has ever kissed you seriously?"

"You," I said.

"I'm not serious, Marisa. I'm dangerous. Don't you know that?"

"I love you, Lars."

"After one kiss"?

"After three years of watching you in school. After dancing with you, and waiting four months for you to come home from the mountain."

Lars smiled.

I began to cry, "I'm sorry, I behaved so badly"! How could I have been so forward, following him to his room, telling him I loved him?

He said, "Are you sure you love me?"

I put my head down, nodded, looked up at him.

He reached down picked me up and held me to him. Still weak, I put my arms around him. He held me. Laying me back down, kissing me gently. He was excited, I was excited. I kept my arms around him. His kisses slowed down, stopped. He sat up.

"Marisa, you trust me too much. You shouldn't be here, doing this."

He reached under my legs, lifted me, sat me on his lap, and spun me around. How did I end up like this? I was bottom up over his lap! His arm not compressing my stomach to his, his arm held my hand behind my back and my stomach pressed to his thigh.

Suddenly his hand was popping my bottom. It started hurting. It burned. He was spanking me!

He wasn't going to hurt me---Well, he was hurting me, but he wasn't going to strangle me and throw me down the stairs. I started to tingle again.

When Daddy Valik whipped me, he was angry, wanted to hurt me. Lars could have hit me hard enough to leave bruises, hurt, but didn't. No force in his spanks, he was gauging them. This was a discipline spanking, a tingling spanking, not an angry one.

As soon as he let go of me, I sat up. My bottom was warm, but I had seen six year old children spanked harder. It wasn't something to cry over. I wanted to kiss him, but he was not in a kissing mood, he was in a sheriffing mood.

A common thing in our era, lawmen often spanked bad kids and sent them home rather than arresting them. Was I a bad kid?

He wasn't smiling. "Marisa, no more following strange men into their houses alone! You don't know me, know what I can do."

If I had gone into a boy's dormitory at the orphanage, I would have been spanked. If Momma Nina knew I was lying in his bed alone with him, she would take me to the wood shed and paddle me.

He said, "You're a virgin, aren't you, Marisa?"

"Yes, Lars." I kissed him quickly on the cheek, hugged him, and put my head on his shoulder.

"Thank you. I was wrong. You were right to spank me. Thank you," I said, "But, Lars, I know you. I trust you. I always will."

Standing up, he took my hand; he pulled me to my feet. I wasn't woozy anymore. As I followed him down the stairs, he held my hand, walked me home.

When we got to the door he pulled me to him, gave me a long lingering kiss.

"Good night, Marisa."

I said, "Will I see you again?"

"It's hard to miss me. It's a small town."

He was gone. I went to my room without supper. I wasn't hungry. Lying down should I cry or laugh? Was he mad at me? Did he like me? I couldn't sleep. I lay looking out the window at the full moon.

Finally falling asleep, I slept in. Doc didn't need me the next day. I woke up at 10:15 AM, starved. Eating a huge bowl of cereal, I wandered into town, walked every street. No Lars, no sheriff, where were they? Where was he?

I went home, tried to read, couldn't. Had I scared him away? I worried all day. 5:16 PM, there was a knock on the door.

A small bouquet of roses, three of them, he handed them to me without saying anything. I smelled them. Did they smell like French sheets? I looked at him.

"No one ever brought me roses, Lars," I said.

I put them in a vase and on Katrina's night stand.

Lars saw it, "Katrina's night---Where did you get it."

"She gave it to me. She couldn't take it with her."

He bent down, touched it, let his finger run down a long black sweep of iron work, closed his eyes. He breathed deep, opened his eyes.

"I'm glad you have it," he said, "I'm starved. Been out in the county all day. You want to have a steak with me at the hotel?"

I smiled, grabbed my shawl, and closed the door behind me.

Finished the first half of his tenderloin, Lars said, "When we were dancing, you had sparkles bouncing off your teeth."

I looked, a piece of steak was stuck between his two front teeth. His others sparkled. They always sparkled. I smiled.

He said, "I thought about you when I was in the mountains."

He looked at sheep and thought of me?

I smiled, thought of saying, *baaaa, baaaa*. But this was serious, dangerous, something to be excited about, not make fun. A distraction, I giggled about the sheep, knew he spent his nights and days on the mountain thinking about Katrina.

He giggled. Neither of us ever knew what the other was giggling about. Did he think about me, or her?

Grinning at each other like opossums afraid of a dog, what was in our minds about each other? Excitement mixed with fear? I was excited, afraid.

Lars remembered me as an immature girl helping the nurse. I thought of him as an older boy in the dormitory next door: a boy smiling at me, a boy who was supposed to marry my best friend. I liked him when we were children, when I was flat chested and skinny, when he was kissing Katrina. A man now with a thin moustache, I remembered a hairless lip. He changed. He was big in high school. The army fed well. Where broad shoulders had been shoulders spread wider, and his chest and arms were broader too. Only his stomach was flat.

I asked, "How much do you weigh, Lars?"

"305," he said, looking down, "but, I'm not fat. You don't think I am fat, do you?"

"No, Lars. You're perfect."

By the pound he was the best catch in Colorado. He was the best catch in Colorado.

Was I a woman about to trap a Danish Berserker and tie him in the yard with a chain around his neck? Yes!

What was he thinking?

He smiled at me.

I smiled at him.

"Hello, Lars"

"Hello, Marisa"

Chapter 7

My Hero

He knew I knew Katrina. No information I could give him about her could change his love. I knew he knew Katrina. Nothing he said about her could give me hope, but his reaction to her night stand did. He was healing, forgetting, separating past, present, and future. He was putting her behind him, and he brought me flowers like he brought her flowers. I was his present. I wanted to be in all his futures.

I had his eye. Was it my pretty eyes? I fluttered them at him. Was it my figure? I swayed my hips slightly. I didn't have a woman's figure in our past. I was a thirteen-year-old stick figure, no hips, no breast. In jeans and work shirt, I could have been a boy. My present, no longer a stick with legs and arms, my breast jiggled when I laughed, my hips wide and full, my waist thin, I was unmistakably a woman. But there were other women. Why me? Was it my pretty smile? The dentist had done a good job of fixing my broken tooth. It wasn't my eyes, my figure, or my teeth he remembered about me.

He said, "You still have enemas every day."

"Yes," I said, blushing.

Lars said, "Momma Nina still gives them to you?"

"Yes!" I was losing interest in this conversation. I stabbed him with a steady stare, my eyes not fluttering.

He blushed, stopped talking.

Not usually embarrassed about my enemas, I was with him? I didn't want Lars grinning at me like a opossum thinking about me having enemas. All the kids in the orphanage knew about me, about my enemas. Whenever a new kid came, they found out. Some asked me about it. Some acted funny toward me. Most forgot about it. Why not Lars?

His opossum grin faded and he didn't say anymore about it. Instead he asked me to go to the Baptist church social with him.

At the social I fluttered my eyes at him, and swayed my hips when he looked at them. Whatever he was thinking, his eyes sparkled. Going to the serving table, I leaned over to get more potato salad and glanced back. He was watching me from behind, liked what he saw. I pouted my hips back, then stood up and smiled at him. He smiled back. I know it was me he liked, even though I was taking him more potato salad.

Men, different birds, feed a man and he will follow. A man with his belly full and belching up a good taste is a man who will sit in the shade on a tree branch with you, chirp nice things at you. If he brings you a stick for a nest, keep feeding him. He is a bird that will spread his feathers and sit on the brood while you take turns gathering worms from the grass to feed your chicks. A good potato salad is filling, and taste good, a good man catcher. I made it. Lars was on his third helping of my potato salad.

I like potato salad, the smoothness of potatoes, butter, and the crunch of celery. Eggs are an acquired taste. The sulfur in them adds a pungency, something that doesn't smell good unless you like eggs. I loved the smell, the taste, and the man. Sitting down across from him, I salted my food, took a bite, and watched him eat. He ate all my potato salad first, then corn.

The corn was beautiful, long large ears, yellow, three shades darker than my hair, with the taste of melted butter, salt, and a basil paste I made for it, it was delicious. He carefully mowed his ears of corn horizontally, from left to right, like written English, like a typewriter taking off four rows at a time from left to right. Broad flat teeth, he was designed to eat corn, cutting the kernels off close to the ear leaving a neat trimmed cob. Eating my corn in vertical strips, not evenly with the rows, working my way down from the tassel, down the ear, like Chinese writing, eating all the immature kernels and finishing with the largest, leaving an ear nipped ragged in alternating layers, we had a difference. A more narrow mouth, my teeth in an arch, rather than a straight line: I was a nibbler, my mouth designed for other things than corn on the cob.

I ate a serving of beans slow cooked on a wood cook stove, individual beans blended into a semi-liquid mass with lumps of deep flavor rich with pork fat and sprinkled chilies. The lightness of corn, the heaviness of the beans complimented each other, filled my hunger. A staple of local picnics and church activities, Daddy Valik's ham was salted, savory, and something my teeth were designed to tear into ribbons and chew. Crushed boluses descended in satisfying waves down my esophagus. The air of food under the shade of a cottonwood tree, I loved picnics.

Watching Lars, I could see he liked picnics too. He ate three plates full, and slipped away to belch his satisfaction. Almost out of ear shot, he almost concealing it altogether, he belched just as Alekeev's Chevy Pickup backfired.

By the end of World War I, country people were trading Clydesdales and Morgan horses for trucks, undependable, hand cranked pickups that averaged two flats per trip to town, and that with breakdowns were not much faster than taking a buggy. The Alekeevs lived closer than other ranch families, but got there last, having had two flats, a clogged fuel line, and two fouled plugs on the trip in.

Coming to town was a serious trip. A church social was an all day and night affair. Most families slept in their trucks, in the church social hall, or with friends in town, going to church Sunday morning before heading back to their farms. Many cool Saturday nights we had three or four families bedded down in our living room.

Ninety percent of the population were farmers or ranchers, and spent every week day alone with their families working their land. Russian farmers were more likely to be friends with Russian town's people than their next door neighbors. Language one barrier, distance another, unlike East Coast farms, Colorado farms are separated by miles. You don't walk to the neighbors to strike up a conversation.

Because you can't talk to your neighbors doesn't mean you don't know them. Few trees on the plains lets you see your neighbors miles away. If the houses line up you know whether your neighbor chops wood in their long johns or their wife makes them wear pants. On cold clear days in still air, hot gray smoke from the chimney rises fifty feet in the air before freezing and falling back to earth. You can see every farm with a fire burning for ten miles around, but if there is the least rolling hill you can't see the light from their windows. You only talk to neighbors on Sunday mornings if you go to Church, or Saturday mornings if you go to town for supplies, to see a hanging, or other event like a Church Social.

Everybody came to every social. This time it was the Baptists, American food and no alcohol at the dance. Next week it would be the Lutherans, Germans with Kraut, snitzel and beer. Skipping a week it was our turn. The Orthodox Russian Church was borsht, wine, and Russian food. Everybody came, a diversity of people congregated with discrimination, neighbors required speaking to, but each ethnic group sought out their own for chatting.

The interactions among farmers coming in followed the same pattern, whether it was a hanging or a church social. The Alekeev's arriving late, it wasn't the food they were hungry for, they brought plenty to share. It was the company. Mr. Alekeev coasted his truck to a stop. It backfired two more times and quit shaking. Throwing two rocks from the truck bed under one back wheel, Mr. Alekeev made sure it would stay put.

His wife was humping baskets of food to the long table and his two boys went one way looking for boys, and his two girls went the other looking for girls. Mr. Alekeev looked around, pulled at his beard, and put one boot behind the other till he was in a circle of Russian men. Men, women, and children hungry for the conversation of their own kind, all headed for their cohorts. Roving packs of boys stopped long enough to gobble corn, woof down potato salad, and swallow a slab of pork before disappearing in circulating patterns among the trucks and buggies.

Different for Lars and I, we didn't belong. The common denominator---family. Almost everyone else was a husband, wife, or child: non mating members of families. A few single adults mingled in their own sexual cohorts, not crossing the public bridge of seeking conversation with those of the opposite sex in daylight. Lars and I weren't seeking, we were found. Not a married couple having spent the last week on the farm with only ourselves to talk to, or children having seen only their brothers and sisters during that same time, Lars and I were openly dating, openly talking to each other, openly exposing night feelings in daylight.

Trying to talk to Lars, the men were insistent. They came to say hello, wanted to talk about the war, pay their respects to a returning hero, but he confined his talk to "Yes," "No," and silence, never breaking eye contact with me. The men drifted away. I stayed. Women more sensitive to social clues noticed that I never looked at them, never sought their conversation. They all stayed away, talked about us, not to us, and smiled.

We didn't leave the church, we kept talking, went back for more food until Momma Nina called me to help. After the picnic, the picnic didn't end, it moved inside. Women began moving the food into the church hall for the evening. Lars waited, talked to the men, and watched me work.

I pulled my dress down constantly making sure the hem was straight and the cloth was not riding up over my hips. Was that what we were talking about? Was that why we didn't fit in any group? My hips? The married couples settled the issue. Last night, or Sunday night, or whenever they wanted, they rolled over in bed with the sexual partner they wed. In public, they as children are, and are again were boys playing with boys and girls playing with girls. A single woman advertises with smiles and solicits with sways of her hips. A single man looks. When he decides and she decides, they shun and are shunned by others until they wed and become a boy and a girl on the church yard again and rejoin their own cohorts.

My hips the prize Lars was thinking of having in his bed, he only watched my hips. With other women he kept his gaze at eye level or dropped it to the ground. He looked in my eyes, when I caught him looking lower, but let his gaze drift lower when he thought I wasn't watching.

Night came. We danced, a mating ritual of its own. Not conversation and distant looks, institutionalized touching, experimenting, and seeing if the curves fit without going all the way. A different kind of dancing for me, I was 17, used to dancing with boys my own age. Growing faster, girls are taller than boys until at least half way through high school. I was taller than the women and most of the men who danced with me. Lars changed that.

He took my hand, it disappearing completely into his palm. Soft, broad, and wide with steel tendons below the padding, I felt the power, the mass. Would this hand keep me safe---or hurt me, spank me again. I had seen and felt what that hand could do. I watched Karl's face fall away from that hand. I had heard what he did to other men. I had felt it on my bottom. Would he hurt me? I looked up. Not used to looking up, my eyes came to his lips, soft lips. They looked gentle, safe, but the deep rumble pouring through them as he spoke to me was hard to hear over the fiddle player and booted feet on the wood floor. I followed its deep rumbling. I followed him, my hand in his. He towed me to the dance floor like a Clydesdale pulling a buggy. I bounced along behind him.

On the dance floor, his arm around me, his other hand on my waist, he pressed me to him like a child, a woman. If I fainted again, I couldn't fall. If I couldn't follow, if my feet didn't have traction on the floor, it didn't matter; a quivering girl attached to the power, size, and strength of a Clydesdale, he held me up. The noise, other feet moving, other dancers disappeared. I saw only him. I felt only him. I was his. His mass, his hand pressing my stomach to his, I glided. My head on his shoulder, I smelled him, a scent like other men, indefinable, stronger, not bad, not good, stronger, something that made me quiver, that made me want him pressing my stomach to his, that made me afraid, an innocent drawn to a flame, fearing, craving, wanting, sensing the danger. My stomach warmed by his, my legs touching and moving with his, my toes hiding, scampering afraid of his, his big, dangerous feet could break my toes.

Eventually when we danced, I always slipped off my shoes, and kept my toes on his for every slow dance, standing on his boots, letting him do all the work, with my toes safe on top of his feet, feet so large that if they had been one size larger, he would have been 4F and not allowed in the army, but they weren't too big for the army, and they moved with amazing grace. This time he danced every dance with me.

He kept asking me out, sixteen times in the next three weeks. Every time there was a dance anywhere, we went. Used to having boys who could not dip or spin a taller girl, a girl heavy with hips and legs. I dipped, spun, and was fluff in his hands. He could toss me over his head and catch me; he could spin me; he made me fly. Now he danced with me.

Why didn't he ask any of the other girls? Four of them, two of them prettier than me, did everything except rob a bank to get him to pay attention to them.

Darla fixed him a cake, one of her best, and she won the county fair blue ribbon for her cake. He ate it.

He said, "Thank you."

He didn't ask her out.

Lavonia knitted him four pair of wool socks and embroidered his initials on them. Colorado winters are cold.

He said, "Thanks." Didn't ask her out.

Mary Sue and Karla smiled at him, waved at him, and walked down the street with him every time they saw him on foot.

He didn't say, "Thanks," nor did he ask them out.

He had eyes for only me.

He took me on walks, came to dinner twice a week, including Sunday dinners. Daddy Valik was nice to him, other than complaining about the size of steaks he ate, talked to him, and kept telling him he considered him a son, one who risked his life for our country, one who honored our house by his presence, and one who would always be welcome in our home. When Daddy Valik moved his gaze from Lars to me, it changed from entreating to impaling.

His eyes said, If you don't make him my son, there'll be hell to pay!

Daddy Valik did not have to speak for me to hear him and obey. I wanted out of his house, and I loved Lars.

There was talk of Lars joining the Grain Company as a buyer for our area if the deputy job didn't work out. His living in the boarding house and being home most weekends would be nice. A small house for sale on the edge of town, I could see myself living there with him. I liked the house; it was only a few hundred yards from the library, a quarter of a mile from the church, and two blocks from Momma Nina. Slipping home for my enema every morning, I would be gone before Daddy Valik woke up.

Lars ran out of places to take me. Walking around town, we knew everyone. No privacy, no place to go, and the urges of youth, we had to do something. Daddy Valik, my step-father, my legal defender, had Lars asked him, he would have turned down the covers for him and thrown me in the bed naked, turned off the lights, and locked the door, leaving me to him.

Lars, a soldier, supposedly experienced in the ways of the world, was attentive, gentlemanly, and shy. My night of following him into his apartment, a night of unforgettable kisses, after dinner the next night, he kissed me goodnight and left. We held hands some, but not always. I never knew whether I was going to be kissed, spanked, or talked to like one of the boys. Four weeks after lying in his bed, not knowing if he had made love to me, we started kissing again. Excited, he tripped backing off the porch and broke the railing. He was sitting in the yard two pieces of broken two-by-four in his hands. I tried not to laugh. Then he had trouble getting up, a twisted ankle. I had him elevate it and iced it. Relaxing in my hands, smiling at me, watching me, he liked this! I made a note to be careful not to nurse him too much, nursing a 95 pound, elderly woman is work. To nurse him a hospital bed in a barn would be a necessity. Someone his size is impossible to turn over without a pulley and mule to lift him.

The next day Lars limped. With a weakened ankle, he moved slower, seemed less of a threat.

He wasn't. A drunk at the pool hall underestimated him. The owner motioned Lars toward the drunk. Lars smiled. A man that never liked Lars, he sneered. Used to people backing away, Lars moved forward. The man jumped at him, not after hitting a much larger man, that wouldn't work, he grabbed Lars' gun, yanked it out of his holster.

"Back off, big boy," the man said pointing the gun at Lars.

"Give me the gun," Lars extended his hand.

An explosion, a pain in his left side, Lars didn't reach for the man, or fall back. His hand slid over a pool table. A pool cue rolled under it, the thinner end. Big fingers wrapped around it.

Frozen, others in the room watched. The pool cue raced through the air, crashed into the man's head and shattered leaving a jagged end in Lars' hand. He grabbed the gun in the man's hand crushing it and pointing it toward the roof. It went off again.

The jagged end of the cue ripped through the drunk's solar plexus and heart. Lars lifted him off the floor carrying him impaled on the cue into the street. He dropped him in the street, the man's mouth open gasping hopelessly at air. His eyes fluttered. He died.

Lars kicked him in rage. A trickle of blood ran down Lars' shirt.

No one moved.

The owner said, "Lars!"

No one else spoke. Doc came, took Lars to his hospital, sent the man to the undertaker.

Lars was hurt. I ran three blocks to be with him.

Doc said, "Lucky he's big, the bullet didn't get below the muscle, no damage to his gut. I'll need to put him out so I can dig the bullet out. You help, Marisa?"

"Yes, of course."

We took the bullet out. Lars would have a little scar on his side.

"He has bigger scars. He's hurt inside," Doc said, patting his unconscious head.

"But he was shot," I said.

"He wasn't cautious," Doc said. "He didn't have to kill Jackson. He had him, could have taken him in."

I asked, "Is he in trouble, Doc?"

"Of course not, it was self defense; but, do you think anyone wants a deputy who kills like this?"

"But he shot him!"

Doc didn't answer, put his hand to his mouth, looked at me, and walked out of the room.

A coincidence that afternoon Lars' captain from the Army was passing through town and looked him up.

Sent to the sheriff's office, the captain and the sheriff came to the hospital.

"Doc, this is Captain Coffman, Lars' commanding officer on the line. Here to see him," the sheriff said.

"Glad to meet you," Doc said. "But, you've come at a bad time. He's still out. I think he'll be coming around in an hour or two. We had to put him to sleep to take a bullet out."

I was in the room, started to leave.

"Marisa, wait, you should hear this," the sheriff said.

I stopped, moving into a corner as the men sat around Doc's desk.

The sheriff said, "Doc, what happened?"

Doc repeated the incident.

The sheriff said, "Captain, you were on the western front with Lars the day he won the Congressional Medal of Honor. You want to repeat what you told me for Doc and Marisa."

Captain Coffman said, "His friend was killed the day before. I think they had been friends for a long time."

Sam, I thought.

Doc said, "They grew up together, worked together. Sam got Lars on with the black smith, his father. They were inseparable."

Captain Coffman said, "A fluke thing, happened all the time. Swenson looked out of the trench for a second. A bullet hit him right between the eyes. Lars was beside him. I asked Lars if he wanted to take Sam's body back to the rear lines, but he had a look, a rage, something I could use, said he wanted to stay.

"I thought about sending him back anyway. He was big, had some talent with guns, but lacked courage, too melancholy, too fatalistic. I would have promoted him, if he led, but he looked across no man's land and didn't see the enemy. He saw death. Did his job, but I never thought he would do anything like he did. Then Swenson was killed.

"Lars was already the biggest man in my command. He seemed bigger. I heard voices in my head, telling me to use him, keep him, that this time he would be different."

Doc and I listened.

"Major Benton told me to be ready in the morning. The war was winding down. The Germans were beat, but not moving back. Across the line was a machine gun nest on a rise. Things were disorganized, if we took that nest; it would give us a clear shot for half a mile down both sides of the German line, could end things faster. Lars could be a leader based on his size alone. If he fought like a tiger and led men when we needed, he'd be a real asset. This time he had rage. I asked him some questions.

"Lars, what do you want to do, go back with Sam's body, or stay with us and get those sons of bitches who killed him?

He got taller."

He said, "Captain, the Germans killed my father and my grandfather, and now Sam. They'll kill me---but this time, I have to go. They owe me, they owe my family, they owe Sam. I need to go. I need to kill them!"

Captain Coffman said, "I could use him.

"I put together a team, pointed out the machine gun nest too them, as if they hadn't been seeing it for their entire time in this trench. Most of the Germans were on the ground in the flat. Those in the nest weren't on flat ground. They had the high ground and the machine gun was elevated by a knob of the hill sticking up behind them. They dug in about four feet into a bank and recessed the point where they mounted the gun. Then they and added about three more feet at the top with sand bags on the edge. A bank dropped straight off about eight feet high in front of it, flush with their line. A bad spot, it had a clear line of fire over four hundred yards of no man's land and our side. I'd called in artillery on it three times. They blew a hole with a direct hit two days earlier, but the Germans moved it over fifteen feet and were in business again the next morning, just a little further forward. That's what made it a good target. Now the nest was out of their trench and forward six or seven feet. Couldn't be protected by the men in the trench. It was out of their line of fire.

"I looked at them: five men, four of them good runners, fearless. I didn't know about Lars. Big men aren't usually the best runners, but Lars would lead them, probably be a sacrifice for them. With his size he would attract all the shooting, one of the others might get through. We put the whole line on, moving up out into no-man's-land, with back up artillery fire. It was a good plan. All along the line, we would break through and end this thing.

"Morning came, dawn, the sun in the German's eyes, the five crept out just as the first rounds of artillery crashed into the German lines for 17 miles along the front. The smell of deep dirt being thrown into the air floated up and into our line. Twenty yards out the Germans spotted them, started shooting. During the night, crawlers cleared a path, a zig zag path to the machine gun nest. Lars knew it. Started running, other men followed him. I could almost hear those big feet pounding the ground. He was a runner, a surprise for a man his size. Of the four men following him, all were down, two dead. The rest of us got up, hunched over and moved forward. Germans shooting at us, there was movement in the nest, the rat-a-tat-tat of machine gun fire. We started taking casualties, kept inching forward. Lars made it through the wire and was on their side, only a dozen yards from the nest, but out in the open, an easy target.

"I shouted, 'Cover him, lay down a wall.' A hundred men opened up with everything they had on the German line. The machine gunners put their heads down, as did the Germans in the trench. Lars kept running.

"He was carrying his Enfield with bayonet attached. Stopping at the edge of the bank below the nest, he swung his gun into his right hand and jumped to grab the top of the bank with his left. Climbing like a lizard he went up, came up looking the gunner in the eyes. Lars couldn't reach his trigger. He popped his gun back and used it like a spear goring the gunner through the chest, left it dangling there and pulled himself up. Grabbing his gun out of the first man he pointed it at the next, but it jammed. He stuck him too. Only one man left that far forward, the officer, Lars grabbed him and tossed him over the front of the machine gun. He fell head first down the bank into our range of fire. One of our boys got him as he tried to climb back into the nest. Lars had the machine gun. Damnedest thing I ever witnessed.

"He did what no one else could have done. I saw him do it at a rear command post once. A machine gun is heavy, bucks. It's hard to hold, needs to be stabilized. Lars picked up one, held it in his left hand and fired it with his right. He was good. He had its rhythm, could handle a machine gun like an ordinary man handles a sawed-off shotgun.

"He ripped the machine gun out of its mount and carried it to the back of the nest, into the trench. Opening up, he shot Germans for a hundred yards down the trench on one side. Seeing him, Germans on the other side got off a few wild shots before he turned on them. Like mowing grass, he cut them down on both sides far enough up that no one could get a bead on him.

"With no one there to shoot at us going forward, we took their trench in a run. Lars saved most of our lives that day. He killed eighty seven men, but he saved at least forty of us, and took the line. We broke through a quarter of a mile of their trenches and left them open on both sides."

Chapter 13

The Villain & the Farm

"I'm a runner, too; I was one of five men who climbed into that nest with him. He was still shooting. I saw what he was shooting at---

"Germans with their hands up. As far as I could see down the line, those still alive were holding their hands up trying to surrender. Lars was shooting them.

"I yelled, 'Stop!' He didn't stop. I grabbed the gun. He pushed me away and turned it on me. 'Stop, soldier! It's done! Stop!' He looked at me. My heart raced. I knew I was dead. He looked both ways. Not a man alive either way, he lowered the gun.

"I put him in for the Congressional Medal of Honor, there was no question he deserved that."

Doc asked, "What about the men trying to surrender?"

The captain said, "I didn't mention that in my report. No one else on our side saw it. Everybody on the other side that could have seen it was dead."

The sheriff asked, "Is he safe? Can he be trusted with a gun?"

"I pulled him out of combat, sent him back to headquarters with the report of what he had accomplished. Shooting enemy soldiers, especially after a friend is killed, soldiers do that, but---"

Doc asked, "Would you want to be drunk in a town with him being a deputy?"

The captain said, "Would you?"

No one said anything. I slinked down the wall, clutching my arms around me.

The sheriff said, "Marisa, you're marrying Lars?"

"Yes," I said.

Doc said, "Are you sure?"

"Yes!" My hands were shaking. *Did Lars do that? Did Lars kill all those people needlessly?*

Doc said, "Marisa, can you control him? Can you stop him? Lars is a hero. We want to help, but don't want you hurt. Do you think you can stop him, if he---"

I asked, "How can I stop Lars"?

Silence.

I began to cry.

Doc said, "Here now, I have an idea or two. First: Lars loves you."
Did he love me? How could he kill all those people and love me?

"He's a soldier, Maria. Soldiers kill people. It's their job. Most men aren't good at it. Lars is. We all respect him for his service, and will protect him, and you, Marisa." Doc continued. "What we have to do is find a way to make you safe, and make the world safe from Lars. Sheriff, can he continue as your deputy?"

The sheriff said, "Bob, he's a danger. He didn't need to kill that man. Being an officer is a people job, mostly dealing with people like that drunk. An officer has to be careful and controlled. Every arrest can go sour. Every contact can be deadly, that's why we carry guns. If a gangster hits our town, whether Lars is in uniform or not, I want him at my side. On a routine beat---no, I don't want him working with me."

Doc said, "What can he do?"

"If he'll do it, I'll always want him as a reserve deputy. There are times we need a hero, when we need a man who can get business done. But, I don't want him around people, people who might do the wrong thing," the sheriff said.

The captain said, "I had him in my unit for two years. He's a good worker, gets things done. Sergeant Swenson, his friend, made him. I never planned to separate them. They were a good team, worked together well. When he was around Swenson, he was controlled. He got in trouble after Swenson died. He was on his own."

Doc said, "You think Marisa will take the wolf out of him?"

"I'd bet on it, sir. If he loves her, he'll protect her. That's a risk. If he's with her, I don't think he should be around many other people. That might be safer," the Captain said.

"Sraelenburg?" Doc looked at the sheriff. The sheriff nodded.

Doc said, "People here respect Lars. The first Medal of Honor soldier we've ever had. Sraelenburg, a Cossack commander, an old Russian officer respects him. He was going to offer him a job, but the sheriff beat him to it with the deputy offer. Sraelenburg owns half the county, has about fifteen farms for sale. He's always setting up some farm boy with his own place and taking payments. He built an empire, but no kids, what can he do with it. Now he's helping, not taking---and he likes Lars---you too, doesn't he, Marisa?"

"Yes Doctor," I was crying, but listening.

The captain said, "What does Lars know about farming, Marisa?"

"We had a farm at the orphanage. Lars worked it. His granduncle had a dairy farm in Denmark, and his father was buying another one here.

Other than the time in the army, he's always done farm work. But wasn't there an opening for him as a grain buyer?"

I wanted him to be a grain buyer. I was ready to be married and live in town. He didn't have any money to buy a farm. Mr. Sraelenburg could set him up as a grain buyer.

The sheriff said, "Gentlemen, I'll go visit Mr. Sraelenburg in the morning." Picking me up the sheriff, hugged me. "He's going to be alright, Marisa. So will you."

Mr. Sraelenburg visited Lars twice in the hospital. Lars didn't tell me what they talked about. Three days later his stomach was healing.

Doc said, "You know around town is all right. If he goes out of town I'll need him checked on, somebody with him in case it bleeds. Can you do that, Marisa?"

I smiled.

Doc took Lars to Mr. Sraelenburg's farm the next day. He stayed two days and a night.

The next day Lars hired a buggy.

Picnic basket beside me we headed out of town. Where were we going?

"It's a surprise," he said.

An hour and twenty minutes later we lurched up a rut road toward a two story house standing alone on the prairie.

Why is he taking me here?

Unhitching the horse and turning it into a well fenced pasture, Lars made clear that we were staying.

"Lars, where do we eat?"

"In the kitchen. I think the table is still there."

I looked at Lars. How did he know there was a kitchen table, and should we be eating our picnic in someone else's house?

The door swung open. A living room with no furniture, no pictures on the wall and no carpets: bare floors, an empty house. A kitchen table and two chairs, why didn't they take those?

My chicken was improving, the first three times he took me on a picnic. Momma Nina fixed the chicken. This was the first time I fixed chicken for Lars myself.

Crunching through his second breast, crunchy breading, Lars smiled. "Good chicken."

I smiled back, beamed. He looked at me strangely. He always said my chicken was good.

My chicken was good! So was Momma Nina's.

The last of the coleslaw consumed, tea drank and it was time for a walk.

Lars said, "This first barn is the main cattle barn, 42 stalls. See these, milking machines, no more hand milking, brand new, state of the art."

Why would I be interested in milking machines? I smiled, a practiced look of interest.

A woman should appear interested in what her man is talking about.

"This barn, the older one, we use as a back up, good loft for hay, storage."

Two more barns, I never yawned. Walking and yawning is hard to do.

"See that, the tree on that little hill?"

"Unhuh"

"That's the southwest corner of the land."

Exciting, the corner of a farm, a dairy farm. I had to yawn.

"Now the house, three bedrooms upstairs, one on the main floor," Lars walked me through the living room. He held my hand and gestured around us with his other. Walking into the hall, he opened various closets and storage areas. We passed the kitchen again. I needed to gather the blanket and basket, but he dragged me on.

As we walked he said, "Four hundred acres of pasture with a herd of milk cows and six hundred in winter wheat."

Was he going to buy wheat from this farmer? Was that why we were here?

Last he showed me the bedroom.

"Faces straight west. Out this window, you can see sunrise on the mountain before it lights here."

Lars said, "Do you like it, Marisa?"

I had to think. Always living in town, did I like farms?

Quiet settled over me. Not a breeze, I could not hear a person, an animal, or any other noise. I heard him breathing. He took me in his arms. I smelled him, the fresh clean of his shirt, the clean sweat of his chest after a bath this morning before we left.

"See, the Mountains are in our back yard."

A cow lowed. Looking toward the window, one thirty, the sun almost straight above, was moving west over the mountain, blue sky above it. I closed my eyes, saw a pink ice face of the mountain reflecting light from far away into the window of the bedroom. Two clouds holding hands walked toward us over the mountains further south, pure white beautiful clouds. A tent flap closed. Was Daddy smiling? Was Momma smiling? Were they watching?

"Ours," I said.

"If you will have me, Marisa, will you marry me and work this farm with me?"

"Oh, Lars!" I kissed him.

But a farm, being a farm wife, was that how I wanted to spend my life?

Chapter 14

The Werewolf

I said, "Lars, I love you, want to marry you, but are you sure. I don't know if I can live on a farm. My colon doesn't work right. I have to have an enema every day, an hour everyday a normal wife would be working with you. Couldn't I be a housewife and you be a grain buyer, so I can be near Momma Nina? She helps me."

"Marisa---," he said. He couldn't finish, something in his voice. There was a question in his speaking my name. He wanted me. He wanted the farm, more---He was afraid. My brave soldier was afraid.

"Lars," I moved to him, held his hand.

His hand shook.

"I can't stay in town, be around people, Marisa. I can't. I need to be here. I need you."

He looked into my eyes. People were afraid of him---but this wasn't the way a dangerous man talks. He was afraid too.

"I can't be in town. be with me here---please."

His eyes were wild, the wild of an animal trapped unable to escape, looking for a way out.

He was sitting, making it easier to hold his head to my chest and kiss his bald spot.

Trembling, he said, "My father farmed in America. Our farm was ten miles from here." He pointed south. "In Denmark both my parents farmed. Before dawn I was up milking with them, in the country, in the quiet, miles from other people. I need to farm. I can't be a soldier or law man surrounded by people. If I am a grain buyer---I can't be a grain buyer. I'll help you with the enemas---Let me help you with them, please."

This time not grinning with his opossum grin, but asking like a hungry child asks for a bowl of peas. He wasn't a predator running down enemy soldiers with his feet thumping or goring an enemy with a broken pool cue, or grinning at me with his sardonic opossum smile. He was Lars, the man who needed me; Lars, the boy who was my friend; Lars the man who loved me.

His grin missing, I didn't blushed this time, wanted to blush, wanted to hold him, wanted him to want me with passion, wanted him to grin at me with that grin that made me feel naked. He had just asked me to marry him. I wanted him to sweep me off my feet, overpower me with love and kisses, and make me say, *"Yes, I'll marry you!"*

Not seducing, not overpowering, asking, showing weakness, he locked his arms around my hips, pressed the side of his head into my chest, held me with a grip tighter than any man ever held me, and quivered like a boy afraid of the dark, made me want him as a mother, not a lover, made me love him as a mother loves a child grown, hurt, and coming home. A side of him he didn't show to others, he showed to me.

His hot breath penetrating my dress, he said, "I love you, Marisa."

I put my arms around his head, my hand mussing his hair.

I said, "You'll give me my enemas?"

He said nothing, looked up at me and smiled. He had a nice smile.

His grip lessened on my hips, I slid down him resting one knee on the floor looking him in the eyes.

"Lars, I don't do well taking care of myself. If you'll help me with them, I'll do better, but---can you do that? It's not messy, but it's the only way I can go."

His grip on me became gentle, imperceptibly lessening, then letting me support myself. His gentle smile fluctuated with the one with his gums drawn back exposing more teeth, his oppossum grin. It was exposing something about him more than extra molars.

Learning him, this was his evil grin, the grin he had when he was up to something he thought was no good. Giving me an enema was something he thought was wrong, wrong in a nasty sort of way.

I said, "Do you want to give me enemas?"

He pressed his face toward mine, kissed me hard.

He wanted to do it!

He had been thinking, planning, hoping, stalking, planning to marry me, to give me enemas, then a mistake, a drunk in a bar with his own gun exposed him, left him naked before the whole town. When he killed he didn't grin, he didn't plan; he reacted; he was calm, clear, lethal, doing something innate in him, something he was designed to do, something he couldn't plan, and couldn't control. Eight witnesses this time, like the times in high school, the whole town knew, remembered. I did. Now he needed me to love him anyway, to hide away on this farm without another soul close enough to hear me scream and be his wife. Worse knowing that, than that he planned to give me enemas, I quivered, kissed him back.

I said, "Lars, I want you to give me my enemas. I want to marry you."

I smiled. I could deal with him having nasty thoughts about me after we were married---depending on what those thoughts were and where they led. If they led to the outhouse, that was good, not bad.

And, I knew him, violence was part of him, a reaction to outside forces, not me, not anything that should come after us on our farm.

He relaxed, kissed me again, stood, picked me up and swung me around the kitchen, then walked carrying me in his arms to our bedroom, stood in the middle of the room with me and kissed me again.

I looked toward the mountains, then back at him. I would marry him, live on our farm. I held him close. He needed to be held close, his hair stroked, to be protected like a little boy and to be loved like a man and have his fantasies fired with reality.

When he needed to be held, he was too tall, too wide and too strong to be vulnerable standing. When he needed to be the weak and mothered would he sit on a chair, look at me with his little boy look and lean his head on me. Would I give him baby love, coo to him, kiss his hair and let him be something no one else remembered him being, a child?

I would never need to give him a clue when I needed an enema, that would be every morning for as long as I lived.

He put me down, kissed me again.

I lay down on the hard wood floor. He lay down beside me. We kissed again, then just lay in each other's arms till the sun lit our faces through the window. He touched my hip once, not running his hand down my leg and lifting my dress, just holding it. I lay with my head on his shoulder. I thought he might make love to me. It would have been uncomfortable on the wood floor, but I wanted him, not from passion or physical excitement, but just wanting him. We slept. Both of us stiff from the floor, the afternoon sun through the window on our faces woke us. He was going to wait till we were married. I would be a virgin on our wedding night.

On the ride home, the horse rocked through ruts on the sometimes maintained road The county was graveling it the next few weeks, making it passable year round with a wagon or a car, but now it had a few rough spots still sinking the buggy wheels in wet weather and making ruts. That ride, the last rough one I had with him on the road to our home, pushed us together with lurches. We held hands as we had never held hands before. We belonged to each other in our hearts, would belong to each other before the world soon.

I didn't tell Momma Nina first. I walked right past her when I went home and went to bed. Why did I do that? She was my mother and my closest friend. Any other girl would have rushed in, woke her mother up and told her she was getting married. I didn't.

Doc asked earlier that week if I were going to marry Lars. I told Doc, the sheriff, and Lars' captain I was going to marry Lars---but Lars hadn't asked me.

The next morning, I went with Doc to deliver a first baby. We would be there at least one day. I would stay for three or four more days, then Momma Nina would spell me, if Elizabeth still needed a nurse around the clock.

Those first few hours were routine. We got everything ready. I boiled cloths, gave her some enemas. Doc rolled her on one side then the other, stretched and popped her back. I shaved her. She had some contractions, far apart. She would deliver, but not for many hours.

In the kitchen, warming up lunch for Doc and me, I said, "Lars asked me to marry him."

Doc said, "You said yes?"

"Of course!"

"You want to talk?"

"Yes," I said, in a whisper.

Doc checked Elizabeth's dilation, popped her back again, and said, "Elizabeth, how do you feel?"

"I'm sleepy, I just feel like resting. Is that alright?"

Doc straightened her covers. "Lay down, get some sleep, you'll need the rest for later on. Marisa and I will be outside for a while. Call out if you need anything."

Doc and I talked.

"Doc, am I doing the right thing?"

"Do you love him?"

"Yes!"

"Then it's the right thing. You worried about the war, the drunk, yourself?"

"Yes."

"Good things to worry about, and get out in the open now. Have you talked to Lars about this?"

"I don't know how, Doc."

"Maybe you shouldn't. He's going to be your husband, not your patient. He's my patient. You want me to talk to him?"

"Would that help?"

Doc said, "Do you mean, will my talking to him change him, make it so he won't kill anyone else?"

I nodded.

"No, it won't do that, Marisa. He is a man, full grown, rigid inside. He won't change who he is from talking to me. It won't change who he is, but he can change his responses, like we all do learning to live. Sometimes that's what a doctor is for, to help someone change something that's not working in their lives."

"I don't understand."

Doc smiled. "Do you think I do?"

"You're a doctor."

Doc laughed. "Sometimes I don't know as much as you think I do---I'll try. Lars is a wolf, a werewolf, Marisa. Do you know that?"

"He's not a wolf, Doc. If anything he is too much of a gentleman."

"I'm not talking about sex, Marisa. It's the type of man he is. He's all man, but he's not tame. I don't think he can be tamed. He's a wild thing, a Kodiac bear living in a rooming house. He doesn't fit. He's too big. He's too good and quick with weapons to live close to people, Marisa."

"Mr. Sraelenburg wants to sell him a farm."

"I know. What do you thing the sheriff and I have been working on since the incident?"

"You made it so he can buy the farm?"

"No, Mr. Sraelenburg did that. He has the money, the farm, and he likes Lars."

"What did you do?"

"Just talked. The sheriff and I like Lars too. Like I say, he belongs away from people, wars, drunks, and trouble. Around people the werewolf in him comes out."

"You keep talking about him being a werewolf. That's an animal, a big, vicious animal."

Doc said, "Yes, one that is a nice man most of the time, then when stressed it becomes a big, vicious animal. Lars is big all the time."

"But he doesn't grow hair and fangs."

"No, but he has the build. You saw him with his shirt off, he has hair, as much as some bears. He doesn't physically change when he becomes a wolf. But this change is in his quintessence."

"But---"

"Marisa, in the war, he got hurt, got enraged and became a werewolf. He killed men, a lot of men. In the pool hall, he got hurt. A man with less gonads would have backed off, tried to get away. Not Lars, he got enraged and killed the man. Scratch him and draw blood and you have a werewolf. Is a man like that safe around other people?"

"No, but---"

"Live in town with him, Marisa, and sooner or later there'll be a fight on the street, something will happen and he will react. Before he realizes what he has done, he'll kill somebody."

"You think living on the farm will help?"

"Yes, I do. You don't store kerosene on the kitchen stove. You keep it in the garage away from the house. Lars being away from town keeps him and everybody else safe. When he's needed in town, the sheriff will send for him. You heard him. The sheriff wants Lars to stay a reserve deputy. That does two things: one, people in the county will call him when they need help, a man with a gun who will use it; and two, the sheriff can call him if he has trouble. Either way, don't expect him to come home without blood on his hands."

Chapter 15

Care and feeding of Werewolves

Doc said, "Another thing, the sheriff and I talked about this, we want you to decide. If the sheriff or someone else calls on Lars to help, you decide if he goes or not."

I said, "Why me?"

Doc said, "Because you'll be his wife. He might do the wrong thing. If the person asking may be wrong, or you don't feel something is right, have them go into town and get the sheriff. There are times when it's better to leave these decisions to the wife. You marry Lars, and that's the way the sheriff will cut the orders. Lars doesn't go off the farm with a gun in his hand without asking you. And God help any man who comes on your farm and threatens you or Lars.

"There was a man like Lars on a farm in Kansas last year. A bunch of deer hunters were hunting on his farm. The farmer told them to leave. They didn't. He killed all of them."

"Why is Lars this way, Doc?"

"Look at him. Some are big, some little. Lars is a Dane. Danes are big, or can be big. It's part of the race, but some things are in the quintessence. If a man has too much maleness in his teens, the bones in his arms and legs thicken, come together faster. This makes them stronger, but shorter, out of proportion. Lars looks like other men, but his back is long, and his arm spread wide compared to the length of his legs. And all that body hair. Men with too much maleness have more body hair than others of their same ancestry---except on their heads. Excess maleness burns through the hair on a man's head. These men, if it is in their quintessence, get bald early. Have you noticed Lars temples receding?"

"Yes. He's going to be bald?"

"Another thing is sex. Men with high maleness are sex addicts. They can't get enough and still want it when other men tire of it, get too old to do it. You marry Lars and he'll keep you happy in bed until you are both old and gray. You want to live with a bald-headed sex fiend, alone on a farm all your life?"

"With Lars, yes!---but, I've never lived out of town."

"Think about it. Think about him. This time, killing that man, he was justified, self-defense. No question about it, and the drunk was a drunk. Nobody misses him. What if he kills somebody important next time? Do you think the sheriff and I could get him out of it? He's a Medal of Honor winner. That gives him slack, not complete slack. Many war heroes finish their lives in prison or on the gallows. If you keep him in the city, more chance of that happening than if you live a mile from the nearest neighbor. The chances of him being bald and gray around the ears and in bed with you are better."

"So you picked the farm?"

"Yes, it's the farm the sheriff and I asked for."

I smiled. "I guess I'll live with him on the farm, Doc."

"Good. He's a good man, will make you a good husband, but when the babies start don't expect easy deliveries. Ten pounders, he'll make ten pounders with a snarl and a bite. But you have baby-maker hips. Probably have an easy time of it."

I said, "I know about having babies. What else? You said you had some ideas."

And I knew about baby-maker hips. Lars wasn't the only man that stared at my hips.

The forth of July parade, before Lars came home, I was standing by Mr. Srealenburg's Clydesdales, big horses. Mr. Srealenburg used them for deep plowing and his heavy hauling wagon.

Sergi, one of the Russian boys talking to his brother passed by and said in Russian, "It takes strong legs to hold up a rear end that big."

Hearing Russian spoken always grabbed by attention, even after all these years in America, Russian sounded sweeter. I heard and understood what he said.

I smiled at the horse and said, "Dah."

Sergi blushed. His brother blushed. To them it was a private language, one they used to hide talk expecting no one to understand.

It wasn't the horses he was talking about. I tried to pull my dress down, but it was down, not down enough to hide my hips.

A few weeks earlier, I had slipped out of a dance with three other teenagers and tried to slip back in through a missing plank in the wall. Missing for years it was a third door to the barn. Katrina and I used this short cut and had used it together the month before she married Abe. A little twist and she went through not breaking her pace. I slid my upper body through easy enough, but had to stop and bring my hips through more slowly to avoid tearing my dress. This time, three years later, my upper body slid through with inches to spare, my hips caught. I twisted completely to the side trying to pull through with only my stomach and bottom touching the planks. Not my stomach, it was flat; it was my bottom. My baby-maker gluteus maximus, it wouldn't fit, wouldn't slide through. A cowboy watching began to laugh. My face flashed crimson; I had to work my bottom loose, backing out of the wall. I didn't go into the dance again for half an hour, embarrassment still in me.

My hips. I couldn't help my hips. They grew, were as broad as Lars' hips, except mine tapered smaller going toward my waist, and were wider than my shoulders. Lars was straight until his chest then he got bigger. Broader than any other girl's in school, the reason I could be slim and weigh one hundred and sixty four pounds was my figure, 38-28-43.

Doc looked in my eyes, wasn't thinking about my hips, and said, "I do have some thoughts. Can you handle his rages?"

"How?"

"You need to pour it down another prairie dog hole."

I said, "Prairie dog hole? What do you mean prairie dog hole? Sex?"

"Some prairie dog holes have prairie dogs in them, others have rattlesnakes. Don't want him killing any more prairie dogs. When he gets mad he can't tell the difference between a prairie dog and a snake. That's what I meant. And yes, sex, if he's thinking about sex, he won't be thinking about killing."

I said, "Is that how I stop him?"

"Yes, but you don't have to strip naked and tackle him. During the war, he learned to react to his feelings with a gun and knife. Unteaching killing is harder than teaching it. If a neighbor or someone gets him going, what do you do?"

I looked at Doc.

Doc said, "Marisa, he loves you, wants to kiss and hold you, have sex with you, that is part of his instincts, just as his killing is, only when he's after you, his instinct is to love you, not hurt you, and he'll protect you. If you get between him and another man, it'll confuse his reactions. When he's confused, you can direct him, just like his captain did. If you hold him, put your head on his chest, and keep telling him to stop, he'll stop, not because you are his commanding officer, or he is afraid of you, but because he loves you."

"Will he ever want to hurt me?"

"Not likely. You're going to be his mate, his sexual partner, not someone he wants to hurt. If a male wolf is unhappy about something their female does, they take her in their mouth and put her on the ground. They don't bite hard enough to hurt her, just enough to make her listen. Don't fight him if he does this."

I said, "Not fight him, if he bites me and pushes me to the ground?"

"Right. He's an alpha wolf, what does a female wolf do when her three-hundred-pound mate is mad at her?"

I said, "Bark?"

Doc said, "Bark? Marisa, have you ever been around dogs?"

"No, we had a dog, but Daddy Valik killed him. You remember."

"Right, so you don't know dogs. Cows?"

I said, "Horns, hooves, and they're bigger than dogs."

"You're going to make a great farm wife, Marisa. Stay close to Lars. He'll keep you out of trouble. Barking might work. He'll think you're crazy and back away from you. An alpha wolf expects his mate to respect his strength, his long, white, shiny teeth. She gets in a submissive posture, doesn't give him a reason to hurt her."

"I don't want him to bite me."

"Then be submissive, A sane female wolf surrenders, puts herself in a vulnerable position, lays down on her back, puts her tail between her legs, licks his feet. She doesn't threaten to fight the dominant male when he's mad, unless he attacks one of her pups. Female wolves are expected to fight for their offspring---You submit!

"I'm supposed to lie on my back and lick his feet?"

"If you do, be sure to bark."

"What am I supposed to do?"

"Didn't he spank you when you went into his room?"

Doc spanked me more than Lars did. I dropped a stack of towels I was holding the first time he did it. When I started working for him, if I made a mistake, he would swat me on the bottom, then complain that his hand wasn't big enough to spank a bottom like mine. It bothered me, but I liked my doctor, my boss, and was a year younger than his daughter. He swatted her on the bottom when she made mistakes too. She and I helped him together until she went away to teacher's college.

I said, "Then I'm supposed to lie over his lap, bottom up, not on my back, and bark? Do you think I am that crazy?"

Doc laughed. "Didn't you say anybody that resisted arrest with Lars was crazy? You could howl. That might take the fire out of his anger, but spanking you was consistent with the sheriff's instructions. Any misdemeanor, the officers spank kids and send then home, no arrest unless there is property damage or someone is hurt. Lars spanks at least one kid a week, and has never hurt any of them, and a spanking is better than broken bones or a criminal record.

"I know, Doc, but---"

Doc would have swatted me on the bottom then too, but I was sitting on the porch swing with him looking out over the prairie.

"When Lars is mad at you the safest place you can be is over his knee bottom up. Suppressing anger doesn't work, Marisa. It goes somewhere else inside and comes out. If he suppresses rage with you, he'll store it and let it out somewhere else. If he storms off the farm mad at you and comes into town, the next man who makes the mistake of saying something to him could end up dead. I think a lot of Lars' violence comes from suppressing smaller episodes of being mad. If you find a way for him to vent it, he may learn to manage it."

"He wasn't mad at me when he spanked me, Doc."

"Has he ever been mad at you?"

"No"

"Then maybe we're talking about nothing. Marisa, we don't know how much anger he has, just the result of it. It may be the sitting around, like in the trenches in France, or being a deputy rather than doing physical work is part of his rage reactions. A werewolf like Lars isn't designed for a white-collar job. He needs to use those big muscles to work off energy. Hard physical work, farm work may calm him, burn off his anger. Strong men are meant to work. If they don't work, they get in trouble. I think Lars will do better on a farm, sweat dripping off his nose, rather than sitting around town waiting for trouble, don't you?"

"Yes, Doc," I smiled.

But a farm. Lars worked for the Blacksmith in town. He liked that work, used his muscles there. Why did he have to farm?

Elizabeth called out.

We walked back in. Doc checked her, said I should give her another enema, get things going. Enemas help women in labor have stronger contractions.

Momma Nina was making me give myself enemas now. Momma never let me do them myself, neither did Momma Nina, until I was fifteen. Then she said I would not have her to take care of me always, and I needed to be able to take care of myself.

I did, but only if she didn't do it for me. I never volunteered. Not wanting to do this alone and in private, was that normal? An enema is a very private thing. Most enemas are self administered alone on bathroom floors or in bed after husbands and children are at work or in school. But, for the first fifteen years of my life an enema was never private or alone. Why should that change?

Was Momma Nina right? She said I couldn't expect a husband to take care of me. It was too personal. I had to be self reliant, take care of myself. If, like most girls, I only needed enemas when sick, with my periods, or if I got constipated, then maybe I could caterwauler and get a husband to do it, but even then it wasn't likely. Most men would rather wear of flower bonnet to town than help their wives with something personal like an enema.

Lars wanted to take care of me.

Momma Nina and the doctor assured him my need for enemas would not affect my marital duties.

Lars smiled and thanked them for telling him and didn't tell them his feelings. He had had a few enemas in his life. Enemas were something drawing him. Like many people who have a taste of something they need, then have it denied, he developed an interest in enemas. He had constipation problems. He would have felt better if he had had more enemas as a child. He didn't. Having a few enemas, and needing more, can cause an increased interest. If enemas needed had been given, how would he feel now? Would he have been as interested in me as he was?

I had no feeling about enemas. Routine things engender no feelings; occasional things engender some feelings and rare things, like gold and diamonds, are the stuff of great excitement. Enemas to me were top soil five feet deep on the western plains: a resource giving me life, comfort and making a system work that couldn't work without them. Enemas were as important to me as the daily jog to the outhouse was to everyone else. To Lars they were veins of gold hidden in the alluvial fan of a mountain: something rare, something wanted, something out of reach, and something unhad in hungry years of growing up wanting to feel good, wanting enemas.

Momma Nina's enemas were clinical, completely lacking in emotion, nothing to feel. My mother's, were loving. I loved my Mother's enemas, but she loved me in other ways too. The enemas were a routine part of her loving me.

I didn't understand why he wanted to give them to me, but was glad he did. Not wanting to do them alone, I wanted Momma to give them to me. She did. Then Momma Nina gave them to me, but it wasn't the same. In winter, with frost on my window, a full moon lighting a pattern in the ice, I shivered under five blankets and a feather comforter and dreamed of being in the tent with my Mother giving me an enema. I was pulled close to her, my cold feet warming on her legs. When I woke up a surge of loneliness, of missing her, filled me. The man I loved was going to give me my enemas. I was happy he wanted to give them to me. Why should I worry about what that grin meant?

I told Momma Nina. She was curious about it, less excited by the prospect.

"Women give enemas, not men," she said.

The next day Momma Nina said, "Marisa, it is better you give them to yourself. If he wants to give them to you because he loves you and wants to care for you that is a thing to be admired. But, if it's not, it's wrong. If he wants to give you an enema because it excites him, you must tell him no."

I said, "Why?"

"God only gives one way of satisfaction for a man and a woman. That's on your back with him on top, nothing else. Anything else that is sexual, is wrong, wrong before God---a sin, a fetish."

I didn't know what to say or think. What was a fetish? Momma Nina didn't explain.

"I'm going to marry Lars, Momma Nina. Don't I have to do what he tells me?"

"Yes, but remember what I said, the only sexual thing he is to do to you is on your back with him on top."

Momma Nina wanted me married to a good man, and Lars was a good man. He had flaws, maybe a fetish, but everyone has faults. He was a hard worker and about to own a fantastic farm. What more could Momma Nina or Daddy Valik want.

"I understand," I said, understanding nothing, then added, "Momma Nina, do we have to live on a farm? He had an offer to be a grain buyer."

Momma Nina glared at me. "Lars has a wonderful opportunity. Mr. Sraelenburg has no children, no family. He is giving Lars the farm with no money down and reasonable payments to help him, to help you. Don't be an ingrate."

"I just thought---"

"Lars loves you, is making you a respected woman: a thousand acre farmer's wife. Be grateful!"

I quit talking.

Lars talked to my step-father. Two minutes later it was agreed. I would marry him in one month and two days, on a Saturday, after we talked to Father Viktor.

Chapter 16

The Priest on Education, Sex, and Obedience

At first when Momma Nina and I were together in the orphanage after my parents were murdered, I was afraid she would not keep me if she knew I was Jewish. I needed Momma Nina. In the camp, sitting on the toilet I had heard her say things about Jews, bad things. I kept quiet and went to church with her not understanding the rituals or the religion, telling her my Momma and Daddy weren't religious, a half truth. Daddy wasn't religious. Momma loved going to the synagogue and believed in our faith. But a lone ten-year-old girl, how could I be a Jew, cut off from everyone of my faith? Maybe if I had been older, I would have kept my faith. An orphan being raised by a devout Christian, I needed to be Christian.

Being a little girl sitting in the Synagogue vanished with my dolls and childhood toys. I sat in church. I followed Momma Nina. Not forgetting my origins, keeping them secret, still Marisa Stratford, not Marisa Jewinski, I became a Christian. Eleven, twelve, and then thirteen and in puberty, Momma Nina and I walked every Sunday to the Orthodox church.

One spring Saturday Momma Nina in a nice dress and I rode to church in a buggy. Daddy Valik was waiting in a suit. Would she have married him if he hadn't been religious? We went to church every Sunday, and I liked Father Viktor, liked the church. Father Viktor had gone to college and seminary: an educated man. Giving me books to read, he shared my love of reading, learning, and education. I followed Father Viktor and believed he was the oracle of God, the voice of Jehovah on earth.

He and I talked about me going to college. A teacher's college fifty-seven miles from our town, I dreamed of being a teacher like my Momma and Daddy. Father Viktor said I should go to that college. Going to him every time I had a problem, or didn't have a problem and wanted a game, he was more than my preist, he was my friend.

We played chess. A legacy from Daddy, no son to teach, he taught me, his girl, to play chess. In our village square, Father Viktor and another old Russian played chess some mornings. I watched Father Viktor beat the older man consistently.

Father Viktor asked, "Do you play, Marisa?"

"My Daddy taught me."

The old man leaving, Father Viktor motioned me to sit down. My white pawn moved out two spaces in front of my king.

Twenty minutes later I said, "Checkmate!"

Not ready for defeat, he was playing easy, thought he would humor me with a game. The priest's beard hung down, and his mouth hung open. A girl beat him.

"Your father was a good teacher, Marisa."

"He placed third in St. Petersburg, Father."

"Again! I placed third in Odessa!" He sat up the pieces, taking forty minutes to beat me.

When we played, we never knew who would win, sometimes he would, and sometimes I would. Chess created a special relationship between a wise, gray-bearded priest and a young girl. I could play with him and talk to him. He respected me, a chess player. I respected him, my priest. From age ten I was his parishioner; we played and talked.

Momma Nina saw me as a child. Did Father Viktor see me as a gifted child, a thinking child. He told me he could talk to me as he did with few men, and never a woman or girl before in his life, that I challenged him. Alone in my home with no one I could talk to as I talked to him, he encouraged, valued my mind, said I should have an education even though I was the only one in my family to reach high school.

Talking to my parents, he raised questions they were not ready to consider. Of peasant stock, none of their people pursued education. My stepbrothers and sisters all dropped out as soon as they reached the legal age to stop school.

My stepfather asked, "Why educate a girl?"

Father Viktor said, "Why educate anyone?"

Daddy Valik said, "Exactly! Education is for doctors and priests. We are working people, don't need education. Marisa is a girl, a working class girl. Wouldn't educating her be a sin?"

Father Viktor said, "Sin is to do wrong, or not do right. To not use a gifted brain is wrong, a sin."

My stepfather said, "Let her marry, use her brain to raise her sons. If they want to be priests or doctors, let them go to college."

My adopted parent's adoration of our priest being less than mine, they thought of him as an educated exile, heard a rumor that he was jailed in Russia before the war for making anti czarist statements, and after the war couldn't go home because of making pro czarist statements. They followed his religion, respected his education, and narrowed their eyes at his social leanings.

Being a doctor or priest required education. 1919 doctors had to have at least two years of college. Men of God varied from self ordained to seminary trained. Nurses? Momma Nina was a career nurse, and could almost read. I tried to teach her. She had the ability, not the interest. Being a nurse in 1919 could mean formal education, far more often it meant asking a doctor. Ask, and if he said yes, voila you were a nurse. Helping Momma Nina in the Orphanage infirmary for six years, I was one of the best trained nurses in Colorado. I officially became a nurse the day I graduated from high school.

The day before the parade for the soldiers coming home from the war, I was up all night.

Doc took me for a birthing, this time two of them, on farms five miles apart. Momma Nina and he delivered one and I delivered the other, a first baby. The doctor thought he had hours to finish the second ladies fifth baby, then come to deliver my lady, but she was quick, an easy birth, After assisting him deliver six babies before this birth and did fine with my first delivery.

Wrapped and nursing when the doctor arrived, the baby was fine. The mother was fine. The doctor was impressed.

"Good job, Marisa. Next time I can sleep in and let you do the work."

He smiled. Said I would have made a good doctor---if I had been a boy.

Doc stayed with me to deliver Elizabeth. He was afraid the baby wasn't positioned right, and he wasn't, a breech baby. Doc turned him inside his mother, and the delivery went fine. If Doc hadn't been there, the baby might have died. I had much to learn from Doc. But, it didn't matter how much I learned I couldn't be a doctor: only a nurse.

Lars thought I would have been a good doctor and knew I was a good nurse.

I said to him, "Lars, I wanted to go to college."

He said, "Why didn't you go?"

My mouth fell open. I stared at him. I was shocked. He thought I, a girl, could have gone to college.

He said, "Why not, you're smart."

I said, "Momma Nina and Daddy Valik wouldn't let me go because I am a girl."

Lars said, "Education is important. If I hadn't gone in the army, and had kept playing football, I was going to go to college. A school back east said I could play football for them. Katrina and I talked about it. She was going to wait for me."

"I didn't know, Lars."

"It doesn't matter, they weren't interested after I got kicked off the team. It's all under the bridge. We'll be farmers."

I said, "Our children?"

Lars said, "They can go to college, girls and all."

"You want girls?"

"I like babies, however they come out is the way they are."

I kissed him.

Lars came into my life. College, being a teacher or doctor, was out of my life, and I had to talk to my Priest about new things.

Momma Nina had talked to Father Viktor about Lars and his fantasies.

Now Father Viktor wanted to talk to me and Lars separately.

The priest questioned Lars first, then, me. He wanted to know if I had normal thoughts about sex.

I had vague thoughts, gray in the dark moaning thoughts, something intimate, consuming, but as unknown to me as neurology or organic chemistry. I had never made love, was a virgin, but I had non-virgin thoughts about males, curiosity about them, unfocused fuzzy curiosity. Were these normal thoughts?

Sometimes I got warm thinking about kissing different boys. Now I felt that way about Lars, but wasn't thinking about different men. I was thinking about one specific man. Wasn't that normal? I didn't have any overt desire to have Lars lay on me, not a specific desire, but I liked being kissed, being crushed in his arms. Kissing had appeal. Being touched privately had appeal, but he never touched me in private areas. With no experience, never having seen anyone make love and having grown up ten years before the first kiss on the silver screen, what were normal thoughts?

After Lars asked me to marry him, he sat on the porch with me into the evenings. His arms around me, out of sight of Momma Nina and my step father, he kissed me. I got warm, hot. I wanted him to lay on me, thought I would like it, like Momma Nina said.

But having him hold me like Momma did in the tent and give me an enema would be nice, a different nice, a more specific feeling. I knew what having him give me an enema could be like, the surging, the warm gurgling, and the holding on. But Momma Nina was right, it didn't have the same excitement as thinking about him laying on me, holding me, looking in my eyes as he was inside me, part of me. Thinking this, I felt something, a phanthom, a fleeting filling, something never experience before, something I wanted. The enema felt personal---sensual, but not sexual. I wanted both, but was too shy to tell Lars or Father Viktor my feelings.

"This is hard to talk to you about, Father," I said looking down at the floor.

He said, "Marisa, a few more questions."

I continued looking at the floor.

Father Viktor said, "Did Momma Nina, your step father, or the teachers at school paddle you?"

"When I first stayed with Momma Nina she paddled me sometimes, not often. My stepfather took me to the woodshed once. I never wanted to do that again, and didn't. At school, I was a model child, never paddled."

He said, "Have you seen other children paddled?"

I said, "Yes. I saw children paddled at school, Father."

"Did you like being paddled, or seeing other children paddled, Marisa?"

"No, Father, it hurts. No one likes being paddled. I don't. I don't like seeing other people in pain. I don't like seeing women in pain having babies. But when a lady hurts having a baby, it's good pain. I like being there when she has her baby in her arms and everyone is smiling. But pain is part of having babies. The rest of working with Doc---Some things are OK; others I don't like. Taking care of people who are dying can be bad. Taking care of children and young people with the bird flu is terrible, so many die. I cry a lot. I don't like that."

"Do you want to have a baby, babies?"

"Yes, Father."

"Do you want to experience the pain other mothers have, or just the holding the baby in your arms part?"

"Just the holding the baby in my arms. I know I'll have to go through the rest, but I don't want to. I don't know any women who do."

"Marisa, you give women who are having babies enemas. Do you like doing this?

I looked at Father Viktor. Why would I want to give enemas?

I said, "Father, that is my job, something I do: something I am ordered to do to help them have the baby easier. The enema gets them into the rhythm of bearing down, makes the baby come faster and easier."

Father Viktor said, "I understand that, but do you like doing it."

"I don't mind, Father. I think I might like it better than milking cows, but I've never milked a cow."

"Then giving an enema to someone else doesn't excite you?"

I said, "No, why would it? I have an enema every day. Enemas aren't exciting."

"To you they aren't exciting. What about Lars?"

I looked down.

"If giving you an enema is exciting to Lars are you going to let him give you enemas?"

"I want him too. I don't like doing them by myself. My Momma gave me enemas, then Momma Nina. If Lars wants to give them to me, what should I do? Momma Nina says---"

"He will be your husband. Are you supposed to do what your husband tells you?"

Yes, but Momma Nina says---"

The priest said, "Nina, do you know about being a wife?"

"Yes, Lars and I have talked about it. I will work on the farm with him. Learn to milk cows, raise a garden and be his helpmate, a farm wife."

He smiled. "Do you know about sex?"

I blushed. "Yes, Momma Nina said he would lay on me after we're married. I know it feels good, or is supposed too. Lars is so big. Will he hurt me when he lays on me?" Blushing more, I talked quicker, didn't give him a chance to say anything. "I heard my Mother and Father, when I was little. Only a thin wood wall between their bed and mine, I heard everything. Momma liked it. Daddy liked it."

The Priest said, "Is that all you know about sex?"

"Yes, that's sex, at least Momma Nina says, and what I heard listening to my parents."

"What about Lars? What does he say about it?"

"He hasn't talked about sex. It makes me blush, then he blushes. I know when he kisses me, he wants me. He'll teach me when it's time. Now we talk about cows, the farm and what living together will be like."

"And he will. That's right, Marisa. You do what Lars wants you too, and you'll be all right."

I thought, *Why does everyone keep telling me that?*

"Momma Nina said I am supposed to lay on my back and have him lay on me, that, that's right and anything else is wrong. She says God doesn't like people doing anything else."

Father Viktor said, "Many people believe that, Marisa. Many churches teach that. Why did Momma Nina tell you that, Marisa?"

"Lars said he would help me with my enemas. Momma Nina thought that wouldn't be right, if Lars wanted to do it, if he thought about sex when he was doing it."

"That's interesting. Do you mean it's wrong to do what your husband tells you to do if it involves sex?"

I looked at my priest. *What did he mean?*

"Marisa, in the Bible is says a woman must obey her husband. It also says you must obey your parents. Who do you think you need to obey after you're married?"

I said, "Lars?"

He said, "Yes, Lars. Once you are married, you and he are a family. You are to honor your parents and obey your parents now, but when you marry you must obey your husband first, and he must cherish you first. If he had parents, his responsibility would be to take care of you and put that above his duty to his parents. Our commitment to parents changes as we grow up, at marriage, and as they grow old. The Bible says *honor thy father and mother*. That never changes, but at different stages of their life, and yours, that honoring changes. You are seventeen, legally a child. The law requires your obedience to them. They are responsible for you. That changes when you marry. Your husband becomes responsible for you and you, for him. In America you are never legally bound to responsibility for your parents. There is a religious duty, a moral duty, not a legal one. One that changes over time. Momma Nina and your step father have less responsibilities for you after you marry. They have other children. All their responsibility goes to them. For years they should not need your help; although, I know if you need help, they will be there for you. In America there is no retirement, when they get old, if they have savings, they will use it, if not it's expected that you will take them in and care for them. If you don't, if their other children won't, they will go to the poor house, or live on the street."

I said, "Father, Momma Nina is my mother, raised me when no one wanted me. Lars and I will take care of her and my step-father."

"I know you will." Father Viktor reached out to me, patted my shoulder. "When you marry you will be a family, a unit. All your responsibilities under the law are to each other. Lars will be responsible for you. You'll be responsible for him. It's a legal unit and a religious one, a unit that's to act as one and must have one head: your husband, Lars, no other. If there is a problem, if Momma Nina tells you to do one thing, and Lars tells you to do another, your duty is to obey your husband. If you can't obey him, you shouldn't marry him."

I said, "What do I do if he wants me to do something that is wrong before God, Father?"

"Then you have a problem. If you are married you must obey your husband, and you must obey God. The laws of God are constant. The laws of men are not. You must always obey God. If you believe your husband is giving you orders that are a violation of God's laws, then you have a duty to leave him, to divorce him, and not to be married to him. But if you stay in his house, remain his wife, you have a conflict."

I said, "Oh!"

Father Viktor said, "Do you think Lars will ask you to disobey God?"

"No!"

Father Viktor said, "Neither do I. Now, if he tells you he's going to give you an enema, and you think it's something he wants to do because it excites him, is that wrong before God, a sin, Marisa?"

"Isn't it?"

"Marisa, in church law, there are things that are wrong. Most laws have to do with hurting others, violating their rights, or doing something that interferes with the operation of society.

"When it comes to sex, God's law is much less specific. The examples in the Bible all have to do with putting your husband's semen anywhere except in your vagina. God's law is not very clear about other things, and that one edict is to assure that you have babies, replenish the earth, something vital to society."

I looked at him, a priest with decades of religious study. He was logical, studied in his conversation, and totally over my head.

"Marisa, in a few places, the Bible condemns people because of putting the husband's semen in the rectum, or spilling it on the ground. People kiss and get excited. People stimulate themselves to sexual release when they do not have mates. God's law doesn't spend much time on these things, and sex between men and women is only approved of once there is marriage. This is because a purpose of marriage is to create babies with a mother and a father. In marrying it's expected that you will have Lars' babies, and religious law is formulated to be sure that you practice sex in a way that puts your husband's semen deep into your vagina so that you have babies. You understand that?"

I said, "Of course, I want to have Lars' babies."

"Good, then do, do what he tells you to do, but if it's sexual, it should end with him putting his male organ in your female organ, putting his seed in you to grow babies."

I said, "It's alright for him to give me enemas?"

"You need an enema every day, don't you?"

I said, "Yes"

"Then what's wrong with him giving them to you, so long as he's not hurting you and he keeps making love to you in a way that makes babies?

"But Momma Nina says anything to do with sex without him laying on me is wrong."

"She has a point. The best way to get your husband's semen deep inside you and for you to hold it may be laying on your back. What if he wants to do something different, or you want to do something different and this means doing something other than missionary prone sex?"

I said, "Missionary prone sex, what's that?"

"What you described is missionary prone sex: the woman on her back, the man on top."

"If it isn't like that, it's wrong before God---Isn't it?"

"The only thing that is wrong, Marisa, is if his semen is deposited outside your vagina. Whatever excites him or you: kissing, enemas, toe nibbling---anything, all that matters is that you end up with him inside your womanhood depositing his seed often enough to give you a reasonable number of babies. If you refuse to do something that is not harmful when he asks because you mistakenly think God disapproves, that is a sin. What is a sin, is for him to refuse to do something that makes sex better for you, that ends up with his semen not in your vagina.

"What's wrong, Marisa, is for you to disobey your husband, or not to please him. That's what obedience is about, pleasing him. That's what cherishing is about, him pleasing you. A good wife obeys her husband and a good husband cherishes his wife."

"Now we know. It is out in the open between you and him. He wants to give you enemas. There is something else, Marisa. Does Lars know what you want of him?"

"Father, I don't know what I want of myself. I want him to teach me."

"It doesn't bother you that Lars wants to give you enemas?"

"I don't mind, Father. I want him to give me enemas like my mother used to give them to me: holding me, keeping me warm, making me feel loved. I want that."

Father Viktor said, "That's wonderful, Marisa. You uniquely may fulfill an important sexual fantasy for Lars---and be an exemplary wife doing this. But you don't know what you want. How is Lars to respond to that?"

"I don't know, Father."

Father Viktor said, "Neither do I. Neither does Lars." He paused, thought for twenty seconds, and looked in my eyes. "Marisa, I counsel people. People know I will talk about sexual problems so they come to me. What I find is that most of the people dissatisfied with sex are women, and that most of this dissatisfaction comes from not having their fantasies addressed. You are a virgin, don't know what you want. When you know, you must talk to Lars. Marisa, I want you and Lars to talk to each other about what you want from each other. This is a conversation that has no end. When you know what you want, or what you want changes, you must tell him. I have no problem with your sharing with me, but you must share with Lars. And I want him to share with you. It's intimate, but you must do this to make sure your dreams are fulfilled in life, in marriage, and in bed, and when you don't want the same things you both must compromise with love.

"If there are differences that you can't resolve talk to me. That's why I'm here. Work out what you can before you marry, set up communication to adapt as you both change, and life will be the fulfillment of both your dreams. Assume nothing, talk to him, ask him. I have told Lars to do the same thing with you.

"Another thing, have you talked to anyone else about Lars wanting to give you enemas?"

I said, "Momma Nina"

"Stop there, Marisa. As long as you bring me children to bless, I'm not interested in what you do privately with your husband. That's something confidential between you and him, not my business. If he likes giving you enemas and you don't mind him giving them to you, that's your business."

I blushed.

"It's no one else's business what you do in the privacy of your home. It is important is that you don't share these details with others without good reason. You may with a doctor or a priest, if you have health or spiritual problems related to what you are doing, but only if problems exist."

I looked at him, what was he telling me?

"Marisa, if you find enemas exciting, or if he does, keep it between you and him---no one else. If he finds hanging by his toes in the barn kissing your feet exciting, or if you do, it's between you and your husband. Other people will not understand. When you find a joy that is different, not usual, not missionary prone sex, other people will find it to be disgusting or wrong. If they find it repulsive, they may say God thinks it is wrong. What is wrong is what you feel is wrong, not what other people think is wrong. Part of marriage is the joy of intimate exploration, you exploring his body and Lars exploring yours. He's a man. You're a woman. His body becomes uniquely yours and yours uniquely his when you marry. God's giving you each other means that you and he should do things with each other that are wrong with any other person of the opposite sex and that those things are personal and private between you, your own unique universe. Do you understand this?"

"Yes, Father."

I said, "In marrying him, must I obey him? It's 1920, Father. Some women say that's old fashion, wrong," I said.

Father Viktor said, "It's in the Bible and all the other religious scriptures of the world and required for a church marriage in every Christian church. Why do you think obeying him is wrong?"

I said, "I'm an adult, well almost an adult. Seventeen---and not sure I want to go from my home, obeying my parents, directly to a new home, obeying my husband."

Father Viktor said, "I understand, Marisa, but you are going to be his wife. Obedience is something required, something none of us escape, no matter how long we live. I must obey policemen, if they blow their whistle or yell at me, and I am an old man."

"But you are a man, when you are inside your house, everyone listens to you."

"That's true, and I insist my wife and children listen to me. It's God's law.

I said, "I am an intelligent woman. Must I listen like a child to my husband, Father?"

Father Viktor said, "Yes and no. You are an intelligent adult, one of the differences between a child and an adult is obeying. I don't ask children to obey. I require it. A child doesn't have authority over their own lives, obeys from necessity, as you obey Daddy Valik out of necessity. If you don't agree with him, or I don't agree with him, like his preventing you from going to college, it doesn't matter. You are his child. You must obey him.

"This time you have a choice.

"Marisa, picking a good man to be the head of your home is the most important decision you will ever make. I believe your marrying Lars is a good choice. It pleases Daddy Valik, your mother, sheriff, Doc, and me. A woman, when she accepts a man, agrees to marry him and follow him. She must agree to obey him.

"And I don't believe in the old way, of forcing sons or daughters to marry. If done in the old way a parent finds a mate for a child, but I believe that child must be asked and agree to the marriage. I think Valik would have traded you for a side of beef years ago, if he could have. But, in America, sons and daughters choose their own mates, as you and Lars are doing.

"You must know him, learn his ways, his heart, love him, know he loves you. A marriage without love can't blossom. A marriage with true love blossoms like a cottonwood tree in spring.

"But, a woman and a man's roles in marriage are different, Marisa. Do you love him enough to be the woman in the marriage, to respect him, to trust him with your life, and your children's lives: to obey him, to respect him as your husband? Do you love Lars that much?"

"Yes, Father, with all my heart, and I know he's a good man."

"Are you willing to be his queen, and for him to be your king?"

"Yes," I said.

He said, "Your heart is a good guide. Lars loves you, will love you and your children as no other man will love them or you. He'll make good decisions. Do you trust him to make those decisions for you, and in time your children?"

I said, "I do, Father, but you know me. I have a good mind. I can think for myself. I'm not sure I want anyone else thinking for me."

"Who said Lars would be thinking for you? The Bible only says you must obey him. And, in our church we crown you, make you a queen and make him a king. Do you think queens do not think? A king and a queen are a team, as a marriage is the pairing of a man and woman. I marry people in the church. I marry kings and queens. My goal as priest is to marry those yoked together, those who serve Christ together as the spiritual head of their home, for the glory of God. Do you love God? Will you serve God as Lars wife, as he serves God as your husband?"

"Yes, father."

"Good. Do you believe in God? Do you believe in our Holy Savior, that he lived for us, that he died for us, that his teachings and the teaching of the Orthodox church are true and right, worth living for and dying for, Marisa?"

"Yes, father."

"Marisa, God gave the church to human kind for our individual benefit. He also gave it to create stable workable societies. The woman is the heart of the family, the mother, the strongest and most vibrant part of the union of marriage, but the husband is the rudder, the stability that keeps the family on course. If a woman is allowed to deny the rights of her husband in the home, to not obey him, then there is no rudder, no stability in the home. The children grow wild without respect for authority, without solid values, values like serving a God that is unchangeable. Can you accept Lars as your rudder in the sea of life, or will you fight his authority in the home, and make your home a place lost at sea, a place where God's love will drown in anarchy?"

"I can follow Lars, obey him, father. I do all ready. He makes decisions all ready, but usually asks me."

"Then I can marry you, but you must agree to obey Lars. That is part of God's law, law that you cannot oppose if you are to be married in any Christian church," Father Victor said turning away from me to light a candle. "Marisa, do you think a farm wife should not think, should go ask her husband every detail?"

"Isn't that what obeying means?"

"Obeying means following orders. It doesn't mean not thinking."

I said, "Father, if I obey him, don't I have to get directions from him about everything I do?"

"Lars is not that foolish, Marisa. He's a man, will work the fields, in the barn, plow, build, take care of the farm. You'll take care of the home, the children. If there is something you don't know, ask him. A farm is a small kingdom. It has many parts, will generate many questions. No one has all the answers. If it is something about the home or children, experienced women usually become the authorities. If it is something about farming, experienced men usually become the authorities. Lars will not know everything about cleaning, fixing food, or caring for the children, any more than you are expected to know everything about his work. As head of the home, he will know when dinner is not ready, when a child is sick, or his Sunday shirt isn't ironed. It's your job as a wife to care for these things---a good wife does this without being told to do it. She does it because it's her duty, because she's is her husband's woman, for love."

"I want to be a good wife, and of course will do these things. It's my duty as a wife, as it's his to care for us. Maybe I don't understand what it is that I'm supposed to obey."

Father Viktor said, "Obeying means watching, listening and observing, then doing what needs to be done, what your husband wants done. If you wait until he orders you, do you think he'll be happy, that you'll be happy, that you will be being his queen?"

I said, "What do you mean?"

"I watched Lars at the picnic last week. He ate corn-on-the-cob until I thought he would burst, but he didn't eat any cheese casserole. If you are going to fix a big summer meal for him, what would you serve him?"

"I like cheese casserole, Father."

"Then you would serve him a big plate of both?"

I said, "Not if he doesn't like cheese casserole."

Father Viktor said, "That's obeying, Marisa. A wife fixes healthful meals for her family. She also fixes what her husband likes and learns to avoid what he doesn't like. I know Lars doesn't like cheese casserole because I watched him, then asked him later. He told me he doesn't like cheese. If he has to tell you he doesn't like cheese before you stop fixing it for him are you being an obedient wife?"

I said, "No?"

"That's right, No. A good wife, a thinking, obedient wife doesn't have to be ordered all the time. She observes and does what she knows will make her husband happy, before he asks, and does the chores of a wife before he asks."

I said, "So that's what my mind is for, pleasing him?"

Father Viktor said, "Yes, as is his for pleasing you. Lars asks you what you want, I've seen that."

I said, "How long do you think he will keep asking?"

He said, "Always. You've been seeing him almost every day for the last month and a half. Does he have to ask you everything now, as he did the first time he took you out?"

"Well, no, Father, he knows me better."

"After fifty years of marriage, he'll know you, as well as, he knows himself, Marisa. And you'll know him. In a good marriage very few orders are given. Good husbands and wives read each other, know each other. Without being asked, most do what the other desires. Some people are harder to read. With them it's best if their mate asks rather than guesses, but if you know, act on your knowledge, be a partner, not a slave, be what he wants, do what he wants. He'll do the same for you. When he must give you an order, or a child an order, he will do it out of love, and you must obey. It's a law of God."

"But what if I don't agree father?"

"If you disagree, does it lessen your responsibility to obey, Marisa?"

"No?"

Father Viktor said, "But, you can tell him how you feel, unless you are in front of others, particularly your children. They must see you obey, or they will not respect you, your husband, or other authorities given the right to order them. In private, you have tears, gentle touches in the night, and his heart. If you obey him, kiss him and tell him what is in your heart, he'll listen. Tell him your opinion with respect, as a soldier tells his sergeant with respect, but with far more power. Because Lars loves you; he will listen. He will judge. He may change his mind, if it's important to you and he sees a way to do it your way. He will bend. If he doesn't, you bend."

Father Viktor said, "Lars was a hero in the war. If it's in an emergency, don't think, do as he asks and talk about it later. He is quick thinking, and in moments of emergency your family needs to respond to your husband without question. Condition yourself to respond when he commands, but when it's something that you have time, talk with each other. Come to a mutual decision when you can, when you can't; he decides.

Father Viktor said, "Trust Lars. I talked to him about this. He doesn't make decisions without thinking when he has time to think, Marisa. He talks to you. He wants your counsel. Didn't he talk to you about the farm before he bought it?

"Yes," I said, thinking about him and our bedroom looking out toward the mountains.

"Marisa, he will always value and listen to your opinions, and your opinions will influence him even when a tornado is bearing down on you. But when he yells to get you and the children into the storm shelter, don't take time to question him. Train yourself to do what he asks. You may question him with the respect due a husband later, if you feel the need too.

Father Viktor said, "Don't think Lars disrespects you, he doesn't. He values your opinion, and I don't think he will make a major decision without talking to you about it."

I smiled. It said this way, made sense. Women talking at the sewing circle complained about having to obey their husbands, but I liked

Father Viktor's thoughts on this. Obeying doesn't mean not thinking, being a slave, it is being part of a team, a woman, a wife, a helpmate, and a counselor.

Father Viktor said, "Obeying doesn't mean you're less than Lars. You're more, the wife always is. The home, your life together, you will make. Lars is a man, he'll always serve you and your children. The children follow you. You follow Lars, and your family is united, a good family.

"In homes where the wife disrespects her husband unity can't happen. The children, confused, won't follow or respect either the mother or the father, and like a ship, a family can have only one captain, one husband. Do you believe Lars will be a good husband?"

"Yes, I do," I said.

"You trust him enough to agree to marry him, to obey him?"

"I do."

"Then marry him. If you didn't trust him enough to keep your marriage vows, then I wouldn't marry you. It's that important, Marisa."

"Father, there's something that the sheriff put as a condition on Lars. He's big. He's dangerous. The sheriff wants him to be a reserve deputy, not a regular one. When they need Lars, they want him. When they don't want anyone hurt, they don't want him. Him leaving our farm to be a deputy, they made my choice, if I marry him. If I don't think he should go, the sheriff said it would be my choice, not his. How do I handle that?"

The priest said, "Telling your husband what to do is wrong. The sheriff putting this on you is wrong, wrong in marriage---but, I know what happened in town. I understand the sheriff's feelings. Putting Lars on the farm lessens the problem because he won't be around people, and won't be around law breakers unasked. People afraid will come to Lars, and people knowing Lars will come to him. Will they be wise enough to know when to go to Lars and when to go to the sheriff? You're intelligent enough to make that decision if you know the circumstances. If Lars is involved and starts to act, I pray God guides you. You will need to act as you think right. You know that in the wrong situation, Lars will kill. You will be his wife, and you will need to stop him. It's not in the Bible, and not part of most marriages. But, Lars has to be stopped from hurting people. You, his wife, will learn to sense it in him, will know when his going is right or wrong.

"In an emergency, if a life is in danger, a crime has to be stopped, or a criminal caught, Lars may act before there is time to think. When things happen to fast to talk, you must follow and support your husband unless you know it is wrong for him to go, the emergency is not an emergency, there is time to get the sheriff, or his going is too much of a risk. The sheriff put you in a position to judge. Judge wisely.

"It's Lars place to protect you, his family, his community, and his nation, but he is more male than other men, more violent. One that is needed in rare situations, dangerous in more common ones, but if he gets in the wrong situation, you know what can happen. If the sheriff doesn't call him, you may have to make difficult decisions.

"Lars won't hurt you, Marisa. I know that, but if you have to stop him, if you block him from doing what he thinks he should, you need to be willing to pay the price. The sheriff is putting you in an awkward situation, Marisa. Giving you the power to say to Lars that he cannot strap on his gun and do what he wills is a problem, a violation of Biblical law between husband and wife.

"Didn't you tell me he spanked you for going to his room alone?"

"Yes, father," I blushed.

"Then you know he will punish you if you disobey social morays or the law."

"Yes"

"If you have to stop him from doing what you know will get someone else or him killed, you are disobeying a marital law to prevent the breaking of a bigger law. Marisa, there's no law that can't be broken, but there is always a price. The price of Lars killing someone is their death, and likely his, if it is not self defense. And we know, even when it is self defense, the killing is not always necessary. What's the price of your stopping him---not obeying him?"

I said, "I don't know, what?"

"Disobeying a husband is not a death penalty crime, Marisa. It's a misdemeanor, like a young girl going into a single man's room and kissing him alone, a spankable crime."

"You mean I can tell him what not to do and prevent him from being hanged, and he can spank me?"

"What do you think?"

"I don't like being spanked."

"It's better than the alternative, him dying. But, he'll need to reestablish his role in the home, if you make him stay home when there is trouble, Marisa."

"You think he should spank me, if I won't let him go kill someone?"

"Rules are rules, one is that disobedience can be punished, whether it is a child or a wife. Is that reasonable?"

"Yes---but"

"Would you rather have a paddling or have Lars hanged for murder? Or if you stop him from being hanged then have him not be the head of your home is that good?"

"I have to let him paddle me?"

"I think that needs to be Lars decision, and yours. It is better he remain head of your home, than to loose those Christian values, Marisa. There are caveats. One is if you violate marriage law and order him to stay home, and he wants to punish you what happens?"

"I get paddled?"

"Yes, maybe, when?"

"After I tell him NO?"

"Yes, if spanking you stops him; if you take the spanking, climb into his arms sobbing; and tell him not to go again, he will listen. If you climb into his arms sobbing before he has the chance to spank you, it can work as well.

"Punishment needs to be a ritual. A crime or disobedience occurring in haste, should be repented and punished at leisure. Rule one: never punish in anger. If you are angry at a child you send them to their room. They wait there until you cool your anger. If Lars is angry at you he should go back to work on the farm and deal with it some hours later. Rule two: have a trial, a family meeting, a discussion between parent and child, or Lars and you. If you disobey Lars by obeying the sheriff, it's Lars right to punish you, and a paddling can be an appropriate punishment.

"Marisa, do you think Lars will ever paddle you?"

"I hope not."

"I don't think he will, but it's his right, and your duty to ask if it is needed to insure the structure of your marriage or home."

"If you stop him from going to a crime scene, or to arrest a criminal, and you know he is angry, is that the right thing for you to do?"

"Yes"

"Is it then his right to paddle you for stopping him?"

"Yes"

"Will he be angry with you?"

"I think so, Father."

"That's a maybe, Marisa. He may be angry at the moment, but when he thinks about it, I don't think he'll be angry. I think he will be glad you were there to stop him."

"So he'll be glad I stopped him and I'll have a sore bottom."

"If he does it right away, yes, but if he follows the rules and waits till his anger is gone, I don't think you will ever have a sore bottom from stopping him once he cools down and thinks about it. Do you see this logic?"

"Yes, Father."

"The next time we meet together. I want you, Lars, and me to lay all this out and agree to it. Doing this before you marry is best. I know Lars is afraid of hurting people, and knows he needs your help. I don't think there will be any problem, and I expect that in the next fifty years he will never paddle you for stopping him from going off in a rage.

"Marisa, pardon me, I am an old man trapped in the cobwebs of intellectual thought. There is the one truth we have yet to talk about.

"Why are you marrying Lars?"

"I love him, Father."

"More detail, Marisa. You are marrying a very large man, considered the most dangerous man in our area---why?"

"I love him, Father."

"Love is the key, without love no marriage works. Why do you love him?"

"I love him because---You ask hard questions, Father."

"Mmmm," he folded his hands, waited for me to talk.

I said, "I was drawn to him, Father. I am Katrina's friend, watched their love through high school. It was very special. She needed him. He needed her, and his consideration of her was unusual, very romantic, very caring. To be loved by him, I knew would be special. I wanted him to love me, for me to love him."

"Those of us who saw them knew they had something special, Marisa. Lars was a dominant male wolf protecting his timid mate with Katrina. She gave him his power, his rage. Love is about giving, Marisa. What do you give Lars?"

"My love is all I have to give, Father. I have no money. Am not beautiful, like Katrina, nor am I as nurturing, as good to him. Have no education or anything special."

"You're wrong, Marisa. Love is all he needs, but you have things you will discover in your lifetime that made you for him and him for you. He is strong. Are you?"

"Yes, I don't have his strength, but I am bigger and stronger than most women."

"Are you smart?"

"Yes"

"Smarter than Lars?"

"I don't know, should a woman be smarter than her husband?"

"Obedience. You must be obedient, smart or not, but Lars is a special case. You have to make decisions that prevent him from getting in trouble. Are you smart enough to do that?"

"I hope so."

Father Viktor said, "So do I. He is a special man, one highly respected, yet flawed. A woman with less intelligence than you could not fill the role he will need you to fill. His heroism, and his anger, make him a man to be watched, cared for, and wifed. I think you are uniquely qualified to be his mate, and your love for him is critical. Love applied through truth is the essence of life.

"Katrina, she will always be special to him, and you. Do you think she could have been the wife to Lars you will be?"

I said, "She would have been better, Father."

He said, "No, my girl, she wouldn't have. Katrina was a girl he loved, adored, and protected. She stood behind him, hiding, wanting him to protect her. How long would he live with a wife like that?"

I said, "A long time, Father. He would have done anything for Katrina."

He said, "That's the point. He doesn't need a wife afraid, standing behind him. He needs a wife standing beside him, one smart enough to understand his nature, one strong enough to stop him, not spur him to violence. He needs a wife competent to guide him when his reactions are out of control. You told me Doc referred to him as a werewolf, Marisa. He is, a very large werewolf, a hero because of this defect in his nature, and he loves you. He needs you, Marisa. A woman with less intelligence and less strength couldn't love him, stand between him and the object of his rage, protect him from himself, then submit to him and stand beside him as an obedient wife. Sweet Katrina couldn't have been the mate he needs, Marisa. She wasn't strong enough or smart enough to be Lars' wife. I couldn't have planned a wife better suited to Lars than you.

"And you have flaws that he matches, Marisa. How many husbands would want to help a wife an hour each day with her bowels to keep her healthful?"

I walked out of the church into full sunlight, light illuminating the ends of my hair and making them glow like strings of gold. I looked down at my wide hips, my long body: hips and a frame too strong, too sturdy to suit most men's desires. I was strong enough, wide enough and smart enough to support Lars. I felt my mother and my father beside me: my mother, a woman, obedient to her husband, a good wife; my father, the man guiding her and me to what he believed was a better future, a good husband who died protecting her. I would be a good wife, obey, and protect my husband. God's sun light warmed the ground around me. God made me perfect for Lars, made Lars perfect for me.

The priest would say again, "...love, honor, and obey."

And I would say, "Yes, I do."

And before we said our, I do's, Father Viktor met with Lars and I together.

Lars said, "Why would I spank her? She's going to me my wife, not a child, unless she wants me to spank her. Do you want me to spank you?"

I said, "NO!"

Lars said, "Then we'll put a sign on the gate to see the lady of the house with any police matters. If Marisa thinks I should go she can come get me. If she doesn't there's no reason to interrupt my work. If anybody comes to me direct, I'll just turn them around and send them to her."

I kissed him.

Chapter 17

Our Wedding

Large formal weddings, the normal for upper classes, were also important to working class people, but less formal, less large. The Russian community in our village was thirty families. The only reason we had a church and a priest was a farmer, a wealthy farmer, Mr. Sraelenburg.

Mr. Sraelenburg had two bits of luck. First coming to America, he went west two decades before the rest of us arrived. Alone in America, he learned English and married an American woman from our village, a widow with a large farm. The second bit of luck was the discovery of oil on the farm. He bought fourteen ranches, seventy-two farms, built one church, and hired Father Viktor, a well qualified, older priest open to a rural parish with a small congregation and parsonage. The rest of the Russians followed the priest growing a Russian community.

Lars and I, orphans, no family except my adopted parents, we couldn't fill the church with aunts, uncles, or cousins. Church members, friends came to our wedding with the local people from our community. Daddy Valik, not a rich Russian, gave me a church wedding. The church gave us splendor expensive to purchase in other churches. Ornaments and Icons, church property, our wedding was ornate and beautiful without being expensive. We were joined in the mysteries of the Orthodox Church, a man and woman united by the Holy Trinity. Father Viktor expounded on the blessing of a union blessed by the Church. He lectured on the grace of God in marriage, on Lars imperfections made perfect through my perfections, my imperfections made perfect by his perfections, sorrow halved by our sharing it and joy doubled by our sharing it.

Orthodox weddings have two parts; betrothal means something different to us: betrothal is the first part, is not something that occurs weeks or months before the marriage: it is part of the ceremony. We were betrothed and immediately married. The ring ceremony starts the betrothal. The priest blessed them, then with the rings in his hand, made the sign of the cross over Lars and my head.

He said, "This servant of God, Lars, is betrothed to this maid of God, Marisa, in the name of the Father, of the Son and of the Holy Spirit"

Taking Lars ring, I placed it on his finger. Had I noticed how hard his hands had become? When he came home from the war, when he was a deputy, his hands were soft. Three weeks on the farm and they were hard and rough.

He dug a water line from the well to the house, six feet deep to prevent freezing in winter, plus doing farm work. He wanted me to have dependable water in the house, didn't want me going outside in the cold for water. In winter, when the temperature dropped to twenty below, he would go outside, bring in wood for fires, keep me warm. He even promised to build an indoor toilet when we had enough money. He was working hard, for me, for us.

I wanted to kiss his leathered hand and did then put his ring on his finger. A new, three interwoven bands gold ring symbolic of the Trinity, a ring Lars expected me to put on his left; I put it on his right hand. We wear our wedding bands on our right hands in Russia. He could change it to his left if he wanted later. All that mattered to me was his being mine.

My turn he took my hand, gently sliding my ring on my finger. I was his. Our betrothal was completed by the ring ceremony.

The second part of the ceremony, our wedding started. Father Viktor handed us the candles. Carrying them symbolized the five wise virgins in the Bible, who because they had enough oil in their lamps, received the bridegroom. The bridegroom, symbolizing Christ, came in the night. Holding the candles represented our readiness to serve Christ, and welcomed Christ blessing to us.

Father Viktor took Lars right hand and mine, putting them together, then read the prayer, "Join these, thy servants. Unite them in one mind and one flesh."

Holding hands, we followed the priest.

A special part of a Russian wedding is the crowns. We were crowned. Lars was to be the king or our home; I, to be the queen. A religious confirmation of the lecture Father Viktor gave me before our wedding, the Orthodox Church recognizes a fundamental truth of life: marriage makes a man and woman the foundation of society. A family is a kingdom, the fundamental building block of human society. An Orthodox Church wedding makes us the king and queen of our home. Kings and queens have crowns. A beautiful crown on my head, another on Lars' head, we were royalty---dressed and recognized as king and queen for one day in our church, and recognized as king and queen for the rest of our lives by the Church in our home.

Father Viktor said, "You are the king and queen of your own kingdom, your home, a domestic church that you will rule with the fear of God, wisdom, justice, and integrity."

Crowning us, Father Viktor said, "The servants of God, Lars and Marisa, are crowned in the name of the Father, and of the Son and of the Holy Spirit, Amen."

Father Viktor said, "Symbols of a king and queen, the crowns are also symbols of a crown of thorns, of Christ: crowns of martyrdom. True marriage is joy and love. It is sacrifice, immeasurable sacrifice, by both the husband and wife."

Lars worked as he never need have worked, had he not married me. I listened to Father Viktor and squeezed Lars calloused hand. Marrying me meant a lifetime of hard, physical work for him. Lars was giving his life for me.

Marrying him meant a lifetime of being loved for me and a lifetime of labor. Labor, childbirth, decades of dirty diapers, child rearing and hard work, farm work, I was giving my life for him.

What hardships lay ahead for us, what sorrow, what joy, only God knew.

Next the wine, the common cup, together we drank wine from a single goblet symbolizing the wine from the marriage in Cana attended by Christ. His first miracle at this wedding turning water into wine, Christ gave it to the marrying couple. Drinking from the cup of better life of sharing joy and sorrow, a symbol of life harmony, a Church mystery, we imbibed. Drinking from the common cup symbolized that we were to bear each other's burdens, that the mystery and miracle of marriage was ours.

Next, we walked. Father Viktor led us around the table holding the cross and gospel: the Word of God and the emblem of Christ's sacrifice. We were taking the first steps of our marriage. Our priest was leading us, representing Christ and the Church. He leading us walking around the table symbolized Christ leading us in the way we must walk. Circling the table with these symbols in the center mirrored the earth orbiting the sun, mirrored Christian living being a perfect orbit.

Singing a hymn to the Holy Martyrs, Father Viktor reminded us of sacrificial love. Our love, as written in St. Paul's chapter on love, I Corinthians 13:

Love sufferth long and is kind; love envieth not;
Love vaunteth not itself, is not puffed up,
Doth not behave itself unseemly, seeketh not its own,
Is not easily provoked,
Thinketh no evil;
Rejoiceth not in inquity, but rejoiceth in the truth;
Bear`eth all things, believeth all things, endureth all things."

Last the blessing, we returned to our place in front of the priest.

Father Viktor said to Lars, "Lars, be thou magnified as Abraham, blessed as Isaac, and increased as Jacob. Walk in peace. Work in righteousness. And follow the commandments of God."

He said to me, "And, Marisa, be thou magnified as Sarah, glad as Rebecca, and increase as Rachael. Rejoice in your husband, obey him. Fulfill the conditions of the law. In doing this God is pleased."

One month and two days from the day Daddy Valik said we could be married, we were.

Father Viktor shared our customs with the guests, as did Momma Nina and Daddy Valik.

My parents bought my dress, a fine white dress flowing to the ground. A peplum wrapped around my hips adorned with the fabric made into white roses flowed in pleats to my feet. White roses at my shoulders stitched into pleats flowing down my back blending with the pleats below, a veil and white lace covered my head.

In the pictures of our wedding, Lars and I stood, so erect, so young. Was I that beautiful? That day was the only time I saw him in a tuxedo, a rented one, one shipped in from Denver, and the only one that would fit Lars in their inventory, and it didn't fit him. The order said he was a large man. Does Large always mean fat? He had to wear it as if it were double breasted approaching a wrap around when it was designed to be single breasted. A seamstress in town tacked the buttons so it would fit, and it still bunched around his chest. And the pants he wore doubled on front and back, the seamstress was stitching him in moments before I was to walk down the aisle.

Lars asked, "What if I have to go to the bathroom?"

He had diarrhea for two days before our wedding.

The seamstress said, "Make it through the ceremony and into the carriage waiting out front for pictures and you can run to the outhouse. I'll have your uniform waiting there and cut you out."

Finishing the rest of our rituals after the wedding in his dress sergeant's uniform with his Medal of Honor around his neck, he was much more impressive than in that tuxedo.

Momma Nina said, "They don't make suits for men like him. He looks like a bear just out of hibernation, nothing but bones and muscle. You'll have to fatten him up."

And she was the one that told me the only way God would approve of us making love was with him on top. I preferred a skinny bear to a fat one. One of my wedding prayers was for Lars to never fit his wedding suit.

For two days before the wedding, Momma Nina and I were baking sweets for the guests. Our friends and the Russians gave us money. Daddy Valik stacked the bills in a cigar box making a careful accounting of it. Our neighbors gave food to us for storage, for the coming winter. We gave them sweets.

Sammy, Lar's friend killed on the Western Front, had a father and mother, people Lars couldn't talk to after the war. People he avoided. They came to the wedding. Sammy's father gave us his Ford tractor.

Lars cried, and between tears said, "I can't take it. I was supposed to take care of him."

It was the first time I saw Lars cry.

Sammy's father hugged Lars and said, "No one can protect another soldier in battle, Son. But, we appreciate that you tried, and what you did. It was Sammy's tractor. We want you to have it."

What was I supposed to do when Lars cried? I held his hand, reached up and kissed him.

He hugged me. When he noticed I wasn't breathing and turning blue, he let me go.

Momma Nina gave me a key to their front door.

She said, "If you need to come home, come home. If he beats you, is bad to you, won't let you breathe come home. You always have a home with us."

Daddy Valik made no such offer. Rid of me, he didn't want me back. If I came home to stay he would turn blue.

The first two months after the soldiers came home, there were five weddings, two in our church. Almost two years after the war ended, we got married. Mixed with continuous music, dancing, and a wagon of wine delivered to the grange by sunset the celebration of our wedding filled the hall. A Russian marriage is longer and more complex than most American marriages. We drink. We dance into the night. We party.

Not a Russian tradition, an American one, the Lutheran minister's wife fixed our wedding cake, but in Russian fashion we did not cut it until well into the wedding celebration. Most of the guest missed me feeding Lars cake and him feeding me cake, but the roar that went up after we ate it got everybody's attention. It wasn't the shock of seeing a bride with white frosting on her nose; it was what Mr. Sraelenburg said.

"I like wedding cake. Had wedding cake my wedding. Want have wedding cake again with Lars, Marisa.

"Lars," Mr. Sraelenburg said, "Ten year from today, you make payments every month on farm; you married Marisa; you stay out of trouble; I eat cake with you, Marisa. I give you title to farm free, clear. You eat cake with me, Marisa, Lars?"

We said, "Yes!"

We both hugged him, then each other. Then, I looked in Lars' eyes. He looked in mine. After eating it, as arranged, instead of staying for the second day of dancing and drinking like a good Russian, I followed my non-Russian husband and his tradition. He wanted to be alone with me, not getting drunk with my father at the grange hall. We left.

Too far out of town, on a road not yet graveled, the ruts were still deep, a hard trip from town, our farm was too far for most of the people in town to come. For the celebration our new home was not used, as it would have been in a traditional Russian wedding. Had it been used it would have required at least a two-week honeymoon to affect repairs. A special place in our marriage, we agreed our farm was private, we wanted no visitors there for two weeks. Our last acts together before the wedding were bringing in furniture and supplies to hold up for a month after the wedding, without going out the gate. I made a sign. Lars put it up. "Trespassers will be shot." Over it my little step brother painted a picture of a machine gun, and below it, I put "Only Exceptions, President Wilson and the milk wagon."

Once the finale of the wedding was taking the bride to a bedroom then sending out a bloodied sheet proving her virginity. Lars would have joined the drinking with the men while I nursed my wounds. If I had no wounds, wasn't a virgin, he could reject me as his wife. Loving husbands had a chicken standing by to do the bleeding if their wife didn't. As civilization spread, this custom was abandoned. Chickens breathed easier. The tradition of my virginity being short lived had not changed. For that ceremony, we planned a week in total isolation.

Traversing ten miles of dirt road, our T-Model truck drove perfectly, no flats, no breakdowns, no problems: a minor miracle in our day. Ten miles on a country road our wheels throwing up a cloud of dust, making the trip without a flat was unusual. Cars and tires were much higher maintenance then. Even by WWII, tires did not hold up as they do now. In the days after WWI, wisdom was carrying several spares. Arriving in the dark alone with my husband, all my things had come out the day before with Daddy Valik. Only me and two changes of clothes remained in town when we said our vows. Momma Nina brought out those clothes the next week, on the day our sign came down.

Kicking up dust, a daily visit of the milk truck broke our solitary honeymoon. We were alone on vacation. Cows, as mothers of all species, have no vacations. Milk is produced every day. Waving at the driver from the porch was prearranged with Momma Nina, but I didn't speak to him. I spoke to no one other than my husband for our first week. The driver reported daily to Momma Nina that I was alive and able to wave. This prevented her asking the sheriff to check on me.

Well into the night, our guest still drinking and celebrating, we were home. Parking our truck in its shed by the first barn, our truck's engine cooled. His body warm next to mine, we didn't cool.

Lars didn't let my feet touch the ground, his first order, my first obedience.

"No walking, tonight you ride in my arms," my husband said.

My arms wrapped around his neck, my knees in the crook of his arm, was I that light? He walked to the house carrying me as if carrying a child. I felt his body? He was hard, hard arms and chest. Muscles tight carrying me were like bones with no fat to pad them, I knew he was strong: I had not realized how strong, and how little fat was on that large frame. I rested my head on the hardness of his shoulder, my powerful husband's shoulder.

"I love you, Lars."

Standing on our porch, he kissed me. I reached down to unlatch the door. His foot pushed it open. Did he put me down? No! His dress shoes sounded their way across the living room and into the hall. For the rest of my life, I could be hearing his step, that cadence, in our house. Where was he going? The door ajar to our bedroom, I felt my bottom touch it pushing it open. My hips settled into our bed. He hovered over me kissing me.

"Can I go to the toilet first, Lars?" I kissed him back.

Running to the out house, I sat for the moment it took to empty my bladder. The open hole beside me for my husband, he could have gone there, but he was shy. I was shy. He, a good farmer, relieved himself in the yard while he waited for me. Taking a minute to calm my heart, I relaxed, heard the screen door close. Lars went back in the house giving me privacy in the silence.

No wind on the plains, I felt the quiet, the majesty, the peace and the love lying over our home. For the first time since I slept with my mother and father in a tent in the canyon in the mountains, I was home. Rising, I went through our yard in the night to my waiting husband. He had been sleeping in our bed for three weeks. He was home. For the first time, we were home.

Walking my last steps as a virgin, I trembled. I walked on the hard, warm earth of home. I opened the door. I walked down the hall, my bare feet noiseless on hard wood floors. A virgin on one knee on our bed, I quivered. Lars lay in silence across from me. I moved over him, leaned down kissed him a long tender kiss. He responded gently, nursing my lips with his love. I lowered into his arms. His kissing was tender, turned passionate.

Between kisses, he undressed me. I didn't help him; limp, I let him, and slid under the covers naked. Shedding his clothes faster than a prairie dog running out of its hole being chased by a rattlesnake, he undressed and slipped under the covers with me. I felt his hard body again; kissed him, kept kissing him. His rough hand with his golden ring held me, ran over my naked hip and slipped between my thighs. Goose bumps covered my body. I shivered.

"I'm sorry," Lars said. "Are you afraid?"

"No---Maybe---it will hurt."

"Maybe once," his hand stopped, He gently kissed me.

My lips turned cold, the warmth inside me turned to a shiver. Fear, anticipation of pain stopped me from relaxing. Dry inside, I wanted to relax, open to him, make love to him, but---

I wrapped my arms around his neck, left my body to his hands. The shiver inside me spread to my skin as I held him.

"I'm sorry, Lars!"

Calloused, rough, hard, how can I describe the gentleness of my farmer's hands? Fingers, not descending to my groin again, floated over my goose bumps striking each one like a match head, lighting each bump with a warming flame. Lars relaxed, warmed, and ignited me, a forest of tinder goose bumps; each one radiated a spot of warmth from my skin to my heart. The ignition continued spreading embers of love over my hip, warming my legs, warming my lower back and warming my soft side and breast into his hard, muscular chest. Not rushing, not pushing, in no hurry, he loved me. Goose bumps afire, flesh quivering, I kissed him. He kissed me. His hand slid over my thigh once more and found a new tenderness, a spot never touched by another's hand. Surprised, my bottom contracted, my pelvis opened. A sliding, brushing, touching he slid his hand back to my hip feeling for goose bumps. Finding a few, he stroked them, drifting back to my tenderness. His lingering touch on my tenderness, stayed. How much time passed? A minute, an hour, a lifetime? Shivering, goose bumps changed, tension passed, passion came.

Tight bands in my legs tensed, relaxed, and spread for him. Rythmic contractions of my bottom propelled me over the gentle stability of his hand. Dry with fear, cold became warm, moist became surrender.

"I love you," I said, rolling slowly on my back not losing his touch as I moved.

Once there, he, supported on one arm, kept kissing me, rough, hard hands began to move easier, more rapidly in a natural lubrication flowing from me.

"I love you, Marisa?" My husband's lips brushed mine.

"Yes, please, paseba" I said, English mixing with Russian, understood in Danish.

An American woman and Russian girl converged on his hand.

Lars was above me. An electric tingle he was on me, in me.

"Oh!" My buttocks contracted, lifted him, bucked him. He stayed tight in my saddle, riding me in rhythm with my contractions. No pain, no discomfort, only pleasure. My virginity was gone. Did I climax? A release of tension filled me. Breathing hard Lars untensed, relaxed and rolled beside me. We kissed.

Lars said, "I love you."

He rolled on his back. I rolled on my side, put my leg over him, kissed his cheek, said, "I love you." I kept kissing his cheek. Kissed his ear, nibbled it.

"I love you," I said.

"I love you," he said, a question in his voice. *What do you want?*

I kissed him again.

We made love again.

Sleeping together, naked body against naked body, in the night he woke, hard hands stroking my bottom, touching my tenderness again, he loved me again. That time an explosion within me rocked us, and again rocked us as I woke a second time in the night, touching his tenderness, exciting another round of love making.

All the worries, all the fears of sex, I lost. Beside me he wasn't big, small or anything other than my man, the only man I wanted. I pulled him, arms, head, and all into me, made him mine, my man, the hope of all my hopes; the faith of all my faiths; and the love, the only one I loved as a woman.

The first night we stayed in our bed on our farm. Lars made love to me as I needed, as I wanted, as a husband loves his wife. Sex didn't hurt: I loved it. The women had told me it would hurt, that it was something I had to let him do, and to do it to please him. I did.

Loving my husband pleased me.

I was in heaven. I understood the sounds my mother made in the night after she and my father put the lantern out when I was a little girl. I loved pleasing him. It was not one sided as the women had told me. Did I love lovemaking more than my husband? He was asleep exhausted. His strong hard body rested by me, spent. My soft, smaller body could have kept going, kept making love. He couldn't. Kissing his shoulder, his semen dripping from my vagina, I put my leg over his, our love ran down wetting the sheet between us. Slipping under his shoulder, I slept my head riding the waves of his steadily heaving chest.

I was a married woman, married to the only man I wanted to ever make love to me.

Chapter 18

Our Honeymoon

Waking the next morning was I tired from days of preparation for my wedding, tired from sleepless nights giddy with expectation? What about last night? Why did I wake up alive and tingling with energy after making love four times and sleeping six hours? Why was he sleeping, tired? Lars preparation for our wedding was a bath, a suit, and showing up. He told me, he had a nap the day before then slept eight hours waking three hours before the service. I was awake, my head on his shoulder rising and falling as he breathed. I uncoiled from him limb at a time. I kissed him. He snored. Looking at Lars, watching him breathe, I felt a twinge of hunger. Would hunger keep me awake and make me nuzzle him and nibble his ear in the night?

With joy in my heart and pain in my side, I had eaten too much, made love just enough, and was ready for more. My heart was full. My colon was full. My stomach was empty. Without Lars my heart would be empty. Without an enema my colon would remain full and hurt. I needed an enema; I wanted to make love again.

Trying and succeeding in not waking him, I slipped into the kitchen. In the middle of the table was a vase filled with wild roses: pastel white, old, simple, rose pedals circled it on the table.

A note trapped by the corner under its base said: *Marisa, I love you. This vase was my grandmother's. My father brought it from Denmark. It is all I have left of my family. You are all I have. You are my family, all of my family. There will be more roses. There will be no more vases from my Grandmother, not another me. We are yours to keep. I love you, Lars.*

I wanted to go back to bed, hold him, watch him breathe, but I had to get the enema over first. Fired up with kindling, our cook stove crackled to life. Adding larger bits of wood, nothing larger than one eighth rounds of cottonwood cut from our farm, I put the kettle on to boil. Not taking long, or needing long, I waited. The night cool, the stove warmed the kitchen. I needed only warm water, not heat to drive cold from the kitchen. By noon it would be balmy, a beautiful day. I used my bath thermometer adjusting the temperature. Water poured into my enema bag. Even though Lars wanted to do it for me and we made love all night in the dark, I was embarrassed to have him probing me in daylight.

I hung the bag from a hook in the cold pantry and lay down on two, folded blankets.

More trouble with it than I expected, why was it difficult to take and hold the enema? A new house and doing all the preparation myself, I wasn't relaxed. I cramped, got in three quarters as much water as usual, and had to go. Without Momma Nina to make me hold it, I bolted for the door and the outhouse. It worked, but not as effective as when she did it. I should have taken another enema, but there wasn't time.

Wishing I was home, wishing for Momma, would any one ever care for me again as Momma Nina or my mother or another woman? Would a man be able to do it like a woman? Would Lars? I never heard of a man giving anyone an enema. Enemas were women's work, like washing dishes, fixing food, and changing diapers.

Happily married, I missed being cared for with this non-sexual intimacy with another woman. But the sexual intimacy of last night, something no woman could have done for me, was imprinted in me forever, like a duckling pecking it's way out of it's shell and seeing her mother for the first time and following her, I followed Lars. Making love a simple thing, a natural thing, my shell pecked open, my eyes open, I followed Lars.

Every bird hatched follows the one laying on their egg warming it, understands who their mother is. The power and love of my man swimming in me, filling me, probing for the egg floating down my fallopian tube, I understood who my man was, who I was to follow. The gentleness of it, the calloused hands on tender flesh, the passion, after the pumping of thousands of gallons of water into my colon a spoon full of male ejaculate filled me. Goose bumps covered my hips, back, and arms. As I sat in the outhouse pouring out an enema a wave of emotion swam inside me. Thousands of tiny, invisible sperm cells breast stroked up my fallopian tubes. A single sperm, flailing it's tail, pecked my egg, filled me as no woman could fill me, impregnated sexually the purpose of my being.

Would I obey him? Would I serve him? Would I bear his children? I suddenly worshiped him, felt the need to be under him, serving him, to give him all of me. I was his woman, his wife. He was my husband. In the cool of the outhouse a gentle vibration spread from my uterus through my fallopian tubes to something deeper inside me. Whatever he asked, I would do. I would materialize his thoughts, would follow my man. How could I have questioned this? How could I have thought that there was life without my husband? If I didn't have Momma holding me for my enemas, I didn't. I had Lars holding me, penetrating me deeper than any enema.

I sat in the outhouse. My enema cascaded into the pit below. Looking down, I saw no blood, my legs unstained. I was a virgin, but my hymen didn't break, didn't prove it. Did Lars believe I was a virgin? I wished my hymen had torn, bled, proving my virginity as nine months later bleeding on our bed I would prove my non-virginity, my worth as a wife. Father Viktor and the guest at our wedding waiting in town those months later, not to see bloody sheets, but a smiling baby, there were no bloody sheets this morning, no proof of my virginity. Lars deserved a virgin, to know he married a virgin. I wanted to be a virgin for him. I wanted to bleed. I wanted to suffer pain, and cry as a virgin for him.

A chicken wandered by the outhouse. Lars wasn't up, hadn't seen the sheets in daylight. Should I? I opened the door and looked at the chicken. The poor thing looked so innocent, sort of like a virgin, chicken for lunch? Suddenly I was hungry, craved filling myself with food, love, and Lars, craved being his vestal virgin his innocent bride.

Heading for our house, I stopped. I looked at the back porch, our kitchen door. I looked beyond to miles of open plain, a wall of mountains, and one peak reflecting a sparkle toward me, a mirror of ice, mist frozen on the cliff unmelted by morning sun. Peace filled me and radiated up from my pelvis, like nothing I felt before. Around him my legs wrapped. Around him my world turned. This was my home, his home, our home.

We didn't have a honeymoon in the city, in a far away place. We had our honeymoon at home making our bed, our house the linchpin of our most special night. For all my life, I was glad we didn't have a place to go, a place to pin my pelvis to another bed, to make my dreams, dreams in a rented room. The bonding of last night bound me to our bed every night sleeping with and making love with my husband, and bound me too it bleeding, bearing our children. Last night was bliss; other nights, labor and delivery. What happened on that bed gave Father Viktor our children to bless and gave me a lifetime of memories filling my universe, all occurring on one bed in one room on the first floor of our home.

I sat in the bedroom watching my husband sleep. He woke up.

Looking at the bed, he said, "I'm sorry. You bled like this?" Blood covered his groin and side, dripped and dried on the sheets.

Looking down, I was a virgin. Didn't he expect me to bleed?

He didn't like cleaning blood off his privates. He was sure I was a virgin and liked my chicken dinner.

I was a virgin. Why didn't I bleed? Why did I fool him?

On this first day, we could sleep in. Walking in before dawn our neighbor and his daughter milked our cows, put our milk in the ice house, and walked home. The silence of contented cows already in the pasture, our mornings work was done. The hum of the milk trucks motor came and went without our rousing. The next day we milked our cows and helped load the truck.

Rubbing his head, Lars held my hand walking to the kitchen, kissing me once before sitting at the table.

I asked, "Are you alright?"

"A headache," he said, rubbing his temples.

"How much did you drink?"

"A bottle, maybe two---more than I ever drink."

My husband was not a drinker. Not a purist he would have a beer with the men, sometimes a glass of wine with a meal, but never any hard liquor or more than two glasses of anything. Last night, our wedding celebration, would Daddy Valik or the other Russians let him stop? Six glasses of strong wine and some vodka, his liver was tender and his head throbbing.

I kissed him. "You need an enema: a large, warm, baking soda enema. You're dehydrated, toxic, and need the alcohol flushed out."

He blushed. He didn't say no.

"I need to give you your enema," he said.

"I did it already while you were asleep," I said.

He looked disappointed.

The kettle on the stove empty, I pumped it full again from the well pump over the sink.

Refilling my bag, I kissed him and helped him to his feet.

This time I undressed him. He didn't resist. I laid him naked on our bed, put a towel under him, and, in a change of roles, slipped something hard into him.

Was that him?

I asked, "What's that?"

I slipped my hand down his thigh to his tenderness.

He didn't stop me, but blushed.

He stammered, "I didn't mean too!"

I didn't let go. I held on, tightening my grip.

I said, "That's my---It's my toy! When it is like this, it's my toy!"

I lectured him. I had his full attention, a quart of water in his colon, not to mention his erect penis in my hand.

I said, "Didn't Mrs. Miller, your house mother, teach you to put away your toys?"

"What---well, yes of course! But---I"

I didn't let him finish. "This is MY toy, and it is supposed to be in YOUR toy box! As soon as we finish your enema, I want you to put it away.

I opened the clamp. More enema flowed into him.

Goose bumps spread over his bottom. I stoked them with my soft hand. They came and went. His bottom began to tighten.

"Marisa,---I," his legs were quivering.

I stopped the flow. He was excited, but my toy had shriveled away. The excitement he felt in the early enema, with no difficulty holding it had changed. Waves of water rumbling to and fro, it was gone. Now he had the excitement of a good enema patient. His energy focused on holding the water in. Sexual pleasure would wait. The trip to the outhouse wouldn't, or would it?

I rubbed my hand over his back, kissed his shoulder.

"I love you, Lars," I said.

"I love you too," he said, relaxing.

I opened the clamp. "I want you to take some more enema."

He breathed hard. Two and a half, maybe three quarts and his legs began to quiver.

"Marisa!"

"It's alright, Honey. I think you're full. You need to hold it a few minutes now to make it work, to let it soak into you and wash out the alcohol." I rubbed his back gently, then lay down behind him, holding him, like my mother held me.

"I love you, Marisa," he said.

I kissed his ear, rubbed his stomach and breathed warm air on his neck as my thighs supported the back of his legs.

Ten minutes of being held and he rolled over facing me. Something was in his eyes, a searching, an urgency, or a peace? I couldn't tell what it was. My toy was coming back to life.

"Lars, you need to go to the outhouse. Let it out slow and we'll deal with this when you get back." My hand brushed his penis.

Footsteps trotting toward the back door then the creak of the outhouse door, he was gone. I waited in the quiet. In broad daylight, I undressed, remade the bed while nude and crawled between the sheets.

Lars came back, climbed in with me. My toy was ready. His toy box was ready. We made love with intensity. I climaxed again looking into his eyes.

I asked, "How is your headache?"

"Gone, as soon as I finished going to the bathroom."

I smiled. I would have been a good doctor, was a good nurse.

Our first day of honeymoon, we had to carry salt and water to the back of the North pasture. Riding together we worked an hour and a half, talked, petted, and walked.

"Marisa, we'll go around the property, walk the property line of our land."

Down the rutted road we came to the turn off and our gate and our keep out sign. I kissed him. The gate: three strands of barbed wire with a loose piece of fence post caught by two loops of wire, attached to a post in the ground, we had to move it out of the way coming and going, a necessary inconvenience. We shared our drive with our cattle. No fence and we would have been sharing our cattle with our neighbors. Walking along the inside of the fence the grass was dry, brushed against our overalls. A blushing bride, I wore typical honeymoon clothes, brogans, overalls, and a cowboy hat, matching those of my husband.

Flat land, good land, dry land, we took most of the afternoon to walk around. Six miles of fence, we shared repairs with the neighbors. Down one arroyo cottonwoods, a sometimes creek and cattle sleeping in the shade, we walked up it, scared a covey of quail.

Around a corner, he led me to them, a row of wild roses on an old unused fence, the border of a property absorbed by our land.

"I got your roses here. We'll plant more along the fence by the gate and on the road to the house."

Did Momma Nina tell him I liked roses? Why did roses always grow best in this little arroyo? We picked a full bushel of rose hips there in the fall. Making six jars of rose hips and honey, the world's most delicious spread for crackers and one of the world's best sources of vitamin C.

"You should always walk your borders once-in-a-while, get an idea of your limits," my husband said, making me, us part of our land.

"My limits are rose covered fences, Lars---with you!"

I kissed him. He kissed me.

Softer, untrod earth sunk beneath my feet. Home was 1280 acres. The land was ours, defined us, ruled us, to the world it was us. The sun began to approach the mountains as we reached our gate again.

Walking back to our house, I went to the bedroom. Lars set our border collies loose to herd our cattle to the barn and went upstairs to watch them work. Looking out the window I watched the sun settle toward the mountain. Happy, I sat down on the bed and watched the sun. Lars joined me. Not saying a word we watched together.

"Let's go to the porch," he said.

The sun set, yellow streaks in pencil clouds. I held Lars hand. More accurately, Lars larger hand engulfed mine, protecting me, warming me. A Cricket pulled out his fiddle and played us a serenade. The sun's yellow painted gold in my husband's red hair. I lay my head on his shoulder, my husband's shoulder. The most perfect twenty-four hours of my life, our sun was going; our son was coming, growing within me.

The second night of our marriage, we ate chicken, went to bed before bright blue sky turned royal blue, and planned to make love into the darkness. We were asleep before the first star twinkled.

Chapter 19

Confessions and Confidences

Dairy farmers, alarm clocks inside our heads, we never needed real ones on a dairy. 4:00 AM every morning, including Saturdays and Sundays, milking, we were up. Milk cows don't take a day off. One day of honeymoon not milking, the next a dairy farm wife, we should have been up, we weren't. No time to think about enemas, 7:00 AM, farm work was to be done, labor performed. The sun was up.

Cows bellowing, three hours late, they were used to being milked before now. Milk cows are peaceful creatures, not bulls charging. Standing in pastures, placidly chewing grass, cows are mellow. Genetically engineered milk producers, huge milk bags, they bellowed, *Milk me now!*

Their milk sacks bloated, hurting, large dark eyes said without equivocation, they were mad at us. A bull would charge, hurt something; a female stands, hurts, and waits, but bellows while she waits.

"Shut up, Bossy," I said.

Lars said, "Just milk her."

Had I milked a cow before? Lars taught me. Head on the cows side, I grabbed two teats, one with each hand, punched up to get her to let her milk down and squeezed, one hand then the other with a gripping downward motion. The first few times I did it, most of the milk went in the pail. By the fourth time, all of the milk ended up in the pail. I smiled pleased with myself.

"You're a natural," Lars smiled at me.

I learned quickly. Hearing the tinny ring of milk squirting into the pail in rhythm with my squeezes, I filled pail after pail. Warm milk went to the ice house, to chill, to keep ice cold till the wagon arrived and took our liquid crop to town. Hours of hard work, my forearms ached, like bands of fire extended from my wrists to my elbows, love making didn't hurt, milking did. It would have taken weeks to get used to the labor.

Then Lars showed me the milking machines again, four of them. Milking in 1920 was much easier than only a few years earlier, but hand milking was still a back up, something I had to be able to do in case the generator didn't work. Milking was first hand cranking the generator, Lars did that, a good use for his strong arms. It kicked over with the second crank, then he checked the voltage as it warmed up. While he did this, I was wiping off the first four cows. Milking was wiping her off and hooking her up and turning on the machine and taking the warm milk to the ice house: a three hour routine of non stop motion.

Our ice house, we still use. A room the size of my kitchen built twenty-two years earlier when the dairy first started; buried next to the barn, eighty percent underground, and packed with ice during the winter from a farm with a lake three miles toward town. Colorado winters and a lake provided all the ice for refrigeration year round for food and farm, and wouldn't be replaced by an electric chilling room for decades, after they electrified all the farms on our road. We had a refrigeration unit added to the ice house and new doors, but electric lights in the house and the little electric refrigerator in the kitchen was an improvement. Besides, I liked going for ice. Going to the ice house in August and going to the lake for ice in January was a treat. Lars and the men worked cutting ice and loading our truck, I skated. Good Russian girls from St. Petersburg skate. Lars never learned.

After all the cows were milked and ambling into the pasture, other chores never ended. Dawn to dusk every day there was work. Haying season came. We worked with other farm families going from farm to farm until all the winter hay was in. One of our barns was stacked to the roof and other stacks lined our pasture under tarps. Till dusk every day until finished, we hayed, after milking. Four teams raked and baled. Men, women and children stacked and gleaned.

A seventeen year old bride, a young farmer, we were junior members of an old club. Wives took me under their wing, taught me. Wives visited me, brought canned vegetables, meat, and other foods off their farms and taught me to be a farm wife.

Trips to the forest bringing in wood for winter with larger trucks from Mr. Sraelenburg, we were part of a community, men, women, and children all working separately on our own farms and together on projects too big for one family. We planted a garden next spring. This year, wedding presents, other farmers filled our cellar and kitchen lauder. Plowing, hoeing, and harvesting were to do. We dried food in sheds and on sheets in summer sun, and I canned. The next year we had extra to share with a new family two farms down.

What time was for us? Night, tired from physical work all day, the first week, we made love and went to sleep and made love again every morning. By the second week, the touch of his naked body comforting in fatigue. The touch of the bed brought sleep first, love making later.

We milked, finishing as sunlight poured over the mountains and lit the house.

Rolling a hand wagon of milk to the ice house, I watched sun rays settle down the east wall of our house, first lighting empty room windows upstairs, then eves of the porch, last our living room and kitchen windows on the first floor. At noon day our house, untreated redwood, was weathered gray board. The gray showed in full sunlight and cloudy days. In morning it was a gold box with onyx under the eaves and only gray roof shingles as the sun played against the walls. Seconds later the light reached the yard. Our house, a glowing chandelier above the shadowy prairie, intermingling, becoming part of the plain. Dawn and dusk the most beautiful times of day, our house was most beautiful at dawn, as we made the short walk from the barn to the ice house storing milk to chill and wait for the truck.

"It's beautiful," I said to Lars, touching his arm.

"It's ours, Marisa," he said. "I love you"

Stopped, not taking the milk into the ice house until the sun reached the yard, he held me. Watching dawn change the colors of our home, his face lit as our house lit, golden, at the same time the yard took light. I nuzzled my head into his chest, saying nothing. The magnitude of our farm overwhelmed me. The cows sated with milking, the breeze not blowing, we were in silence, a silence of love, until unmilked cows, unsympathetic to the view or our love, bellowed. With the empty hand wagon, we headed back to the barn.

This would be my life, my husband's life, and our children's lives. Our farm was our life. A city girl, sore and tired after a day's work, I would toughen, harden in a few weeks, move in the routine without pain. I would prepare the meals, my husband would do most of the hard work outside, but I was his wife. I worked beside him most of the time, especially milking. Our hands hard, and our faces tan, we would be like most Americans, farmers. Never a real vacation, winter brought other chores and then spring and summer and fall. Unending, it got better every month and every year.

Working the land I loved, I would pity my friends who lived in town. Nothing---nothing is as fulfilling, as working the earth, watching calves born, listening to the quiet of the country at night, seeing things grow in the day, and harvesting, making it all happen with your own hands. My husband gave me, taught me this and more. We learned together.

All this happened through weeks, years, and decades yet to come. That day, the second day of our marriage he reached for my hand.

"Now, it's time for your enema, Marisa," my husband said to me.

I followed him to the house like a cow about to be milked. I was full, needed emptying, but I wasn't bellowing. A shy young heffer, I was blushing.

I prepared the enema, slipped off my clothes and lay down on the bed. Lars hands shaking, he spread my bottom. The nozzle quivering, he stabbed at my anus.

"Lars, that hurts!"

I grabbed his hand steadying it, and helped him slide the nozzle in me. Why was he shaking holding the bag up? Was he going to drop it? He lifted me with ease. Why did a little bag of water make his hands shake? Holding on, I made sure to get the water in at one go. Finished, full, I rolled over looking at my husband. His hands quivered. The bulge in his overalls was unmistakable, with a wet stain at the end of the bulge. His opossum grin, glued to his face, was mixed with a beet-red blush.

I reached up and slipped my hand inside the side of his overalls. A small, slick explosion had happened.

"Lars?"

"I didn't mean too!"

"Why?"

He ran into the kitchen, taking the enema bag with him.

That evening he kissed me more passionately and we made love several times before falling asleep. The intensity of his lovemaking was greater than our first night, this after a hard day's work. I was totally exhausted. I didn't wake up early the next morning. When I did, he was out milking. I ran to help without thinking about my enema. We finished three hours later getting the last of the milk in the ice house. 7:30 AM, back in the house, my hands were sore. I was tired.

He said, "Marisa, did you have your enema?"

"No!" I looked down. "I'll do it after I get your breakfast."

I was going to be a good wife and take care of, before being taken care of.

He said, "Can I do it for you?"

Rubbing my sore arms, I stopped. I smiled at him.

"Would you? I'd love for you too, but you don't have too!"

He smiled back at me and pulled me to him and gave me a kiss. His opossum smile quivered, alternating with loving crinkles.

I said, "You know how to do it?"

"Not really. I know about enemas, but the enema I gave you yesterday was the only enema I've given, and you fixed it. I just gave it."

He started the fire. In a few minutes, the kettle was boiling. Laying the enema bag and thermometer on the table, I showed him how to check the temperature, fill the bag, and add baking soda to the water.

I asked him, "Are you ready?"

Nodding, he was embarrassed, excited, nervous.

I unsnapped one shoulder strap of my overalls, then the other. They tumbled to the floor, and I stepped out of them and draped them over a kitchen chair, adding my work shirt, bra, and panties. Lars watched.

Naked with him in daylight again, did I see a bulge?

I said, "What's that?"

My hand slithered inside the slit designed to open to his blue jeans pocket, Not wearing blue jeans, only a tee-shirt and underware under his overalls, I explored. I grasped a well developed sausage pointing up at me.

Not stopping me, he blushed.

He said, "I'm sorry!---"

Did I let him finish? "This is MY toy! It's to be in YOUR toy box!" Gripping my toy, I put the kettle to the side of the stove, off the fire box, and led him to our bedroom.

After lovemaking was over, he said, "You're---you're---," then he kissed me a long tender kiss.

Kissing him back with the same tenderness, my toy was gone, shriveled away, an appropriate time for a tender kiss. A day or hour later, hard passionate kisses filling our bed, he would put his toy away again. A good boy about keeping my toy in his toy box after that, we were children, playing, exploring, loving.

Lars, learning to give enemas, checked the water in the kettle. My enema water cold enough to put me in shock, he poured it back in the kettle and reheated it.

After I ran to the outhouse and released my enema, we talked.

I said, "It excites you, giving me an enema?"

Unsure of himself, he said, "Well" and clamed up.

I said, "If it excites you, that's fine with me, but I want to know how you feel."

"Well!" He was like our Model T on bad gas. A good, black truck, like all Model Ts, good gas or bad, if you kept cranking it, it sputtered, turned over, warmed up, and ran.

Pushed back against the wall, trapped my arms, I cranked words out of him.

My head buried in his chest, my hands on his bottom, I said, "Tell me!"

He sputtered, said a sentence, said two, gas exploding in his cylinders, his motor was running. He talked. He told me a story, one I might have observed, yet never saw: one that could have happened any day to any boy in the infirmary as I stared at Momma Nina working on them. Stripped naked, prodded, probed, treated, no privacy, boys and men were different then. Women and girls expected to be modest had privacy curtains. Men and boys closed their eyes and hid behind their lids as others freely watched as enemas and other personal procedures were done to them.

Colds and flu required enemas, lots of enemas. In the infirmary at the orphanage for a cold when he was 15, Momma Nina gave him a series of enemas lying on his left side, bare bottomed facing six other boys open eyed, open mouthed and silently watching him and her. Closing his eyes the other boys were gone. It was him and her. Wonderful for him, all the surging, holding on, and the good feeling afterwards, he was a teen age boy getting physical attention from a woman. It opened him. He loved it.

Eleven boys in his dormitory room at his residence and one dorm mother and an occasional visit to the school nurse, he craved maternal touches, missed his mother and his grandmother, two women that gave him enemas when he was little and could cuddle on their laps when the enemas were done. The only touch from a woman for over a year, Momma Nina held his hip as he quivered taking the enemas. The memory of her touch lingered on his hip as he held back the rumbles of the enema holding it, waiting for permission to run for the toilet.

The next morning waking up thinking he was in his dorm room in a double row of beds, he woke in a single row of beds in the infirmary disoriented. He listened. Time for my enema, he heard my high pitched ten-year-old voice talking to Momma Nina. We went on the girl's side of the room. Open eyed, not seeing through the curtain, he heard. I didn't talk once my enema started, but he knew what was happening, knew I was ten feet away, my panties off, my dress up, and a hose doing magic in my bottom, as it had done magic in his the previous evening. I stayed on my side on the bed for five minutes holding it and ran to the toilet. He heard me sputtering, releasing, going to the bathroom. I was a child having an enema. He felt empathy, wanted to be me.

At sick call one of an older girl came in, a girl his age, constipated, needing an enema, Katrina. She complained in a soprano melody as two and half quarts filled her lovely bottom, a bottom he had began to notice as lovely. Exciting listening to her enemas, to her moans, to her begging, Lars was becoming a man. She, a fifteen-years-old girl was a woman to him. He liked her, liked her curves, liked the sound of her voice, liked her. She smiled at him, kissed him that morning between enemas. Her first kiss, his first kiss, Lars mingled kisses and sex and enemas.

He blushed telling me this, but never used her name.

I kissed him. He didn't have to tell me it was Katrina, I knew he was talking about her, that he loved Katrina. Holding him, I wanted him to love me as he loved her I wanted him to give me my enemas, all of them.

I told him.

He said, "After what I told you?"

I smiled.

He smiled.

If I had said he had a fetish, an abnormal fantasy; if I had told him I would be giving myself my own enemas; what would that have done to our marriage? Knowing I was having my enemas without him, knowing I knew he want to help me, and knowing I knew he was a pervert, would he have been hurt, have been sad, have been thinking of me---or thinking of her? Would his fantasy have drifted away from me, back to Katrina? Would his dreams and hopes and heart have left me? A fetish of love denied is love denied. A hunger unfed from an empty heart seeks another heart.

And did I have a reason to deny his love? I wanted him loving me filling every nook and cranny of my womanhood. Momma gave me enemas with love, out of necessity. Momma Nina loved me and gave them out of necessity. Lars loved me and wanted to give me my enemas. I needed to have an enema every day. A necessity to me physically, his love was a necessity to my heart. I didn't want his heart dreaming of other hearts and making love to me in our bed.

I needed an enema every day, and wanted them given to me, wanted him giving them to me with the gentleness he gave me my enema this morning. But, he wanted me excited like Katrina. Did having an enema excite me? Of course not, having an enema every day, an enema was part of having a daily bowel movement, not exciting. But, why was I excited after my enema this morning? Why was I in a hurry to return from the outhouse to be with my husband, other than the fact that this was the second day of our honeymoon, and I had a new hunger, a hunger that two days before was an undefined want, today was a necessity that filled my heart---it wasn't the enema. It was him.

The only one excited about giving me enemas was Lars. Could his being excited by giving me an enema excite me? Could Tom Sawyer's excitement about painting a fence excite Huckleberry Finn? What pleased Lars pleased me, excited me.

Chapter 20

Pleasing my Husband

We worked and we ate and we kissed and we went to bed, and if we made love it was with Lar's red hair on fire lit against the ceiling's shadows of crimson above me. My only love, my man, he gave me life in a rose colored room. Closing my eyes, sight, sound, touch, and movement became forever set in the dried oil pigments of time. Our sunset lovemaking lasted only the few months between our marriage and the birth of our children. It was my honeymoon, my special time. The sun pulling the covers of light onto the Front Range and looked back at us beaming straight down on his head like the noon day sun without blues or full hues, only passionate pinks and reds, and in slow increments turned off the lights and said good night.

In the dark we woke: both of us at the same instant looking but not seeing until Lars or I struck a match and lit the lantern. Barely time to kiss, we dressed in overalls, tee-shirts, and undies in midsummer; in midwinter, coats, gloves, Eskimo hats, and lined pants: arctic gear for the coldest hours of days that never climbed to zero on the Colorado plain. Temperature varied. Time, never: a routine marking the rest of our lives, we lived in synchrony with cattle, with the tenderness in their milk sacks, their need to be milked, to be emptied?

Milking over, enema time, my turn to be emptied!

Lars hammering a nail above our bed to hang the bag, I had my enemas in bed from that day on, another part of our routine.

"Lars, are you comfortable getting it ready? I'll wait for you here, if it's all right with you."

Too tense the last few days to have the enema and hold it best, I needed to be relaxed, warm, and snuggy---to prepare myself.

I heard what he said about Katrina. He was excited listening to her having enemas; not excited listening to me have mine. Did he look for her first when he came home, then after knowing she was married and gone, keep company with me? What would happen if I let him give me my enemas, acted as excited as Katrina, and wanted him to make love to me afterwards? What would that do?

He smiled, took the bag, and headed for the kitchen.

I undressed and crawled in bed.

Ten minutes later, leaning over me, he hung the bag on the nail. It quivered. I quaked under a sheet drawn from my toes to my nose covering myself like a virginal, Arabian bride with only my eyes showing above my veil. I uncovered myself, slowly, first my lips, my pouting lips, then my trembling chin. Glancing down taking quick glimpses of his eyes, was I blushing? A crinkled sheet slid off my shoulder revealed a breast. I jerked the sheet back up covering it, pouted my lip at a him, looked at him with little girl eyes, feigning shyness, and lowered it again. By the time the sheet collapsed in a bundle covering only my bare feet, Lars was breathing hard; his hands shook; a bulge grew in his overalls.

Lars, then remembering why the nozzle was in his hand, it flew at me and dove for my most private spot. Making insertion harder, I yanked my bottom forward, then pouted it back at him. He shook. The nozzle making small looping motions trying to find home, he was rubbing the grease on my bottom and around my anus, not in it. Steadying my hip with his other hand, controlling my gyrations, the loops spiraled to the bull's, or should that be the heffer's eye. I sucked it in.

"Ooh," I said, a quiet sultry ooh, enough for him to hear like a teenage girl half room away with a privacy curtain between us.

I heard the clamp click.

He said, "It going in alright?"

I smiled and cooed at him, "Muhuuu! Better in bed like this---with you holding me."

I rubbed my hand over the sheet, touched his finger, and rushed my hand to the pillow under my head. "Oooh!"

Used to enemas, I saw many given to girls who were not used to enemas, Katrina being one. Copying her 'oh' was a challenge. I practiced while in bed waiting for Lars to return from the kitchen. My voice deeper than Katrina's, I tried, was never perfect, never a petite high-pitched, young, lovely voice like Katrina's.

"Please, please---I have to go," I said two times, just as I had heard Katrina beg to Momma Nina. I dug my feet slowly under the sheet.

Lars said, "Are you all right, Marisa?"

Of course, I was all right. The water, barely filling my rectum, had not reached the blocking point in my side. Was he all right? I looked at him.

I said, "I'm all right. It's the enema. Keep giving it to me."

I pouted my lips at him then buried my head in the pillow with repeated furtive glances.

His eyes were sparkling as they were after I kissed him when he asked me to marry him.

"Oh, it's warm. So warm. It feels so good inside me!" I breathily whispered to him, batting my eyelashes.

Warm water gurgled in my rectum, he perched behind me watching me, watching me contract and roll my buttocks. The nozzle gripped tight in my bottom, the bag hanging on the wall, he had nothing to do with his hands. Nervously he removed the one from my hip. It flapped, confused, and lost, circling his knee. He flew closer to me perching on his bottom on the bed. The hand flying with the deliberation of a homing pigeon headed for my hip and landed there, gently rubbing. Another landed on the center of my low back, rough calloused palms and fingers rubbing me. Obediently a carpet of goose bumps met them, ignited. Not acting, I enjoyed it.

I took about half of it then, when the pressure was building as the water blocked at that point in my left side, I started to beg. "Please, I can't take anymore. Please stop!"

HE DID!

I stopped begging. "Honey, you aren't hurting me! You're filling my colon with warm water, a good enema. You have to be strong. Make me take enough to do what the enema needs to do, or it won't work. Don't stop unless you see my calves quivering, or I grab your hand, Ok?"

"Dah, Marisa," Lars said answering me in Russian, the language of my childhood, or was it his. Danish.

Nodding his head, he enjoyed my enema. His opossum grin, where was his opossum grin? He had a look of joy, a little crinkle at the edge of his lips, his mouth was closed and his eyes sparkling.

My hip pulled back, I sent out new goose bumps in waves with the enema, with the rubbing, and with his eyes. Was I getting goose bumps from looking over my shoulder at his eyes looking at my naked bottom?

He opened the clamp again. My enema continued.

This time, I did have to go, but on cue, the wall broke and enema flooded higher as it always did. "Honey, I am so full!! You are giving me such a good enema! Ohh, Ohh!"

He kept it flowing.

Did my eyes sprinkle sparkles on him?

Almost three and a half quarts, the amount I needed to have in my colon, my legs quivered. Me quivering, he was supposed to clip the clamp closed.

"I'm full, Lars. I'm full!"

Could he tell the truth from fiction? I grabbed his hand. The nozzle continued to vibrate building pressure from my anus to my cecum. He smiled at me. I didn't smile. My eyes dilated.

His hand slid off my hip like a bird diving to the ground for a piece of bread. He had the clamp.

I heard it click.

Then Lars did something as surprising as an eighty degree January day in Denver after he took the nozzle out. He lay behind me and warmed me into him, his chest covering my back, his thighs supporting my thighs, and his arm around my chest touching my face. Momma held me like this, never Momma Nina. Momma Nina never touched me during the enema except to put the nozzle in. Seven years since anyone held me as I held an enema, "Oooh," I said, without meaning too.

I melted in his arms.

It came back! I was in the tent, secure, happy, my mother holding me as I rested ice cold feet against her legs. She pulled the blankets over us as the enema surged through me. I closed my eyes. My mother was holding me. She wasn't dead. But, she had big hard arms and something pressing against my bottom that she never had before, something so hard, it didn't feel like human flesh, but was.

I sobbed, cried, and wanted him to hold me like this forever! I loved Momma. I loved Lars.

Two nights before, he made me feel the love of a woman the first time in my life. That morning he woke up the love in me of a little girl. A love not felt since that morning in the mountains, my Momma giving me the last enema she ever gave.

Lars said, "Am I hurting you, Marisa?"

I said, "No! My mother used to hold me like this for my enemas. No one has done that since she died. I love you---I love you so much."

I kissed his arm.

Completely in his arms, tears streamed down my cheeks wetting the pillow, his breath warm on the back of my neck, I couldn't move. So full, so emotional, I wanted to disappear into him, to turn to him, to be his forever. But, my colon full, immovable, tight as an inflated tire, I couldn't move.

Crying for joy, I had no idea anyone would think of doing this to me as being exciting, or would hold me like he was holding me. My husband engulfed me in his arms, brought back my life, the life I knew as a little girl, the life I expected to have forever that morning in the mountains with Momma and Daddy, the life I had in the plains mixed in an omelet of sexual, motherly, unconditional love: true love, the love I had forever with him.

After my enema, holding my enema, I ran to the outhouse. Running back to bed faster than I ran away from it, I had to be with my husband.

"Lars?" *Where was he?*

"Here," he said, from the bedroom.

I stopped in the kitchen about to grab some grease and massage it into my vagina. I stopped. Loving the enema, that enema so sensual, I didn't need grease. I needed Lars.

He had my toy ready for me.

Pouncing on him, I kissed him, a long passionate kiss then sucked his lips into the air and inhaled them. They followed mine until they pinned me to my pillow. Looking at each in other full daylight, we made love. Locking my legs around him, I grabbed him like a milking machine, a one hundred and ten volt milking machine plugged into a two hundred and twenty socket. I rocked milking him in rhythm with the spasms of his buttocks. When the muscles locked holding him deep in me, I set my milking muscles on sixty cycles per second spasms sending a magnetic current through my toy. Lars rose off me, his arms straight like trunks of young oaks rooted in top soil, only touching me with his pelvis, his back stiff, his weight, his 305 pounds of muscle and bone crushing into my pelvis. I felt the pump, that rhythmic pump, my toy, my husband, pumping into me.

"Uhh, uhh, uhh," he made noises, collapsed. His every muscle limp, his chest compacted me into the bed. His head motionless, his eyes open, dilated, not moving, was he dead?

"Lars, I love you," I said, checking.

"I love you, too," he said in a weak voice.

The only reason we stopped, my toy went dry, went away, and wouldn't come back.

That day as we worked together, Lars was not as strong as he was. Weakened, he was at peace, the peace a man only feels when bathed in the raging love of a woman. A contentment remained fixed on his face: the little crinkle at the edge of his mouth stayed. He looked at me, watching me with a different look, a look I had never seen, a complete look.

In evening we ate. As I washed dishes, he came behind me, lifting me, sweeping me off my feet. I was in his arms again, the back of my knees in the crook of his arm. He carried me to our bedroom.

"Lars, can I go to the outhouse first?"

Did he put me down? He carried me, sitting me down on the bench, then sitting beside me.

"Lars, I have to tell you something," I said. He had told me things private, trusted me.

"Lars, when I bled after you made love to me---"

He looked at me.

"I was a virgin. I was, but I didn't bleed---I killed a chicken."

He looked stern, disappointed.

"Marisa, you fooled me?"

I said, "Yes, I'm sorry."

"All that blood, those feathers, weren't yours?

I sobbed, "I'm sorry!" Then I thought, *Feathers?*

I said, "Feathers?"

He said, "Not many, a few."

"You knew?"

"That you didn't have feathers? I didn't see any, but you said you were different."

Our outhouse, traditional, we had a pile of corn cobs. I hit him with one. He ran. Throwing, I hit him with two more.

The big man, the war hero was running away from a woman throwing corn cobs. I kept them sailing through the air.

Turning toward me, he had a look in his eyes, the same look 87 Germans and one American might have seen seconds before he killed them. I ran. He chased me and caught me and pinned me to the ground.

My heart was racing. Fear gripped me.

"I know you were a virgin, Marisa." He kissed me hard, then gentle. "I don't want you out of my sight, Marisa. I need you. I love you. For the next few days, where you go, I go. Let me fill myself with you until my heart runs over, is full, then you can have yourself back. All right?"

"All right!" I kissed him. Doc told me not to argue with him, and I didn't want any space between us either.

For three days he dressed me. I dressed him. The only time my hand was not in his was when work required all our hands. We were one, two people, one existence. Gradually we began to breathe again on our own, but we remained one. House work was to be done. Work on the farm was to be done. For that we separated, performed our roles: husband and wife.

I asked, "You aren't doing your opossum grin when you give me enemas anymore. What's the matter?"

"I know you love me, love me doing it. I don't feel ashamed anymore about my feelings, not with you."

After a few months, something else happened. He stopped getting erections when he gave me enemas.

I asked, "You aren't excited giving me enemas anymore?"

Did he see disappointment in my eyes?

"Marisa, I love giving you enemas, but at first, before we were married, before you made a game of love making, made if fun, pleasure, I thought it was wrong, that I was a freak, a pervert. You didn't make me feel like a pervert. I love giving you enemas, watching you quiver as I filled you, listening to you react to the enema, but I don't feel dirty about it anymore. I feel love. I love you!"

His eyes misted. I held him rocking him. We kissed, a soft gentle kiss, not a passionate or erotic kiss, one of union, bonding, love.

He said, "I love you so much, Marisa!"

Something changed between us. He wanted to give me enemas and was afraid to ask, afraid to make me do it. He persuaded me. Our priest said he had the right to order me, make me obey. He didn't, he asked. I gave him what he wanted. I wanted to please my husband.

After that there were times when we disagreed, when I thought of telling him no, but that look of love he had that morning permeated my mind, my soul. He gave me everything, I let him give me enemas and made it sexy for him. How could I refuse to do what he wanted in other things?

I kissed him as he kissed me. The love I had for him made me follow him, watch him, learn his ways, predict his movements, his smiles and thoughts. Rarely did he have to ask me anything after the first few months, I anticipated his wants, his orders, was obedient to him before he knew what he wanted himself. We were one, a team. Did he do the same with me? Of course. In cherishing me he searched my soul and brought out in me my best, the parts of me that longed for his touch, his husbanding.

We had a real marriage, not one of orders, submission, or manipulation by partners each seeking their own gratification, but a marriage of two people seeking the union of love. In a great marriage there is only one person with two heads, two bodies and two souls seeking to be perfect mates for each other, one unity. My need of enemas was complemented by his desire to give them. My work on the farm was his left hand, his was my right. My life, his, together were ours. After I was seventeen and married Lars, I never had a life. My life was his, he woke it up, stroked it, played with it, and made it fly above the plain every morning. Looking in his eyes, I saw him. In all the decades we had together, his life was mine, he didn't have a life either, he gave it to me.

He told me when he asked me to marry him that this farm would be ours. He never spoke of it as his, it was ours. The land, the sky, the reflection off the distant mountain, his life and my life were one. When a man and a woman unite in Holy matrimony, it is a blending of body, mind, and soul. We became one. An old four-quart enema bag facilitated that with a filling of love. A routine experience for me, an excitement for him, made our lives exciting. Milking cows, working the land, missionary prone sex routine for him, exciting for me, made our lives exciting.

I was in heaven, heaven for two, to be three in nine months.

Then winter, cold less work, more love, more throwing up, my first baby, Lars loved me, put up with me. Spring, high country, still snowing, past the sick stage, I got hungry. I wanted food, something leafy, fresh, green.

I said to Lars, "What do you mean you can't plant greens? Build a fire, thaw the ground. Then you can plant."

He kissed me, rubbed my low back.

"I'm not waddling. I don't waddle," I said.

He kept rubbing my back. One more month and I'd have my waist back. I felt the baby kick.

"Lars, feel that. Is that a boy's kick, or a girl's?"

Lars snuggled me under a quilt, kissed me, and brought me some pea soup with flakes of dried parsley and basil.

Chapter 21

The Visitor & the Werewolf

I was a virgin, innocent, sexually naive. He wasn't. He had specific, perverted sexual thoughts, thoughts acceptable to me, thoughts that made my life better, not worse. He was my man, the only man who ever husbanded me. My sexuality plastic, the callused, gentle hands of my husband sculpted my passions. He defined me as a woman.

I wasn't his first love. Katrina was. When he was a boy forming sexually he thought of her, her hourglass figure, her beautifully formed body; he fantasized about her; and on becoming a man he sought out women who looked like her. He dreamed of her slim hips, her perfection, but married me, a larger, big hipped woman, a woman not physically the image he sculpted in his mind in his years of youth. Not his first choice, not even his second, I studied him. Reaching the passion of his mind, I touched exquisitely tender, virgin areas of reality. I touched his dreams and made them real. My hands hardening with farm work reached in his mind, rubbed his goose bumps, and sculpted his passionate dreams into reality. I defined him as a man.

I needed to know every path, village lane, and main street of his mind; to know how to obey him into being the husband I was defining; and to be who he needed me to be: to love him into being everything I needed him to be, to be his first and only choice.

A month into our marriage, we sat on the porch watching sunset. A hum in the distance vibrated the silence into sound. A green truck moved toward town.

"Limbaugh," Lars said. "On his way into town to get drunk again."

"You were friends before the war," I said.

"We should be now," Lars said, "My fault."

Then he told me the story. It was after basic training. They were waiting to be assigned to a new base, hanging around the barracks, nobody else around.

Limbaugh said, "You ever think of doing it with a man, Lars?"

Lars said, "NO!"

Limbaugh stopped talking. Lars put on his dress uniform and headed into town to a brothel.

A week later Limbaugh and another man in their company were caught copulating in the toilet and dishonorably discharged. Lars shared this with me, telling me to say nothing about it.

"No use making life harder for him, Marisa. He was a friend. I said too much to him as he was leaving the base. Things I shouldn't have said. Things I wouldn't have said, if I'd thought about it. It was something in me. The thought of him wanting to do it with me made me sick. He cried, Marisa, and he's never talked to me since I've been home."

I didn't tell him what Limbaugh had told Katrina when she asked about Lars. Lars feeling guilty about making a hard situation worse for him, Lars didn't need to learn that Limbaugh lied burning away the last hope Katrina had of having Lars back. I held him to my chest and I cried.

Lars said, "Why are you crying, Marisa?"

I hated Limbaugh for what he did to Katrina and was grateful to him for my husband at the same time.

I thought of Katrina's slim beautiful hips. Lars should have been making love to them, but he shared more.

He said, "I'm sorry, Marisa. It's only you I want now. I won't ever go to a whore house again. I don't want any other woman, but you. I didn't know you then. It's something men do, soldiers do. I won't do it again."

I wasn't thinking about brothels, but I did want to please him, did need to know what they knew to please him. What did they do that pleased him that I wasn't doing? What could I learn to please him more?

"Tell me about those women, Lars. Tell me everything."

"No other woman can please me like you do, Marisa. Only you," he said.

As I lay under him making love with my head to the side beneath his chest breathing, I had his experience in the brothel to thank for the joy and security I felt.

His first prostitute, a Katrina substitute, having Katrina's figure, small frame, and smile; she kept slapping him on the arm until he let her up. Lars thought she was excited. Almost suffocating, she was. Gasping for air, shaking, crawling from under him, she was terrified.

"I'm sorry," Lars said.

"It's not your fault," She said, regaining her composure. "We need to do it a little differently."

She wanted him to partially stand on his knees as well as support his weight with his arms. Under this bridge, she crawled under him carefully like a mechanic going under a car on jacks, checking each leg and arm to be sure he wouldn't fall on her again. With her feet on his shoulders, she worked his pelvis into hers and gave him ecstasy. She was his girl the entire time he was in Kentucky.

In France there were more women. One night, none of his Katrina models available, his sergeant noticed him.

The sergeant said, "Boy, you big over grown SOB, come here!"

Lars, expecting to be cussed out for some indiscretion, meekly went to his superior.

"Boy, I seen you with these little women. Ain't you got the sense God gave a June bug? You're gonna slip and fall on one of them and kill her---Here!"

The sergeant shoved him in an open room with a woman he had never met, and called in after him, "Inga, I'm payin'. I expect you to take better care of this boy than you done anybody since you been whoring."

Lars got another Dane, a larger woman, one as tall as him and as broad in the hips as himself. She didn't put her legs up to get him inside of her. She wrapped her legs around his, locked him into her. Better than standing in a yoga cat pose to make love, he remembered her as he watched my big hips moving at the church social. I would be able to take him laying flat in bed.

Ideal lovers are more similar than different. With the widest hips of any girl in town, I was made for Lars. My big hips handled Lars' big hips, but his massive upper body too large to lie comfortably on any woman, he stood on his elbows to love me. Making love sandwiched to the bed by one large man my entire life, I was always satisfied and never knew anything else, never made love to a little man, or man my size.

A reason for virginity, I would never know the penetration of a smaller man with smaller hips settling deeper into my pelvis his organ rubbing my clitoris harder providing me more clitoral stimulation, nor being more comfort being under a lighter body.

I would never know the ride of a small man, miss it with my broad, heavy husband, nor would I frustrate a smaller man disengaging him at a crucial moment pulling his shorter legs downward with my longer ones, or bucking him off with such force that he would bounce off me and the bed and onto the floor.

Lars massive body would crush into me and keep our physical contact as no smaller man could, and my well developed buttocks would rock and lift him with a sexual power that no smaller woman could.

He wanted Katrina, dreamed of her, but knew in bed she could not have loved him with the power I did. But, he never forgot her. Teenage dreams, unrealistic, are the stuff of fantasy, fetish, and formation. None of us ever completely replace those hopes and dreams.

And the danger of those dreams, their power in memory always there, make little men and big women, and big men and little women have long happy marriages adapting, doing what needs to be done to please. The reality of physical match never exceeds the reality of matching dreams.

I knew Katrina was in his dreams even when he was in mine.

Then she came back.

"Marisa, I've had a letter," Father Viktor said. "An old friend wants to visit you and Lars."

"Of course, Father."

"It's Katrina," he said.

A knot formed in my stomach. Why now, why at all? None of us had seen Katrina in several years. She lived the next town over, not much to an Easterner, but we were Westerners. Next town over meant 92 miles to us, and with no reason to go to Denver, Lars nor I ever went to her town. I had not seen her since she graduated from high school, married and I visited her three months later.

Why now, when my belly was watermelon size and I was into the nesting phase of being pregnant. Why now when Lars couldn't lay on me as we both liked best and we were adapting to positions that didn't put pressure on my abdomen. For six months I had either been throwing up or throwing things. Lars had been patient, kind, forgiving. He didn't need an old love waltzing into his life. Well, maybe he did. I didn't!

No phone, no way to know exactly when she would arrive, I knew it was to be Tuesday.

I watched our road. No signs of a car coming, I washed dishes in the sink, then started the clothes on my wash board outside. A flash caught my eye: sun on chrome. She wasn't in a car. She was on a bicycle, an unusual one, shorter and lighter than most, with smaller wider wheels, and the mid bar lowered so she could peddle in a dress!

I squinted to see her. As she got closer I could see. A pretty dress, a blue bonnet, that same slender waist she had in high school, she was beautiful! Why was she beautiful? She was married, had two babies. She should have been fat, a good, broad Russian peasant.

Her bicycle, a good means of transportation, brought her sailing toward the house. Not waiting, I went to the porch to meet her.

"Katrina!"

"Marisa!"

We hugged and made do over each other like the old friends we were.

"What is this?" I pointed at her bike.

"My husband made it for me. It's wonderful, only took me an hour and a half from the bus stop to here."

I looked at it, shiny chrome wheel guards to keep water off. Chrome handle bars and a metal guard over the chain. It was special. Was there another one like it in Colorado?

"No, it's the only one of it's kind," Katrina said.

Holding her arm, we walked into our kitchen where I had a kettle boiling on the stove for tea.

Katrina said, "How long, Marisa---one or two months?"

"One, my first." I rubbed my belly.

Katrina said, "Abe Jr'll be three, in two months, into everything, and his sister is walking. Children are wonderful, Marisa," she said, smiling with her warmest smile, the one that caused women like me to become jealous and men to swoon.

I looked at her, why was she here?

"Marisa, this is hard for me…"

She stopped. I stopped, looking her in the eyes. What was she going to say? A fear boiled up from my bloated belly, caught in my throat. I had been afraid of Lars, of loving him, of him hurting me. Now I feared losing him. Was Katrina here to take him from me?

"Marisa, Abe sent me. He said I had to see Lars before we left."

I asked, "Left?"

"He's a mechanic you know, actually designs parts for engines now. Henry Ford likes his work, sent him a train ticket to go to Detroit and talk to him. Abe is going to work for Mr. Ford. He's not a mechanic anymore; he'll be designing cars, with his own shop at Ford. We're moving to Detroit."

And? I thought.

"Marisa, do you remember how I cried when Lars left?"

I said nothing, waited for her to keep speaking.

"Marisa, I love my husband, but Lars' ghost is there at night, during the day, anytime I close my eyes. I know he is yours, and I have a wonderful family, but Abe said I need to see him, know he is all right, before we move to Detroit.

"I wanted to see you too, and am glad you have each other---I just needed to see him one last time before I move away, before I die!"

There were tears in her eyes. She still loved Lars---my husband! I sat down.

"Can I see him, Marisa. I'll go if you say to go, and I won't ever be back. Please let me see him, please!"

A tear rolled down her cheek.

Standing, trembling, I put my hand on her head, held her to me as I did Lars when he had one of these weak moments. I didn't answer straight away.

"He's in the barn," I said.

Katrina hugged me then walked with an unsteady gait picked her way toward the barn. She went in.

My heart sank.

Was it ten minutes, an hour, two hours? I couldn't tell. She and he came out of the barn. Lars was holding her hand!

I knew them. My angel, my friend, Katrina had been there when my parents died, helped me at the orphanage. She spoke English for me and hovered over me until Momma Nina took me in. I loved her. I watched them fall in love, watched them, two orphans, lock into a total commitment, never looking at anyone else, watched Katrina build her whole world around Lars, and him build his around her. They were inseparable, until he hurt Karl.

As they got closer to the house, I saw---They were crying. Katrina cried for two months when Lars left for the army. Lars never cried. In the years I had known Lars, he only cried at our wedding over Sam. He was crying.

I had lunch ready. I sat down hard in my chair, not hungry.

In the kitchen Katrina said, "Thank you, Marisa."

Lars hugged me, crushed me. I couldn't breathe.

"I love you, Marisa," he said.

"I have lunch ready," I said.

"I'm not hungry, Marisa. I'll eat later," Lars said.

Leaving us alone, Lars walked back to the barn, his head down.

Katrina said, "Marisa, you're a wonderful wife for Lars. You're my friend, my best friend." She hugged me.

"Marisa, thank you for letting me talk to Lars. You know how I feel about him and how I feel about you. I'm sorry, Marisa, I've never been able to stop loving him. I had to see him. I'm leaving forever next week. We'll never see each other again. Abe and I---Will you do something for me? Write me? I'm your friend. I want to know you're all right. If you need anything. We've done well, now in Detroit we'll do better. If there is anything you need." She wrote down an address.

I didn't know what to say.

She didn't want to eat, started back to town.

Before she reached her bike, I waddled after her.

"Katrina, I love you too." I hugged her. "Thank you for not taking my man!"

She smiled. "No one will ever take Lars away from you, Marisa. He loves you."

I said, "But, he loves you!"

"He loves us both, Marisa. I was his first love. He was mine. That love will always be there, but it's different for a man. Men can love more than one woman, at least most men can. It is harder for a woman. Abe has a cousin. She has been crying ever since Abe went for the interview in Detroit. She doesn't want him to leave. They grew up together. She hasn't married, I don't think she ever will. I know she loves Abe, but they don't talk about it. He's a good father, a good husband. I'm happy, but he knows how I feel about Lars."

I said, "Let me show you our house, Katrina."

We walked from room to room. Katrina touched the walls, held the towel in the bathroom to her face, smelled Lars. She didn't move for two minutes. We went to the bedroom. Our bed was made, a quilt on it. She looked longing for a minute. She never slept with Lars. Having seen him, touched him, and walked where he lived, she closed her eyes, breathed deep and opened them looking at me.

Katrina said, "I'm hungry now. Can we eat?"

We ate.

Commenting on how good my chicken was, she smiled.

"Marisa, I'm happy now. I love Lars. I love you. I imagined you and he having a good live. Now I know. Had he written me, I would have waited for him. I gave up, but I never stopped caring. Knowing he married you---Love means something more than having, it means joy in the happiness of those you love. When Abe Jr. and Missy grow up, I have to let them go, watch them have their own lives. Lars and you are like that to me. I can't have him as we were. He can't have me. Abe's my husband. I married him. I'm glad Lars married you. I am happy for him and you.

"Do you understand how I feel, Marisa?"

Did I understand? I didn't have a high school love. I had never loved a man before Lars. How could I understand? Lars' baby was in me. In all my life, I had never desired a man like I desired Lars. I knew I wasn't his first. Katrina was. I wanted to better her, be a better lover, a better wife than she could have been. Now she was sitting in my kitchen telling me she loved my husband. Did I know how she felt?

"Thank you for not taking my husband." I began to cry.

"No one will ever take Lars from you. He adores you, Marisa. I don't know what you have done to him, but he worships you. I have a good marriage. We care about each other. We share each other. We respect each other, but you and Lars are special. I see it. Something about you, you opened something deep inside him and let him feel a love that I couldn't have given him, Marisa. Whatever it is you are doing to him, keep doing it. I know Lars. He would never be as satisfied with any woman, as he is with you. You're his wife. The only one he wants to be his wife."

I could have told Katrina about Lars giving me enemas, my making it special for him, but that was private between us. Would she understand how we felt?

We smiled at each other, talked. The tension relaxed, we were girls again chattering about boys, life, school, Momma Nina. I missed Katrina when she left.

She peddled away down our drive, more beautiful than she was riding up it.

I wrote down the address. I would write her, tell her about our life, our baby, about Lars.

Three hours later a car came up the drive. We didn't have many visitors, who now?

The priest? Why would Father Viktor be coming to see us now?

"Marisa," he said, a sad look on his face. "It's Katrina."

"I know; she was here, Father. She still loves Lars. He loves her, but he loves me too. She's leaving, moving to Detroit with her husband." I smiled at him.

"She's dead, Marisa!"

"What?" I sat down on the step.

"An accident, before she reached the main road. A car or a truck hit her. She died."

He said, "Do you want me to tell Lars?"

"I'd better tell him," I choked through my tears. My friend and I were just talking. How could she be dead?

We followed the priest back to town in our truck.

Passing the spot where she died, the priest stopped.

"It was here," he pointed out some skid marks, gouges in the dirt road, and a redden area in the dirt.

The smell of fresh blood still tainted the air.

Lars picked up a bicycle fender. He hadn't cried like I cried. What did he see?

I asked him, "Are you all right?"

"Green," Lars pointed out a streak of green paint on the bicycle fender. "A skid pattern. See here, the front wheels locked here. The back ones are more to the side. Too wide a space beween the front and back wheels for a car to make."

He was doing what he did. He didn't mourn Sam, he killed Germans. He didn't look to see if he was bleeding when he was shot. He took down the drunk. This time I heard him; I saw him. His voice deep, smooth, unemotional; his face calm, not a twitch, no sign of sorrow; he was Lars, the Medal of Honor winner; Lars, the cold blooded killer; Lars, the man I married, the man I feared.

He said, "Limbaugh. Limbaugh is the only one on our road with a green truck."

Limbaugh was a drunk, a bad driver when he was drunk, a drunk sent home after only four months of service in the military. People wondered what happened. He limped, said he hurt his leg. A couple of men said something about his cowardice after he got home. Limbaugh knocked both of them out, drank down a jar of whiskey and passed out himself. He didn't do any more fighting in the war, but he kept drinking. Weaving his way home day or night in a complete alcoholic haze, this was his normal driving. Would he or anyone else expect, or be looking for a bicycle on our country road? Was it his fault? If he had been sober would he have missed her? Had he been more of a man would he have stopped and helped her rather than running away? Would she still be alive?

Lars had seen his truck passing by earlier that afternoon, after Katrina had left. Limbaugh weaved down the road faster than usual.

The earth shook with the thumping of Lars' feet.

I shouted, "Lars, where are you going?"

He was moving toward our truck.

"After Limbaugh," he said, a steady stare in ice gray eyes.

I ran between him and the truck.

"Lars you can't go. You'll kill him. YOU CAN'T GO!"

He tried to side step me. I moved in his way. He dragged me.

"You can't go! You can't go! I love you."

My orders weren't working. The 'I love you' slowed him. He stopped a second when I said that.

"He killed Katrina," Lars said.

"I know. You have to tell the sheriff. That was our deal, don't you remember. It's my decision whether you go or not when there is trouble."

I kissed his shirt.

He stopped.

"I love you, Lars. You can't go!"

"You can't tell me what to do, Marisa---He killed Katrina!"

"That's why you can't go. You have to get the sheriff," I kissed his shirt.

"You can't tell me not to do this, Marisa."

"I know. I'm your wife. I obey you, but this time you can't go." I was crying.

"And what if I go?"

"I'm your wife. I love you. You can't go. Take me home first and paddle me, blister my bottom first, before you go. I'm telling you not to go. I'm disrespecting you. You have to paddle me before going to Limbaugh's place. You can blister me for telling you what to do, but I'm doing it---you're not going!" I kissed his shirt.

He was moving forward. How could I stop him? At half his weight and a quarter his strength, I put my arms around him. I was skidding back. He was pushing me, carrying me toward our truck. I put my head against his chest, it slowed him. I kissed his shirt again. All that muscle, all that power, stopped by a kiss. Was I that strong? Was the chain I tied him with that strong? Was his love for me that strong?

"Marisa, I love her."

"I know you do, Lars, but I can't lose you."

"I know you and the baby need me, Marisa. I love her. I love you. But, Limbaugh killed her."

"Tell the sheriff. Let the sheriff handle it, please for me, for our baby."

Lars lifted my hand kissed it, then let me go, stepped backward. He picked up the bicycle fender, fumbled with it.

He said, "The sheriff'll need to see this."

We drove to town.

Chapter 22

The Legacy

I kissed him. I tried to obey him. Knowing his limits, and as part of our growing together, as Father Viktor said would happen, he came to entrust me with decisions he didn't want to make. Rather than play the bull and charging off bellowing when he needed a second opinion, my husband wanted my second opinion first.

The decision not to avenge Katrina was one of the hardest in his life, one I was proud to be part of. Had he paddled me, I would have taken it without objection. I offered when we got home. He never answered. He took me in his arms, kissed me for five minutes, and went back to the barn. I cried for an hour then thought of him crying alone in the barn. A worn crinkled piece of paper taken from its hiding place in my Bible, I went to him.

Lars had written, "Katrina, I will love you till the day I die. If in the rage of battle I die, I will die loving you. If I die old and in bed, I will die loving you. I will die loving you. I will always love you."

Katrina had written, I won't live without you. The day I die, I'll be holding your hand, loving you. Without you, I don't live. I can't live."

He burst into tears on reading it. He cried in my arms as the sun sank below the mountain range where Katrina and I first met in the mining camp. He and I both fell asleep still sniffling. I put the note in a cigar box with all our other important papers in a drawer in our bedroom.

The next morning, both of us in the barn, our milk cows had seen Katrina, but needed to be milked on that morning as they did every morning. Our routine didn't change. We had to be up every morning at four---cows. Coming back to the house a few minutes before he finished the milking, I got the fire going, the water heating, and went back to bed. When Lars came in, he got my enema ready and gave it to me and held me then I rid myself of the day's waste. When I crawled in bed with him, I started doing everything I knew to please him. Making love before we got up for the rest of the day was our breakfast.

Our lives, routine, were never boring! Every time he gave me an enema, he held me, cherished me and made me glory in being his wife. After the first months of marriage, he stopped becoming sexually excited during my enemas, but sprang to life when I came back to bed.

I asked him, "Giving me an enema doesn't excite you anymore?"

"It does, but we do it every day. It's routine, and it isn't sex. Your enemas are about keeping you well, making you feel good. Giving you an enema doesn't do anything for me. Making love to you does. I know how that is going to feel and anticipate it. That excites me."

I kissed him.

"Marisa, I know my thoughts, they are there, as they were. An enema's a fantasy when it's associated with sex. If I gave you enemas erratically that would excite me, but I don't. I do it every day. Giving you an enema has lost the sexual part." He kissed me. "I hope you don't mind. I'll always love making love to you and giving you enemas, but they've become different to me. Enemas will always be sensual to me, but not as sexual as they were."

Strangely, things were not different at home after Katrina's death. The sheriff arrested Limbaugh. Father Viktor was right. After that time Lars never even alluded to his right to make decisions as to when to get his guns and go deputying. He always told people to ask me first, give me the facts, then I would say whether he was going, or they needed to go to the sheriff. More conservative than he could have been, many people went to the sheriff that might have been as well handled by Lars, but he never had another hard arrest. Everyone went with him peaceably when he went out, except years later when one gangster holed up on a farm with his gang.

Lars was with the sheriff on that one. They killed two of the gang members, but no one from the sheriff's department or citizens were hurt. Lars helped plan the assault on the farm house and was a hero again. I worried about him going, but took it to him, told him I was worried. I knew the gangsters had a machine gun, and didn't want him to go but knew they needed him.

I said, "Lars, you're not a soldier without a family. Your grandfather left your grandmother pregnant. I'm pregnant. You have me and an unborn baby waiting for you to come home."

Katrina said, "What about us, Momma? Alexi, Sarra, Sammy, Junior, and I will be waiting for Daddy to come home."

Lars hugged us and said, "It's my duty."

I said, "I know!"

Sarra and Junior cried.

Lars sat with them on his knee loving them. "It's my duty, Junior, Sarra. If I didn't do my duty, others wouldn't do their's. Bad men would hurt innocent people. No one would be safe in Colorado. You wouldn't want that would you?"

"I don't want you hurt, Daddy," Junior said.

"Living, son, has to be done with honor, respect. A man has to do what is right. I have too, and someday I expect you to, too. This is one of my jobs, protecting you and your brothers and sisters---and Momma. You want me to do that don't you?"

Junior couldn't answer him. A five-year-old all that mattered to him was his daddy.

I kissed Lars and helped him getting his things ready to go. The children prepared their parts for their daddy's trip to town. Junior gave him his toy gun.

There was no spanking of me for telling him no. In fact, there never was another spanking or paddling of me. The kids weren't so lucky, or perhaps that was part of their good luck, having a father that made them obey the law. Their father wasn't strict, but they knew their limits and respected his authority and knew he loved them.

Our statistics: in fifty two years of marriage, my husband didn't spank much, if it was once a month when all seven kids were home, I'd be surprised. He never hit or hurt me in anyway, he gave me one spanking, but that was before we were married, and he gave me more than 19,212 enemas, one a day and extras when I was sick or had a baby. I have no idea how many times we made love. I'd have a better idea, but we didn't do that everyday, and less as we got older. We made love everyday for the first month. When I wasn't able to make love, during my period, a baby, or I didn't feel like it, I'd tell him. If I didn't want to make love, he would be out working on the farm when I left the outhouse. If he didn't feel like it, he would tell me, and I would go from the outhouse to work, otherwise after my enemas was love making time.

Before our children went to school, our routine differed from most farmers. We kept them up, read to them, and fell asleep with them in front of the fire on a big bed we made for all of us. Sleeping in, the little ones were asleep while we milked, asleep when the older kids and my husband had breakfast, asleep while I had my enemas and asleep when we made love. After they grew up enough to go to school, our routine was the same. We did my enemas after they went to school, having recruited them into our early morning work routines. School nights, from first grade on, were early bed nights for us all. Saturdays and Sundays, we made love at night.

A wonderful life, of our children, all of them went to college and five graduated. Momma and Daddy made me value learning. I couldn't fulfill their dreams for me without them. I could for my children. I lived to be behind them, to read to them all winter when they were little and to do mathematics with them when we were working.

Peas in, Katrina and I were shelling them. Row after row of peas in bowls, a bushel basked of hulls in between us.

I said, "Katrina, what is the square of three?"

"Nine," She said.

"The cube?"

"27"

"There, over the horizon is Wichita, Kansas. Is it colder there or here?"

"We're higher. It's colder here," She said.

"How much," I asked.

"We're at 5, 300 feet. Wichita is below 2,000 isn't it?"

"Around that," I said.

She said, "Ok, more than 3,000 feet difference, at 5 degrees per thousand feet, its more than 15 degrees Fahrenheit colder here. Right, Momma?"

"If the same conditions are here, as there, yes," I said, hugging her.

She was my girl, one of seven children. We kept talking.

I encouraged them to read and learn on their own. Lars approved, he wanted them to work the farm, learn from nature.

Two of the boys graduated from agriculture college. Our oldest, Alexi worked the farm with us, although, with his education, he bought two more farms and managed five others. He lived in a bigger house on one of his farms, a farm three times the size of ours, but connecting to ours on the west side. We saw lights in the distance in his and his wife's kitchen when we got up to milk the cows.

A problem persisted, I got sick when we went off our farm and I had enemas somewhere else. Why? Decades later, a doctor told us that it was because of chlorine. Towns began putting chlorine in tap water. Our well was never chlorinated. Chlorine kills normal flora, should be avoided in enemas. Drinking it is different, no essiential bacteria in the stomach that is needed, it doesn't cause that problem. If you put chlorinated water in the colon it affects the function of the colon, can cause B12 deficiencies and other floral problems.

Not understanding why I got sick, I learned to stay home. Why should I ever leave our farm? I had all my babies at home in our bed. I wanted to be home every morning for my enemas. Everything I loved and needed was here. In our time, when farm people went to the hospital they usually died. I didn't want to die; I wanted to live forever on our farm. If my husband went somewhere overnight, I wasn't happy. I worried about him. He felt the same about me.

Having a wife like me, one wanting him so much, would have been hard for some men. I stayed home, and took care of myself on those days that he had to be away, but I didn't sleep and barely ate. He never left me long, and when Alexi came home from college, Lars put him in charge: meaning that any business off the farm was his responsibility. Lars and I never slept a night alone after that day.

Wanting Lars to take care of me, wanting him to make love to me mornings, I wanted to fix his breakfast, do my part, and be his wife. I needed to know he was on the place and see him in the fields or barn for glimpses as I did my work in the house. As soon as I could, I went to the fields to help him. Every day with my husband was filled with love, happiness.

Townspeople and our children thought we had a boring life, never leaving the farm for more than half a day, but it was our life, every wonderful minute of it.

When well into my forties, a chiropractor was engaged to our daughter. He wanted to find out why I couldn't go without an enema. He did a barium enema, wrinkled an eyebrow and sent me to another doctor who took a small piece of tissue from my colon. I had a thing called Hirschsprung's syndrome; a disease inherited or just happening to some people. My son-in-law to be wasn't sure which. A segment of the colon doesn't work, usually low in the colon. I had that, except higher, in my descending colon. Nothing could get past that point because the muscles in that segment didn't work. The chiropractor recommended I go to a gastroenterologist, a surgeon. All he had to do was to cut out that piece of my intestine and reconnect it, then I would be able go on my own.

We talked about it, but why change? I had been having enemas every day for more than 45 years. I was healthful, and Lars giving me an enema everyday bothered neither of us.

The gastroenerologist was surprised that I had Hirschsprung's syndrome when he saw me in person. Most people with this have big abdomens. I didn't. My husband and my children were pleased with how I looked. I had big girl hips, but a slim waist all my life.

My colon was smaller than most people's. People with Hirschsprung's have big colons. I didn't. I had an enema every day. If I had had them occasionally, or not at all and waited until my colon was full and pushed past the segment of bowel that did not contract, I would have had a huge colon.

Colons, like everything else, get bigger when stretched for long periods of time. The enema filled me, stretched the colon for a few minutes then my colon shrank to its normal size for the rest of the day. The enlarging problem can happen to people who don't have the problem I did, especially children who stay constipated and don't go regularly. These people get bigger colons. Those who have enemas keeping the colon from stretching for long periods of time don't.

The colon, like any other part of the body, grows to accommodate as a child. Girls in Africa, who put ever larger rings under their lips and leave them stretched, develop huge lips, a sign of beauty in their culture. American's help their children develop huge colons and large abdomens by letting them remain constipated as children, stretching, and expanding their colons. On X-Ray, the doctors said I had a healthful colon. Many people had some colon problems by my age. I didn't.

Happy to have this knowledge, I knew why I was different. It had not made my life worse, only better. Lucky enough to have parents, lucky enough to have a husband, and lucky enough to have a family that loved me as I am and caring enough to care for me as I needed, my handicap made my life perfect.

We got old.

Did Lars love me? Was ours an ideal life? It was, but that didn't change the pain we both had when young. It didn't change the tragedy that happened to our families.

"Lars, we haven't been to Momma and Daddy's grave in four years," I said.

Lars folded his newspaper, looked at me, finished his last bite of breakfast. He said, "Now?"

We went to the mass grave where they were buried every year or two, straighten it up, put in some flowers, made it look nice. I trimmed a rose, I had put there a long time ago. He watched me.

"Marisa, we've never seen Katrina's grave. I'd like to see it, check on it."

I said, "Now?"

It was a little out of our way going home, but only an hour and a half.

Last Sunday we had our 52nd wedding anniversary. All those years we worked on the farm, never taking a break. Of a sudden, we were free, all of our kids grown, one running our farm. We went places, to town, to movies, we even went up in the mountains to near where Lars herded sheep. Once a full day trip up the mountain to his herding camp, it took forty minutes after we reached the turn off. Another few hours away from home and no one would miss us, including the cows.

Katrina was buried at her church in Denver, a long trip for us, then. We could have gone to the funeral. But Doc said I was too far along. That was a good excuse.

It would have been good for Lars to have met Abraham, but it would have been an awkward meeting, two men who loved her, they would have shaken hands, been cordial. But, Abraham knew Katrina loved Lars, sent her to Lars to help her get over their love and be closer to him. The trip killed her. Katrina an orphan, only his family at the funeral, all that was known was that she went back to her home town to visit some friends and was killed in an accident. It was better left at that.

I wrote Abe that Katrina loved him, was coming home to him. He didn't write back.

Did Lars ever forget her?

He wanted to see her grave, see her one last time before---He was sick, had been having pain in his arm for a week. His color wasn't good. I wanted him to see a doctor.

"Lars, you don't look good. I want you to go to Doc Smith when we get home."

He nodded, started the truck.

Denver was an easy drive, but we had hunting to do. We knew she was buried there and found her in a small church cemetery. It must have been forty years since anyone did anything with her grave. We dug up the weeds, planted some wild flowers, Mountain Gold. With no one to care for them, maybe they would survive, maybe they wouldn't, but cultivated flowers wouldn't.

I looked back at her grave as we walked to the truck.

"Lars, it looks so lonely." I cried.

He started crying too. He cried at movies too, sad ones. Lars not a crier when we were young, in his seventies, he cried often, was old. White hair around his ears and freckles all over the top of his head, he wouldn't wear a hat. I kept buying hats for him; he kept going bareheaded in the sun. Bald men should wear hats. Even men with hair wore hats working in the sun. Not Lars.

Not many young people paid any attention to him now. People feared him when we were young, now they went around him. Still big, he moved slow. The excess testosterone that made him dangerous was gone. It didn't even show in his walk when they dragged him out to make him lead the veteran's day parade every year. He shuffled along with his medal of honor around his neck looking down afraid he would trip and fall; and in bed---no kids, no cows to get up and milk every morning, we had more time for love making than we had in our entire lives. But, his interest was fading and there was some danger that he might break some of my osteoporotic bones. We hungered when we were young. Now we made love occasionally, but it was like eating a second breakfast, when your stomach is full, you do it to make the cook happy, but you'd rather not.

I looked at him again. He opened the truck door for me, stumbled.

I said, "Are you all right?"

"A little tired," Lars said.

We started to drive.

"Lars, do you still love her?"

"Marisa, she was my first love. I still love her, the teenager, the girl who gave me my first kiss, was everything to me until I kissed you."

I slid over sitting in the middle beside him.

Lars said, "What the Jim Fiddle are you doing sitting in the middle like a teenager?"

I said, "I'm a teenager, sitting by the boy I love, the only one I've ever loved."

We smiled.

Another hour and we would be home, maybe we would make love tonight. We would stop at the diner in town and eat, a couple of steaks. We always did that when we went through town.

Lars said, "I really don't feel good, Marisa."

He down shifted the truck, and started to pull over to the side of the road. He rubbed his left arm.

"My throat hurts!" His face was pale. Then he relaxed. "That's better."

Slowed, almost stopped, he started to put the truck back in second, pulled back out on the road. Not getting it in gear, he veered across the road and ran off into a field. We plowed through a few yards of wheat. The truck stopped still running.

I froze. I looked at Lars. He slumped over the steering wheel. He never regained consciousness. The doctor pronounced him dead as soon as we reached the hospital in Denver.

Lars and I had agreed, we wanted to be buried on our farm, but burial laws prevented that. The option was to be cremated and scattered there. That worked for us. We made the arrangements twenty years before Lars' death.

Leaving the undertakers we had talked about Katrina then too.

"Lars, you loved Katrina?"

"You know I did." He gripped my hand.

"If you go first, would you mind if I put a scoop full of your ashes on her grave? She loved you too, probably as much as I do."

He said, "Do what you want, Marisa. You're my wife."

I smiled. She gave him to me when she was young and loved him. She loved him. He loved her. A common cold, constipation, a few enemas, a kiss and the first wave of puberty made him hers. If the rage of manhood had not been flushing through him one morning at school, he would have been her husband, not mine.

The fetish developed in him listening to her have enemas made him mine. A fluke, something unintended is that what fetishes are made of, always made of? No one intends to grow up with abnormal sexual fantasies, fetishes, but almost everyone does. If she had not had those enemas from Momma Nina in the school infirmary would that have happened? What would have gone into Lars's mind at that moment of readiness? If she had not had them would Lars have wanted me, a girl who had to have enemas? Prettier girls, brighter girls, girls with better personalities, they would have taken him. But I had something he wanted, desired, thrashed in the night thinking of, something that made him mine. Would he have married me, made my life the life it was had he not known I needed daily enemas? Katrina, Momma Nina, and a rhinovirus came together to make Katrina his lover. A defect in my colon made him mine. She was my friend. Her first love, she loved him all her life, died on the road from our farm crying for the missing of him.

I had him for fifty-two-years; all my life. She died alone on the plains. I didn't want her bones forever alone and unloved. Her family, her children, gone, never came back to Denver, never visited her final resting place. I sprinkled part of him over the patchy grass where her body lay. I kept most of him.

Books by J G Knox

Love Thine Enemas and Heal Thyself
An Enema, A Birthday Spanking, A Love Story
For the Love of Amber
The Good Enema

Books available through special order at book stores and online bookstores worldwide

Novellas by J G Knox

Momma's Tears, A Story of Love and Overcoming Grief

Other short stories by J G Knox

Mrs. Smith, the Boarding School Enemas
Caught and Spanked
Tall Dark and Handsome
Honey, I'm Home

Novellas and short stories available at Amazon kindle, e-book stores, or in pdf at http://www.e-lovestories.com

To be placed on the mailing list for new publications, to obtain order prices direct from the publisher to any location in the world (We offer a substantial discount on direct orders and bulk orders, usually 40-50% off book store price), or to share observations about this book, or other books we have written, please write:

Love Truth and Life Publishing
PO Box 65130
Vancouver, WA
98665
Telephone 360-690-0842

We reprint books with corrections periodically, and appreciate anything that will make future editions better. Those submitting corrections we use will be sent a new copy of the next edition.

Kriloff's Original Fables, translation by I. Henry Harrison, London 1883

CPSIA information can be obtained at www.ICGtesting.com
Printed in the USA
LVOW131944110912

298391LV00003B/151/P